Tryst In The Dark

An Omega Lottery Novel

Grace McGinty

Also by Grace McGinty

Hell's Redemption Series: The Redeemable/The Unrepentant/The Fallen

Damnation MC Duet: Serendipity/Providence

The Azar Nazemi Trilogy : Smoke and Smolder/Burn and Blaze/Rage and Ruin

Dark River Days Series: Newly Undead In Dark River/Happily Undead In Dark River/Pleasantly Undead in Dark River

Black Mountain Mates: Hunting Isla

Eden Academy Series: The Lost and the Hunted (Prequel)/Heart of the Hounded (Prequel)/ Rebels and Runaways (Book 1)/Sweethearts and Savages (Book 2)

Shadow Bred Series: Manix/Frenzy/Feral

Stand Alone Novels and Novellas: Bright Lights From A Hurricane/The Last Note/ Inside The Maelstrom Part 1 and 2/Eight Seconds To Fly

Editing by Aubergine Editing

Cover by DAZED Designs

For all the readers who've been sent to the naughty corner. You know who you are.

G x

Tryst In The Dark

Chapter One
Tryst

I hadn't felt this much rage since Topher Johnstone told me my boobs were small and he'd rather eat sand than be my boyfriend when we were in the second grade. Granted, I'd caught him eating sand more than once, so to this very day, I wasn't sure if that was a yes or no.

I'd still punched him in the gut, though. I'd been a hot-tempered kid.

As I stared at the trashed room around me now, it occured to me that while I'd grown boobs, I hadn't outgrown my temper.

I sat on a bed that was made for luxury. Thousand thread count sheets that cost more than an average month's wages, a comforter probably stuffed with thousands of baby geese, and pillows that were the very definition of fluffy clouds. But I'd never felt more uneasy in my life.

I alternated between anxiety and rage, and it was definitely one of those emotional roller coasters that made you want to throw up.

The door to my room was firmly locked and bolted from the outside, yet they still insisted that I was a guest, and not a prisoner. I snorted. I was sitting in a gilded cage, waiting to be kicked off my perch.

My mother had said I was just unlucky. I preferred to think that I was Fate's bitch, and she was just edging me until she finally released me from this goddamn torment.

An unlucky quirk of my DNA meant that when I'd turned sixteen, I'd revealed as an Omega.

No one knew why it occurred in some women and not others, even between siblings. Some suggested it was some kind of genetic glitch resulting from the nuclear fallout of the Last World War, while others thought it was evolution. It didn't matter, not really. The results were the same. I was special, and I was a prisoner.

I guess it was the same for Alphas, except no one thought they were incapable of caring for themselves. Alphas were bigger, stronger, and more compelling than the non-designated humans we called Betas.

No, Alphas became CEOs and politicians with far

too much sway. Instead of taking away their rights, the government and private corporations plied them with money and responsibility. Instead of telling them who they could see, what they could study, what jobs they could have—like they did Omegas—the government let Alphas roam around, amassing fortunes and females.

Other countries put limits on Alphas, like Canada, who said Alphas weren't able to become cops or lawyers, or hold any role where they could have undue pheromonal influence on a jury.

The US just left them completely unchecked.

What everyone conveniently seemed to forget—or purposefully ignored—was that if Alphas were truly left unchecked, they sometimes became cult leaders and despots, powerful and cruel. They led mass suicides and oversaw pyramid schemes.

Yet it was the Omegas whose lives were monitored and controlled by the government, right up to the year of their first heat. They insisted we were slaves to our baser instincts, that we were a danger to ourselves and others if we went into heat around the general population, like a ticking sex bomb waiting to explode and cover everyone in various bodily fluids.

I wasn't stupid. They kept up this 'Omegas are mentally deficient' ruse for a very specific reason, and everyone knew it.

The general reproductive health of humans had

gotten all fucked up at some point. Beta women couldn't really have babies anymore, not at the olden day rates anyway. Don't get me wrong, there were still plenty of women in the country, and some normal old Betas who could still have a baby. But those children were rarely girls, so population rates were slowly declining.

And so they invented the Allotment. Originally, it was just for Alphas, but when there were riots and shouts of eugenics and genocide, they'd expanded it to all male citizens of the US. It was a lottery system, and every unmarried man went into the draw. Alphas and Betas alike, almost like conscription.

It was bullshit. I snarled, standing up to pace.

Today, there'd be a televised lottery. One unlucky man would get his social security number flashed up on the screen, and his life would change forever. Next week, the same deal. And the week after. It would continue until the Department of Designation Associations decided that I had enough.

A knock on the door had me spinning toward the only entrance to the room. It opened, and a younger guy in a nice suit entered. "Sorry, Omega. The Allotment is about to begin. Would you like to watch the draw?"

It didn't help that these things were a massive damn event. Somewhere between a public execution and the old school lottery. Luckily, I wasn't paraded about like a prize mare at auction.

"No."

The DoDA Official's face tightened, maybe with pity or maybe with annoyance, but he nodded respectfully.

I'd give them that, at least. They gave us more reverence in these Allotment houses than we got in the outside world. People were naturally drawn to Alphas, almost against their will, but Omegas were weaker, easier targets. Somehow, we got blamed for every small societal problem, from the fertility crisis to the economic crash that almost put us back to the Dark Ages.

It made no fucking sense, but whatever.

I shifted my focus back to the suit in my doorway, who was still speaking to me softly, like I was a spooked wild animal. "I'll bring up your dinner. The draw will be held in five minutes, and we'll be along with more detail for you as soon as we've verified the number. He should arrive by tomorrow evening, or earlier, depending on his location."

They could guarantee this because someone would be there immediately to collect the lucky guy. Or unlucky, depending on his feelings. I mightn't have a choice in this charade, but neither did they. If you were picked, you had to come when directed. But at least they had a chance at a normal life. Omegas were never even given a glimmer of that hope.

I'd already tried to run once—hence the locked door—so they'd make us bond immediately. Give me the old ball and chain, both figuratively and literally, because once an Omega was bonded to a mate, any large distance between them was physically painful.

I cleared my throat and tried not to eye the open door like a caged tiger waiting for its freedom. "Thanks." He gave me another tight smile and left.

Less than twenty minutes later, the same guy returned with a tray of food and a paper file tucked under his arm. It was done. There was nothing I could do now but deal with the fallout. There was no longer an escape.

He laid down the tray on the small table beside the window, but I didn't care about the food. His eyes were soft as he handed me the file. Paperclipped to the front was a driver's license photo with some basic details scrawled below it.

I looked at my soon-to-be bondmate. He was... attractive. Not that it mattered; he could look like a mountain troll with a voice like he'd eaten Mike Tyson and was trying to gag him back up again, and I'd still have to bond with him.

This guy had brown hair, and a shadowy beard with a ginger tinge to it. He was tall-ish, around six feet, and had laugh lines around his eyes, but also two small wrinkles on his forehead like he'd frowned a lot.

He was a Beta. He looked blissfully average.

I'd take it.

I looked at the rest of his details. He was from the Midwest, a mechanic by trade. He was raised by a single mom and had a tiny nest egg in his bank account. I already knew he didn't have a wife and kids, or a criminal record, because both of those things exempted you from the Allotment proceedings.

Grady Davis. He even had an average kind of name. I didn't get my hopes up, because maybe he was a prick. Or a psychopath who liked to kill kittens. There was only one way I'd find out.

The Official excused himself, and I began to pick at my food as I opened the rest of the file and devoured everything I could about Grady Davis.

Chapter Two
Tryst

As much as I wanted to meet my future Packmate caked in mud from being crash tackled during my escape, I knew it would be redundant. They'd make us bond anyway, and I'd hate my first impression to be that I was unwashed and gross. So despite my hatred of this whole ritual, I found myself getting up early and heading to the ensuite to scrub myself until I shone in preparation for Grady's arrival.

Maybe he would be on my side. Maybe I'd finally have someone who had my best interests at heart. The Omega in me wanted to make a good impression, because we'd been alone for so fucking long.

The Official who came up with my breakfast said we were expecting Grady around lunchtime, which meant I'd finally be getting out of this goddamn room.

Both Grady and I, as well as my other new Packmates, would stay at this house until the Allotment was complete, and then they'd give us our own place, probably somewhere nice with a bit of land. In addition, all our medical expenses for life would be free, and any children we had would have their education paid for.

That's how they sold it to the public, to the social justice warriors who sometimes got fired up about the treatment of Omegas. In a world of struggle and hardship, what they were providing was a good and easy life, at least on the surface. Until you remembered that it wasn't the life you chose.

I barely touched breakfast, and by the time lunch rolled around, nerves and hunger were making me feel a little ill. I paced up and down until another Official came to collect me—the same suit from yesterday.

He unlocked the door and stood to the side. "They should be about ten minutes out. I thought you might want to receive him in the living room."

"So we can pretend that you haven't kept me cooped up in here for four days?"

The suit frowned. "Yeah. I'm sorry about that. Unfortunately, when you tried to escape that first night, they decided on harsher measures. We've managed to secure the whole house now, so we won't have to lock the bedroom door anymore. You won't feel so confined." He winced, even as he said the words.

I gave him a venomous look. "Thanks for making my cat run bigger."

Squaring my shoulders, I walked out into the house that I'd only seen briefly when I arrived. It was nice, in the way all show houses were nice. Bland. Impersonal. There were beige-looking bureaucrats bustling around everywhere, prepping for the arrival of bondmate number one.

I looked back over my shoulder at The Suit. His hair wasn't as slicked back today, the strands a little messier, like he'd had a stressful morning. My Omega liked this Official better than the other ones; his energy didn't make my skin feel like it was crawling, and he didn't act like I was stupid. Well, not so far, but the day was still young, I guess.

Maybe I was the idiot they expected me to be, because the human part of me was desperate to believe that someone was on my side, and this guy, with his nice suit and pleasant face, was apparently it.

"Do you have a name? I've mentally been calling you all Doucheweasels or Fucksticks, but if you're going to be my primary jailer, I should at least be able to curse you specifically."

He rolled his eyes, but I saw the ghost of a smile as he held out his hand for me to shake. "Riley-James Hicks. You can call me RJ if you want." It suited him.

He sounded like a NASCAR driver or a Prom King or something generic.

"Tryst O'Sullivan."

RJ gave me an actual smile. "I know." He wrapped his warm, dry hand around mine, shaking firmly. I liked that he didn't give me a limp shake, as if he thought I was breakable or weak, which a lot of men did.

Yep, he would do as a pseudo-friend for now.

I realized I was still holding his hand and shaking it like the simpleton everyone believed me to be, and dropped it quickly. He lifted a brow but didn't comment. Point one for my friend RJ.

He ushered me through the archway into an open plan living room. The couches looked hard and the art was generic, like a glorified hotel. I sat down on one of the armchairs, trying to look self-assured. Inside, I was freaking the hell out.

RJ disappeared almost immediately. Dammit, so much for my pseudo-friend. Figured, though—if being an Omega had taught me anything, it was that you could only rely on yourself.

I was basically thrumming with nerves by the time the front door slammed, signifying the arrival of our guests. RJ reappeared in the room, a small glass of water in his hand. "For your nerves."

I frowned, but my mouth was dry, so I gulped it

down. Then I resisted the urge to spew it back out through my nose. "Holy shit," I gasped. "That wasn't water."

RJ frowned. "Why would I give you water for your nerves?"

I was saved from answering by the sudden appearance of several higher level Officials. I could tell, because they looked like the sticks were further up their butts.

I stood, smoothing down my sweater. I didn't want to meet my new bondmate in a position of weakness. Who said sixteenth century battle strategy wasn't required Omega reading?

Behind all the pen-pushers was a man in faded jeans and a button up shirt. His driver's license photo hadn't really done him justice. He was broad across the shoulders, his hair shining under the downlights, hinting at a touch of auburn in those brown waves. He looked tired, though.

No. He looked tired *and sad*.

His eyes met mine immediately, and I watched them widen a little. I forgot that this would be his first time seeing me at all. He wouldn't have gotten a profile rundown the way I did. Girls with Omega designations were kept out of the social security register, ironically, for our own security.

His eyes flicked downward, but shot back to my face. Points for not being a lecher.

Agatha Danvers, the DoDA Official in charge of Omega Relations during the Allotment, smiled beatifically between us. "Mr. Davis, may I present Tryst O'Sullivan, your Omega."

I clenched my back teeth at the way she was presenting me like a prized cow. Grady Davis frowned slightly, though the friendly light never left his eyes. He strode past all Officials until he was standing right in front of me.

He smelled nice, like metal and strong soap. Both quite sharp scents, but somehow blended together on this man, they created a scent that was oddly comforting.

He put out his hand. "Hi." His smile this time was reassuring, and he stood close enough that his shoulders blocked out the rest of the room. "It's nice to meet you. A bit of a shock, but nice all the same."

A small smile stretched my own mouth, and it felt brittle on my face. I hadn't smiled in days. "I bet. It's nice to meet you too."

We fell back into silence. What the hell did you say to someone you'd just met but were meant to spend the rest of your life with? Not to mention the other stuff. Had I mentioned that to bond with a potential mate, you had to have sex? Yeah, they didn't put that in the brochures.

My heart thumped harder, panic rising in my throat at the thought. I would never be Tryst O'Sullivan again. If an Alpha was drawn, the Pack would take his name. If I got all Betas, we'd take Grady's surname as the first bonded mate. But no matter what, as of tonight, Tryst O'Sullivan would be gone.

Grady must have sensed my rising hysteria, because he looked around, his eyes falling on RJ. "Maybe we could have privacy to get to know each other?"

Agatha huffed. "I'm afraid, Mr. Davis, that at least one Official will have to be in the room, for security purposes."

"I'll do it," RJ jumped in, and Agatha gave him the stink eye but nodded. He lifted his chin at Grady. "RJ Hicks. Come on, you can use the library. It's quieter."

Ten points to my pseudo-bestie.

I followed him out, very aware of Grady at my back. As I did the exercises my therapist had suggested for when I was on the knife's edge of a panic attack, I took stock of my emotions, dissecting them.

I was attracted to Grady—that was obvious to me—and it was the blissful attraction of a woman to a man. I was worried about the bonding ceremony. I was absolutely terrified of the next Allotment draw and the possibility of getting an Alpha.

Maybe I'd get lucky and get all nice Betas like Grady?

Even as I thought it, I dismissed the idea. They might like to pretend that the Allotment wasn't rigged, but I wasn't stupid. There'd be at least one Alpha in my new Pack, and I just hoped he wasn't an asshole who'd bend me to his will for fun.

The library lived up to its name, except for one glaring problem. All the books were facing spine in, to create a wall of beige. The aesthetic look was probably pleasant, I guess, but it was a literary travesty.

"I don't know who the interior decorator was for this place, but they need to be charged with crimes against books," I grumbled, and Grady laughed.

"Do you like to read?"

"Yep. All my best friends are fictional." I found an armchair beneath the window. It was a really nice room. Maybe now I was out of my bedroom prison, I could spend time down here getting lost in other worlds.

I could almost hear my therapist's voice now. *When you feel an anxiety attack coming on, what do you do?* I'd learned the answer was never, 'Dive into a book about Orcs who steal plain country farm girls and fill them with their seed.'

"What do you like to read?"

Uh-oh. How was I supposed to tell him I liked terrible, spicy novels filled with giant appendages and swoony book boyfriends who pounded pussy like they were born to do nothing else in their life?

I cleared my throat. "Uh, fantasy." My cheeks flushed, and for the first time since his arrival, the sadness that pulled at Grady's features seemed to lift. "I'm sorry about all this." I waved a hand at the house, and at RJ, making the man in question glare. I glared right back at him.

Grady shrugged. "It's not your fault," he murmured, turning the books around one at a time like he was Vanna White.

RJ cleared his throat. "Most people would be honored to be in your position."

"To most people, this will only be an entertaining dream, like being a rockstar or becoming President. This is my life," I snapped. "One that I've had no choice in since I was sixteen."

He had the good grace to look chastised, at least.

Grady's eyes bounced between us. "I *am* honored, Omega. A little part of me might even be happy I was chosen. It's just that I had to leave everything behind." His eyes told me that 'everything' was a person.

"You had a girlfriend?" I thought they exempted

people who had listed themselves as in a committed relationship.

"No. Well, kind of. I had a partner. He's not recognized by the government."

He?

Oh shit.

"You're gay?" That was probably an awkward thing to blurt out, but I was about to be tied to the guy forever by bodily fluids, so there was no point treading gently now. "Not that I care if you are; I'm no bigot. It will probably make the rest of today's events uncomfortable for you, though. I'll... do something. Maybe a simple blood exchange would work? You can't help if you aren't attracted to me." It all spewed out in one embarrassed, run-on sentence.

The tips of Grady's ears went pink. "Uh, no, we don't have to worry about attraction. I'm bisexual, so the bonding won't be a problem. Unless you don't want to..." This had officially become the most awkward conversation of my life, and I'd once had to have the birds and the bees talk with my mother.

Covering my face with my hands, I melted back into the armchair. I peeked out between my fingers, and while Grady looked equally as embarrassed by our conversation, there was an amused curl to his lips too. His soft features made me feel... safer somehow.

Maybe it would be all right.

Chapter Three
Grady

I watched the Omega, Tryst, squirm around on the armchair that seemed to dwarf her. She was a tiny little thing, but man, she was a spitfire. Blonde wavy hair and pouty pink lips, she was the textbook definition of what an Omega should look like, but as soon as she opened her mouth, she blew away the stereotype.

She shifted on her seat again, and the scent of her gusted toward me, making my dick stir. Which made me feel like shit, like I'd forgotten him already. I couldn't even think his name without a stabbing pain in my chest, and I focused on breathing through the pain.

Cutting him off completely was what was best for us both. We couldn't live a half-life of stolen moments. It wasn't fair on either of us, and it wasn't fair on Tryst.

She oscillated wildly from looking like a lost lamb,

to looking like she wanted to scratch someone's eyes out. Her dress was a pretty pale yellow thing that looked more like fancy wrapping paper than a dress.

I was turning the books around on the bookshelf like an idiot, just so I had something to do with my hands. Plus, I liked how pleased she looked when a spine was revealed. I had the feeling not many people ever took her preferences into account.

"So, uh, they didn't tell me much about you on the way over here. Could you tell me a bit about yourself? You're twenty-two?"

So fucking young. Granted, I was twenty-five, but I could have been sixty-five and she would have been stuck with me. The idea burned, and maybe it was her uncertainty that made me feel protective, or maybe it was because I was feeling less than charitable toward the DoDA.

She shrugged. "Yeah. I wanted to be an architect, but that wasn't on the prescribed list of Omega approved courses. So I was studying literature." She gave me a crooked, self-deprecating smile. "Books are more dangerous than a weapon, and far more dangerous than getting a job in a man's profession, but they didn't seem to understand that. So I'm out here reading *Animal Farm* and *Little Women*—even *Boudica,* of all things. Yet they're worried I'll somehow get ideas about independence if I get a 'man's job.' Idiots." She looked over at the Official, who was trying to be unobtrusive in the corner. "No offense."

"None taken."

I had no idea what books she was talking about, but I liked the passionate way she talked about them. I'd never been a big reader, as I preferred building things with my hands. Maybe I'd ask her for book recommendations; it'd be nice to be able to talk to her about this kind of thing. I couldn't imagine spending an eternity with a person who I had nothing in common with, and if that meant I was going to have to read a book for the first time since high school, so be it.

I mean, I'd learned all about famous artists for— No. I needed to forget about him. I was only hurting myself.

Sure, dumbass. It's just that easy, forgetting the man you loved.

I cleared my throat. "It sounds interesting, at least?" I wanted to tell her that once we were mated, she could do whatever she wanted. I'd make sure of it, even if I had to fight every single one of her other mates. I mightn't have a choice, but I could make sure she did from now on.

"It was. They unenrolled me, of course, because it was time for the Allotment, and all my focus needed to be on... well, I'm not sure what. Being pretty? The fucking part is second nature, right? Shouldn't take too much mental energy?"

I blinked at her plain talk, but she was looking at me quizzically, like she was waiting for an answer.

"Uh, sure. I've never bonded another person before. Or been bonded. I mean, I'm Beta. We don't bond. We get married."

Her face folded into sadness again, and I could have kicked myself. "Omegas don't marry, though I like the idea of a wedding." She gave me a tight, fake smile. "I guess the matebond ceremony is kind of like that, but you skip the big dress and the food, and go straight to the wedding night."

I looked over at the Official, and I swear, he was staring at her with the same pity that was welling in my chest. I'd never tell her that I pitied her, though. I pitied all Omegas, though up until this moment, it had been an abstract kind of pity. Like the kind of pity you felt for climate refugees and abused animals. You hated that bad things happened to them, but you didn't go out of your way to think about it unless it directly affected you.

Well, guess what? It affected me now.

"Do you like animals?" Okay, so not my best conversational cue, but hey, I was working with nothing right now. No one had ever prepared me for a conversation with the woman who'd be tied to me for the rest of my life. The woman I'd be expected to have sex with in hours.

I mean, I'd had my fair share of hookups, with little to no 'getting to know' you conversations. But I wasn't about to fuck and forget Tryst O'Sullivan. She was forever, and I couldn't screw this up. I didn't want us both to be miserable forever.

She smiled, a genuine one this time. "Yep! I have a goldfish. Huckleberry Finns." Her smile dimmed. "*Had* a goldfish. I don't know how long this will take, and they didn't give me time to find someone to take him. I gave him a holiday feeder block thing, but I don't think he'll still be alive when I get home."

I shot an accusing look at the Official in the corner, like he'd been the one to drag her away personally. His face was now impassive, and I didn't understand how he could be unaffected by those big, blue eyes that seemed to dominate her face.

I covered her hand with mine, giving her what little comfort I could as a near stranger. "That's a good name for a fish. I'm sure he'll be fine, and then we'll go and get him. I promise." She gave me another smile, but it still didn't reach her eyes. "I don't have a pet, but I do have a garage cat who kept the mice out. Her name's Morris."

"*Her* name is Morris?"

I pulled out my phone and scrolled to the right

photo. It was Morris with four little fluffy lumps around her, which all looked oddly like every tomcat in the area. "She seemed to multiply herself one night last month. Worked out that I knew shit all about sexing cats. I can't pet her, and she scatters if I even go within five feet of her, but she let me rehome those kittens, like she knew I'd find them good families. Now each one of my brothers has a cat, and I got Morris desexed." I showed her the scars on my hand that I got for that humanitarian effort, sucking in a breath as she traced the silver lines with her soft fingertips.

"You did a good thing."

I nodded. "I wouldn't change it, despite the war wounds. My mom or Cor—" I broke off and swallowed hard. "Or my friends will feed Morris. She'll be fine."

She gave me that turned down smile again, this one making it to her eyes. "You're a good man." I didn't miss the relief in her voice, and it made my heart clench in my chest.

"I try to be." I sucked in a deep breath. "I'm going to try to be a good bondmate to you, Tryst. I'm going to try and make you happy, because everyone deserves that. I don't think this was what either of us had in mind when we decided what to be when we grew up, but that doesn't mean we can't make the best of it. Together." I reached out and covered her hand with mine. "So if you want a whole menagerie of pets, get them. You want to be an architect? I'll support you every step of the way. You want to drive a Honda..." I screwed up my nose. "I mean, I wouldn't say no, but you can do better. What I mean is that I'll support you, no matter what decision you make."

She threw back her head and laughed. "I don't even know how to drive!"

My mouth unhinged. Who, in this day and age, didn't know how to drive? It was almost unsafe not to be able to operate a stick shift.

"We'll fix that first thing. I'll teach you." I mean, I'd happily drive her wherever she wanted to go, but she needed her independence, and not to be reliant on me or any person. I'd give her that freedom, even if I couldn't give her my heart.

"I'm sorry that you were torn away from your life, but I'm really glad you got called up first, Grady Davis."

I gave her a crooked grin, reaching out to cover her tiny hand with my much larger, calloused one. "Me too."

Something raced between us, a tingle along my skin, just a prickle of awareness that I recognized was arousal. What was it about her that made me feel like this, when my heart felt like it was breaking?

Maybe the old newspapers had been correct when they talked about the original Omegas, the ones who ran away from home and were all found in hand-dug dens in the woods. Mud Maidens, they'd been dubbed by mainstream media, but others had called them witches. Sometimes they still did, and every now and then, a hate crime committed by extremist groups would show the word 'Witch' emblazoned across a building, or outside an Omega home.

It was bullshit, of course. Witches didn't exist then, and they didn't exist now. But there was no denying the pull of her Omega pheromones on me, even if she wasn't trying. I felt relaxed and happy, like I'd drunk half a bottle of wine under a soft blanket with my lover.

She was like a bandaid on my broken heart.

Chapter Four
Tryst

We spent a few more hours talking, getting to know each other, and I felt myself relaxing a little. I had built up the Allotment in my head, like I was going to be unfortunate enough to get monsters in my draw. But Grady was blissfully sweet. Now, the whole thing didn't seem so scary, because I'd have Grady with me, on my side.

It was selfish as hell, especially considering I could see his heart breaking slowly in front of my eyes. He'd smile and laugh, and then his face would shutter like that was a betrayal. I couldn't help him, though. This was non-optional for us both.

Considering the insanity of the Allotment draw, and the buzz that went around it, the bonding itself was a pretty intimate affair. I went upstairs and changed into something sweet and almost bridal that they'd provided me with. Like this was the equivalent of a planned marriage, rather than a shotgun wedding.

Still, I touched up my makeup, and curled my dirty blonde hair with my fingers. I looked nice, and not nearly as freaked out as I felt.

Fifteen minutes before the ceremony was to take place, there was a knock at the door. "Come in." I was no longer surprised to see RJ. "Did you make a bet and now you have to babysit me permanently? I haven't seen any of the other suits all day."

"Basically, yes. You made an impression when you first arrived, especially when you kicked Denozo in the balls."

I had been a bitch when I arrived. I came in spitting fire over being dragged from my life like it didn't belong to me. Like I was government-issued property. I'd kicked several officials in the dick, and made one cry. Probably Denozo. RJ just looked amused at the memory.

"Was I the prize or the punishment?"

He winked. "You'll never know." His gaze swept over me. "You look nice. Are you ready?"

I flushed a little at the compliment and shrugged, not bothering with shoes. "As ready as I'll ever be, I guess. I can't persuade you to sneak me out of here and cover for me until I'm halfway to Bermuda?"

He jokingly looked like he was considering it, but then shook his head. "Sorry, Omega." His face showed real regret, though. Aw, was RJ softening toward me? He stepped back through the doorway, and swept a hand toward the door. "After you."

I sucked in a big breath. This was it.

Despite the fact I liked Grady, the walk to the living room felt a bit like walking to the gallows.

Researchers had realized fairly early on that Alphas and Omegas had slightly different pheromones or something, both to normal humans and to each other. When an Omega had sex with a Beta, or exchanged any kind of blood or sexual fluids, we essentially bound the Beta to us for life. It was why I'd never had a boyfriend of any kind. A Beta would never risk being permanently tied to someone they couldn't have, just to get their rocks off once or twice.

My heart clenched. With Alphas, it was a little different. They were less likely to accidentally bond a person, though they could tie themselves to Betas and Omegas with blood and bodily fluids. But it also took a bite. A claiming mark of teeth during sex. So there were rarely any accidental bindings with Alphas.

Another reason why Alphas were revered and Omegas were diminished. We played right into the old Jezabel narrative from a thousand years ago.

We stepped into a large room in the back of the

house, and my nerves began to take hold. "Someone has to witness this, right?"

RJ nodded. The idea of Agatha watching me have sex made my stomach roil.

I looked up at him. "Do I get a choice who?"

His whole body tensed. "I think so. As long as it is someone within the DoDA."

"Could you do it?"

I liked RJ. He wasn't cloyingly fanatical like some of the Officials, who fawned over me just because I was an Omega. On the other side of the fence were the Officials who considered me a prized cow, and treated me as such. Then there were those I'd personally put offside, the ones who hated my guts.

RJ treated me like a person, and if someone was going to have to watch me having sex with a stranger, I wanted it to be someone with whom I was at least a little comfortable.

He stared at me for a long moment, like he was trying to decipher what was going on in my head. Finally, he nodded. "You can request it. I'll tell them it's fine by me. You sure you don't want Agatha or one of the other women in there?"

I didn't want anyone at all in there, but the female Officials had been the worst so far. It was like half of them were jealous of me, and the other half were relieved they weren't me. They got to go home to their spouse at the end of the night, knowing they loved each other, and that made them feel guilty.

I didn't like the second group. I looked at them and saw what could have been my life, if it wasn't for a freak accident of birth.

I shook my head. "I'd prefer you. You treat me like more than an Omega."

He let out a long breath. "If that's what you'd like, Tryst."

I was saved from responding by Grady appearing in the room. He had his own attendant, and he looked so handsome. He was in soft gray slacks, and a white button down. His brown hair was styled back haphazardly, and he'd shaved off the stubble, leaving him fresh-faced. He had a square-cut jaw that just made his face look hard, at least until you got to his eyes.

His gaze was like a caress, and there was empathy there. His eyes took in my pretty sky blue dress, and my legs that seemed extra long because it hit me mid-thigh, and then back to my face. He gave me a crooked grin, and I flushed again. He smelled like some kind of woodsy cologne, which instantly made my mouth water.

"You look beautiful."

"Thank you. You look handsome too."

Agatha pushed her way into the room, thrusting

forms and papers at us, watching with eagle eyes as we signed away our lives.

When it was done, and Agatha had gotten all her documents in triplicate, she nodded toward the bed I'd been studiously ignoring in the middle of the room. "It's time to undertake the bonding." She walked to a chair and perched on the edge of the seat, like she was at a circus. The rest of the Officials in the room also moved to the walls, like we were nineteenth century English royalty and the consummation of a marriage was a spectator sport.

"Uh. No. Thank you," I said, making the other woman frown. "I am legally entitled to only have one witness, who may be chosen by me, as long as they have the proper authority from the Department of Designation Associations."

Agatha's frown deepened, and she looked around at her compatriots, as if trying to find out who'd been giving the Omega too much information.

I glared at her. "Sorry, I know how to read. I looked up the laws that directly affected me as soon as I became an Omega." Well, that was only a small lie. I'd been looking for a way out of this whole sham, not for information about bonding night.

Agatha sighed, pinching her nose. "Fine."

I shot a look at Grady, and he nodded encouragingly, giving me permission. "I choose Official Riley-James Hicks."

"Miss O'Sullivan, I would prefer you chose a female Official," she said, like she was patiently explaining something to a child.

I gritted my teeth. "Why? You don't think Official Hicks knows what a vagina looks like? Think he might get confused?"

RJ coughed behind me, like he'd gasped and sucked it in the wrong way.

"Miss O'Sullivan—"

"It's Omega Davis now, since we signed those papers," Grady interrupted. "My Omega has chosen, ma'am. I'd like to get on with the ceremony, and then our lives."

Agatha looked like she wanted to stomp her foot, and she gave RJ an imperious look that probably meant trouble for my new pseudo-friend. Then she stormed out, the rest of the Officials following her, leaving just me, Grady and RJ.

Chapter Five
Tryst

I grimaced at RJ. "I'm sorry if this'll cause problems for you."

He shrugged. "Agatha knows the rules. Let her try and raise hell; there were half a dozen other witnesses here who'll back me up." He looked around the room, his gaze awkwardly bouncing off the bed. "I'm going to go over and sit in the corner. Just... pretend I'm not here. I'll try and give you as much privacy as possible."

Oh sure, he was basically a ghost.

I looked up at Grady, and he was smiling a little. "Good for you." He cleared his throat. "I guess we should, you know..." He cupped my cheek, stepping closer.

I looked up into his warm brown eyes, mesmerized. I'd never kissed a man before. There was a false rumor that even kissing an Omega would create a matebond. No matter that it was bullshit, people tended to avoid me at all costs, but especially when it came to kissing me.

I held my breath as his head dipped, and he swiped his lips across mine. They were softer than I'd imagined, pillowy even. He deepened the kiss a little, and a soft sigh escaped me. But when he sucked my bottom lip between his teeth, I moaned.

The hand not holding my face was firm against my spine, and he gently moved my body toward his until I was pressed right along his front. Grady was fit, his body hard and muscular, but my curves seem to mold to him perfectly.

He kissed me until I was breathless and forced to move away to gulp in oxygen. Probably should get the awkward shit out of the way now.

"I think you should probably know that I've never actually had sex before."

"Not even Alpha lovers?" Grady asked with surprise. The moral standards of society had become more lax for the sake of species survival. Virgins were no longer revered the way they were once upon a time.

No, now it was seen as almost selfish not to fuck around a little.

I shook my head. "Way too bossy. And Betas weren't interested in getting locked down just to ride the tilt-a-whirl, you know?" I grimaced at his shocked expression. "Don't make it weird. Me and Mr. Squeaky, my dildo, have had a grand old time for a lot of years now."

RJ snorted, making me look in his direction. He had his body pointed toward the window, giving us privacy, like he said. Rolling my eyes, I turned back to Grady.

He was suddenly looking nervous as hell, and that kind of made me feel better. Now we could both be anxiety-ridden messes.

Finally, he squared his shoulders, and his eyebrows dropped low into a serious expression. "Don't worry, Tryst. I've got this." A sudden grin lit up his whole face, making my breath freeze in my lungs. He was really, really fucking handsome. How had I forgotten? "By the time we're done, you'll be a certified sex maniac."

He picked me up in his arms, his lips capturing mine again. I guess he'd made a plan of attack, and quite frankly, I was happy to hand over the reins to him. Normally, I clung to control with an iron fist, but I was out of my depth in this room. As he deposited me on the bed, I let go of the fear and anxiety. It would do me no good here.

"Tell me if I do anything you don't like. Doesn't have to be words if it's too, uh, awkward. Just like, I don't know, smack me upside the head or something, okay?"

I laughed at the idea of taking a swing at him during sex, but nodded, because it was so fucking ridiculous.

He kissed over my cheeks and down my neck. "And if you want to stop, say so. I'll deal with Agatha and the Department." He looked over at RJ, his face challenging, but then dropped his eyes back to mine. Reaching behind me, he dragged down the zipper of my dress, pushing it off my shoulders until it pooled around my waist. He made a low noise in his throat as he took in my white lace-covered breasts, then reached around and undid the clasp, sliding my bra off my shoulders too.

I was topless in front of a man for the first time in my life, and it was oddly liberating, the way his eyes ran over me like I was the most beautiful thing he'd ever seen. I lost a little more of the nerves, and the rest disappeared when he moved down over my collarbone and sucked one of my nipples into his mouth.

"Oh my god!" It came out as a shocked squeak.

Don't get me wrong. Masturbation was fun. But I wasn't endowed enough to suck my own nipples and let me tell you, I'd been missing out.

Grady moved to the other breast, and I buried my fingers in his soft hair. He pushed me backward until my shoulders hit the mattress, then he tapped my hips. I raised my ass and let him wiggle off my dress, leaving me in nothing but strips of black lace that were masquerading as underwear. Mismatched lingerie had felt like a 'fuck you' to the Department this morning, but now I kind of wished I was wearing the matching white ones, like I somehow had my life together.

One quick look at Grady's face told me I could be wearing granny panties and he wouldn't have given a damn.

His eyes ran over my body, like he didn't know where to taste first. He crawled back between my knees and kissed his way down my stomach. "Let me show you what Mr. Squeaky can't do," he said softly as he hovered over me. The feel of his breath between my thighs made my breath hitch. He ran his face over my lace-covered core, his nose nudging my clit and making my thighs clench. Hooking his fingers under the waistband of the lace, he tugged them down, pulling them off my legs until I was completely naked before him.

"Why am I naked but you're still fully dressed?" My voice was rough, and Grady looked up from where he was gazing at my body like a just-revealed birthday cake to raise an eyebrow at me. He sat up and slowly started to strip off his clothes. I wondered briefly if he moonlighted as a stripper, because watching his fingers nimbly open his buttons, exposing the hard expanse of his chest, was an erotic experience.

Finally, he slipped the shirt from his shoulders and let it fall to the ground beside my dress. Losing the slow, methodical movements, he thrust his pants down his legs like they were on fire.

He was hard. And naked.

And hard.

I swallowed the lump in my throat as he took his dick in his hand and stroked it once, letting me look as much as I liked. When my eyes finally shot back to his face, he smiled softly. He kneeled between my thighs again, lifting one of my knees until he could hook it over his shoulder, and sliding his hands beneath me, cupping my ass in his hands with a soft squeeze.

"Remember to tell me to stop if you don't like anything," he said, inches from my fucking vagina. Honestly, the word stop was not even in my vocabulary right now.

He swooped in, and I could only assume he was giving me a test run, like he was finding out what I liked by trying a little bit of everything. He did long strokes, quick flicks of his tongue, eating me out while his nose bumped the Devil's Doorbell. All of them drove me crazy, but when he moved up and sucked my clit, I thought I saw Jesus. Apparently, the wrong person was answering the doorbell these days.

I let out a sound that would have set off a car alarm, and he pulled back, his eyes wide and concerned. I grabbed his head before he could move away.

"No, don't stop," I gasped. "I'm sorry, I'm sorry, but please..." I dragged him back toward my core, and the panicked look on his face turned into something inherently more smug. He sucked my clit again, and I tried to swallow down the noise, but it was too much. My orgasm hit me like I was being electrocuted, and I bowed under the force of it.

Grady chased my orgasm with his tongue until his face was wet, and I was panting as I dragged him up my body. He kissed me, spreading my come from his cheeks to mine. His cock nudged between my folds, and something inside me came alive at the sensation. At how close I was to something I'd been yearning for, but was too stupid to realize I was missing.

"Please, Grady. Now," I gasped.

He kissed me softly. "Hold on, baby. Remember what I said, okay?" He rubbed his cock up and down my slit, and each time the head stroked over my swollen clit, I felt like I was about to leave my body. "Fast and hard, to get it out of the way like ripping off a bandaid? Or slow?" His jaw was clenched like he was holding himself back, and his eyes were luminous pools of desire.

"Fast and hard."

He nodded and thrust into me in one quick movement, burying himself balls deep. I gasped again as his body stretched mine, and he stayed still, letting me acclimate until I was rolling against him, wanting him to move. He dragged back out before slamming in again. And again.

I was moaning something incoherent—maybe it was his name, maybe it was mine, though that would be weird—as I clung to his back like he was my lifeline. He moved inside me, hitting places that I, and Mr. Squeaky, could never.

He was still kissing me when he snaked an arm under my back and rolled us until I was on top, looking down at him. He was giving me control, and I smiled at him. Fate had been kind, giving me Grady first. I held his eyes as I rolled my hips, trying to find that rhythm that I was just supposed to instinctively know. He dropped his hands to my hips, helping me move, until he was discovering places inside me that made my eyes roll back in my head as another orgasm shook me. But Grady didn't stop, and neither did I.

I rode his dick like that pony I'd always wanted, until we were both panting, heaving messes. I threw my head back, but halfway up, I caught sight of RJ on the other side of the room. I'd almost forgotten he was there.

But not anymore. Every vestige of the privacy he'd

been trying to give me was gone, and he watched me with open hunger on his face. He was staring at me like I was a work of art, or a cake fresh out of the oven or something.

Logically, I knew I should be offended that he was so intensely watching this intimate moment, but instead, I found myself clenching around Grady, making him moan. I met and held RJ's eyes, grinding down harder, until Grady's thumb pressed into my clit and sent me over the edge yet again. My eyes slammed close as I rode the powerful orgasm, my body shaking until I fell onto his chest. Gripping my hips, Grady held me still as he pounded up inside me, coming with a curse.

I felt the bond snap into place on the tail end of the pleasure.

Our respective orgasms left us wrecked. I just lay on his chest, and his arms circled around my back, holding me tight. We were silent for a long time, and I vaguely heard RJ stand and leave. He didn't acknowledge the fact he'd eye fucked me good.

Grady rolled us over until we were both on our sides, facing each other. "I know Omegas don't do the marriage thing the way Betas do, plus you barely know me. Just know that I promise to love, honor and protect you to the best of my ability, Tryst O'Sullivan, for as long as we both shall live."

Emotion welled in my throat, and I whispered out a strangled, "Me too."

He huffed a little laugh, dragging me up his body until I was splayed over his chest, my head tucked beneath his chin. He reached for the blankets, pulling them up over our naked bodies. For the first time since I'd arrived at this house a week before, I let emotion take over. My tears slid over my cheeks, and Grady held me tight through it all.

Chapter Six
Tryst

Apparently, the whole first bonding thing was a little bit anticlimactic for the Officials, because over the following days, half the workers left, leaving only a skeleton crew to make sure I didn't abscond.

It was fine by me. I was happy that I didn't continually feel like a bug on display. But I was a little hurt that RJ was one of the people who left, without even a goodbye. He'd just watched me fuck Grady and then disappeared. I told myself he was actually an Official, not a real friend, so he didn't owe me anything. He barely knew me, and I barely knew him.

I was sitting in the back sunroom with Grady, an Official watching me carefully from the corner in case we were about to make a run for the border. He kept sighing and looking at his watch.

"You know, you can go and do your other tedious jobs, which I'm sure are more riveting than watching me drink coffee. I'm resigned to my lot now; I'm not about to make a break for it. I promise." I crossed my heart messily, and the guy narrowed his eyes at me in annoyance.

"I don't care either way, except I'd lose my job if you fucked off. I think this Omega worship is bullshit."

My hackles rose, and I glared at the aging guy. His dark hair was streaked with gray, and his cheeks were beginning to droop into jowls.

"Worship?" I said incredulously, but Grady was already standing.

"You better watch your mouth, before I close it for you permanently," he growled in a low voice, looming over the pen-pushing douche.

"Whatever, *Beta*," the man snapped back, which was dumb since they were both Betas, but Grady took a threatening step toward him. I grabbed Grady's arm and dragged him back into the house, all the while silently fuming.

The fucking audacity of the man to assume that I *wanted* this. Like it was me being high-maintenance, rather than them basically stealing my life from me, making me prance around in this three-ring circus.

I realized quickly that Grady had led me to his room and not mine. It was basically identical in layout, though the decor was a little more masculine. On the dresser was a group picture, and I found myself drawn to it.

There were two older people and half a dozen younger ones, all crowded tightly together to fit into the frame. Everyone was smiling, and I spotted the similarities between several of the men, with the same brown hair and square faces. Definitely brothers.

Only one stood out. He had blond hair that was long at the top and short at the sides, a wicked grin stretching his cheeks. Clearly not a brother, so that must mean... "Is this your partner?"

Grady stopped behind me and cleared his throat. He picked up the photograph, and the look of longing on his face broke my heart again. I held myself stiff, feeling guilty despite their separation not being my fault. How did Grady not hate me and everything I stood for?

As if he could feel my thoughts—and maybe he could now we were bonded—he curled a hand around my waist and pulled me back into his body. For a moment, I held myself taut, but eventually the soothing presence of the matebond had me relaxing into his arms.

"Yes, that's Corrin." He put the frame back on the dresser. "That's my mom and her partner Terrence, and those are my brothers." He pointed to two men on the left side of his mom. "And these are my step-brothers." He indicated the other two smiling men who looked so similar, I'd never have known they weren't blood relatives.

I didn't comment about the amount of sons. It was too common these days to have only boys. It was considered miraculous to have a girl baby, especially one who survived to adulthood.

"They look nice." I ran my finger over the smiling blond man. "He looks nice."

Grady snorted. "He's a fucking shithead. He's mischievous, and has this dry sense of humor that could cut you if you didn't know him. Sometimes I don't think he ever grew up, or at least he's not trying to." His smile was wistful. "He loved hard, though. Once he was sure I was right for him, he dug in his heels and laid his heart out there for me. You never have to doubt if Corrin loves you."

I laid my hands over his, trying to blink back the tears. "I'm sorry I stole you away from him." The more I stared at that handsome face, the more determined I felt. "I'll find a way to get him back for you, I promise."

Squeezing me tightly, he kissed the top of my head. "He'd like you, I think. You'd definitely like him. He's impossible to hate." He cleared his throat again and pulled me away. "Come on, Tryst. Let's take a nap so I can enjoy this time before I have to share you with someone else."

The reminder of the upcoming second draw made anxiety trickle back through my veins. I was happy with just Grady. What if next time I wasn't so lucky?

With the next Allotment day approaching, all the Officials who had been gone during the week returned. I didn't really understand what skills they brought to the whole event, but I guess even bureaucrats needed other emotional support bureaucrats.

It also meant the return of RJ.

I was finishing off my outfit, Grady lying on my bed in his sweats looking kind of delicious, when there was a knock at the door. Expecting it to be Official Douche-Knuckle from the sunroom the other day, I almost gasped when I saw RJ. He was in his normal suit, but his face looked guarded.

I gritted my teeth, feeling kind of hurt all over again. "Official Hicks. Nice to see you back."

RJ tilted his chin. "Thank you, Omega. It's good to be back. Unfortunately, I got called away to the Head Office."

I frowned. What the hell did that mean?

RJ didn't allow me to ask, though. "Would you like to see the draw?"

I shrugged. "Okay, why not?"

It wasn't a particularly exciting thing really, unless you were the unlucky person who got called up. I looked over at Grady, and he looked pensive. I guess a week ago, he'd been that unlucky person.

"Did you watch the draw last week?"

He shook his head. "No, I had the transmission on a 1978 Mustang to replace. First thing I knew about it was my brother calling me up and telling me. We have each other's social security numbers memorized, you know." He shrugged. "Then the DoDA turned up, explained that I was Allotted, gave me twelve hours to pack up some stuff and then I was shipped here."

"They didn't even let you say goodbye to your family?"

He shook his head. "They don't live close by, and besides, it's not forever. Just a couple of months at most. Then we can go and visit."

I nodded, trying not to think of my own family. We'd never been close, though I thought they'd loved me once. I guess it was hard going from having a miracle daughter to having an Omega teenager. Knowing she was no longer yours—she was the property of the US government. All the hopes and dreams you'd instilled in them to be a ballerina or a paleontologist went out the window with an Omega designation.

Grady wrapped his arm around my shoulder and smiled. "Let's go and find out who's joining us, hey?"

We made it to the living room, where half a dozen people were on laptops, someone was talking on the phone over in the corner, and generally speaking, the whole place was a hive of activity. It looked like a space launch rather than the televisation of a stuffy-looking man pressing a button and watching spinning numbers appear on a screen.

A countdown sat in the corner of the broadcast, and I watched it warily. I cuddled close to Grady's side on the couch, unable to tell if he was supporting me or needed the support himself. We were silent, just watching the numbers decrease rhythmically. RJ perched on the other side of the room, his eyes bouncing around at everyone doing their job.

Finally, the countdown turned red.

Ten.

Nine.

Eight.

Was it hot in here?

Three.

Two.

One.

A long number flashed on the screen. No other identifying information. Just the number.

"Kudos to your brothers for remembering all those damn numbers," I whispered to Grady.

He leaned close so his lips brushed against my ear. "Trick is to only remember the last three numbers and then panic."

There was a flurry of activity, as people tapped away furiously on their laptops, checking the person attached to the number. Finally, RJ presented me with a nail in my coffin. Well, a tablet with my next bond-mate emblazoned on the screen.

"This is Remzi Hart. Your second mate, but your first Alpha. Congratulations, Tryst Hart."

Chapter Seven
Tryst

Remzi Hart was an Alpha. And like most Alphas, he'd climbed to the very top of his chosen field. In Remzi's case, it was technology. Most of our technology had failed when things like power stations shut down after the Last War, thanks to nuclear bombs having been dropped across the world as countries fought in ways that were completely unnatural.

The following year was a dark one in our history, but eventually, humanity marched on. Green power grids focused on lighting houses and running homes, and advancing technology fell to the wayside for another fifty years.

Until people like Remzi Hart came along. They managed to restore cell towers, and with them, mobile communication. With that technology came the internet, which had been buzzing along just fine in other countries that weren't so hard-hit as the US. When we were once again connected with the outside world, life got just a little less barbaric. Remzi Hart was lauded as one of the saviors of civilization. He was richer than a god, and treated as such.

And now he was going to be my bondmate.

I rolled over onto my back in Grady's bed. Sensing my nerves, he'd brought me back to his room to sleep. Well, to have slow, lazy, comforting sex filled with three orgasms and then to sleep. Grady had been right; he had turned me into a bonafide sex addict. Bless his cock.

I mean heart.

We were both nervous about tomorrow. Remzi Hart was an Alpha, and they were intimidating at the best of times. But an Alpha of Remzi's standing? He was going to be a self-important prick, and I'd be forced to lay down on my back for him.

Grady's arm wrapped around my waist, and he pulled me tightly back against his body. "You're thinking too loud," he mumbled against my hair. "Go to sleep." His thumb rubbed over the exposed skin of my hip gently, and I sighed. I closed my eyes, trying to force myself to sleep. There was no point in borrowing tomorrow's trouble yet. Besides, this time I'd have

Grady beside me, and I knew enough about my first bondmate to know he wouldn't take my mistreatment lying down.

I focused on Grady's soft breathing and soon enough, I dozed off too, dreaming of a faceless Alpha who made me submit. The weird thing was... I liked it. Even though I couldn't see his face, I felt the burn of his gaze.

I woke up with a start, sucking in air. I took a moment to orientate myself, my face pressed close to Grady's on the pillow, his body warm against my back.

Wait, what?

The eyes looking down at me weren't Grady's. There was a stranger inches from my face. Wide awake now, I opened my mouth to scream.

His hand whipped out, covering my mouth. "Hey, shhh," he whispered desperately. "I'm sorry, I didn't mean to scare you. Hush."

My hands reached behind me, grabbing at Grady. He rocketed up behind me, his gaze bouncing around the pitch-black room for an intruder, until they dropped to me.

"Get the fuck away—" He gasped. "*Corrin?* What the fuck are you doing here?" he hissed, grabbing the other man's wrist and pulling his hand away from my mouth.

I scrambled away from the man in the bed with us,

but now that I wasn't so panicked, I recognized his face from the photo on Grady's dresser. Still, I jumped out of bed, moving to the other side of the room and turning on the floor lamp in the corner. I looked between the two men, my eyes sticking on Grady's face. There was relief, and fear, and joy, then anger, all in quick succession.

Corrin sat up on his knees, not moving from the bed. "I didn't mean to scare you, Omega. I'm sorry," he said, looking genuinely repentant. "There was no other way to get in touch with him, and I was in the bed before I realized you were in here too, but by then it was too late."

"For fuck's sake, Corrin, they could throw you in *jail* for this," Grady whisper-yelled, but his fingers reached out to brush the hand of his lover, like he couldn't help himself.

"What was I supposed to do? You said goodbye, then blocked my number." I could hear the pain in Corrin's voice. "I had to basically beg your mom for any information she had—which was not very much, by the way. Call your mom. She's worried about you," he chastised gently. "Then I had to wait it out and follow what I assumed were boring government sedans, hoping that they led to you and not some homeowner who'd call the cops on me for trespassing. Honestly, I should be Sherlock Holmes, all because I love you too fucking much to let you go like this."

Grady darted his eyes to me. Well, this was awkward. "I'll just go..."

It was Corrin who got up and grabbed my hands. "No, stay. Please." He turned to Grady. "Did you hear me? I love you, Grady Davis. More than I could ever hope to love another person. I refuse to give you up just because the government took away your choices." His blue eyes were fierce as he moved his gaze to me. "Yours too, Omega. I say we take those choices right back."

Grady was off the bed and in front of us. "You're talking crazy. There's nothing we can fucking do. Go home; find someone else who can love you." His voice broke a little. "I'll never forgive myself if you end up in prison because you chased me here. This is out of our hands."

Corrin shook his head. "You're right. It's out of our hands—but it isn't out of hers." He tugged me forward, his face softening a little. "Sorry, Omega, to put you on the spot like this. But *you* can take the power back. Take the choices back."

"Tryst. My name is Tryst," I squeaked out.

"Pretty name." He smiled, and it was like I'd been slapped. He was fucking beautiful. How had Grady managed to drag himself away from this man? "If you bonded with me, they'd be forced to let me stay. They're hardly going to throw you in prison for breaking the rules, right?" He snorted at the preposterousness of it. "If you bonded me, I would get to be with the man I love, Grady would be happy, and we could all say a giant fuck you to the Department of Designation Associations."

Grady hissed. "Corrin, no. You can't ask that of her."

Corrin's face was fiery. "Why? How is it different from what the Department is *making* her do? At least I'm asking, and she gets to make a fucking choice here." He squeezed my hand. "If you say no, I'll respect your decision. I refuse to be as bad as them." He hesitated. "But I really hope you say yes. It would be a point in the favor of love, rather than this farce." He waved a hand around the room, or the house, or society in general; I didn't know exactly.

I stared at him, at his angular face and soft white blond hair. He looked like a fae from a children's tale. Or a smutty fantasy novel.

"But you're gay."

Corrin threw back his head and laughed. "Sweet Tryst, I don't believe in labels, but I promise that bonding with you won't be a hardship." His eyes raked over me, obvious desire in their depths.

I flushed bright red, and gently pulled my fingers

from his. I couldn't think when he was touching me, looking down at me with those electric blue eyes. I dropped my eyes to the ground, desperately trying to corral my whirling thoughts. Corrin was right; he wasn't asking anything that the DoDA wasn't already demanding of me.

I looked up at him from beneath my lashes. It wouldn't be a hardship sealing the bond either. His body was sleek and muscular, and he had the sharp cheekbones of a fashion model, which might have made him look cruel if not for the imploring expression in his eyes. But it was the passion with which he spoke, the fierce tilt to his lips, that made him so damn alluring.

I would get shit for this, I knew it, but I kind of wanted to take back a little control. If I could make Grady happy in the process, that'd be even better.

I looked between them. "Okay. If it's what Grady wants too. But it has to be tonight. My—uh, *our* new bondmate is an Alpha and..." I paused. People thought all Omegas were weak and happiest on their back, so I was loath to generalize Alphas in that way too, but... "It will be one more person to ask permission. Better to present them with a *fait accompli*."

Corrin looked at Grady, whose wide eyes looked worried. I could see the cogs turning in his head, weighing and measuring all the possible outcomes.

"Are you sure?" he whispered, and from the tremulous note of hope in his tone, I knew his answer would be yes. I nodded, and he reached out, grabbing my waist and pulling me to his chest. He buried his face in my hair, squeezing me tight. "Thank you."

Pulling back, he kissed me softly, and I had a feeling that maybe it was a test for Corrin. Grady's lips were soft, and the kiss was wonderful, but I could feel his mind elsewhere, watching his lover for hints of jealousy.

Instead, Corrin clapped his hands together. "Think of all the amazing threesomes we can have!" Tugging me softly from Grady's arms, he clutched my cheeks and kissed me hard. A desperate kind of kiss, filled with emotion. So different from the way Grady kissed me, but no less amazing.

He reached into his pocket, pulling out a pocket knife. Opening it up, he held out his hand to mine. "We could have sex, but I kind of think it's barbaric making you sleep with a man you've just met. Treating it like doing the dishes or putting on your tie to go to work. Just another step in the process." He scoffed, his nose screwing up in distaste, though I wasn't sure if it was at the idea of ties, dirty dishes or having sex with strangers. "You should have a chance to get to know me." He slit open the palm of his hand. "I've done my reading. This works just as well at binding us together."

My brain was stuttering on one key point. "You don't want to have sex with me?" Immediately, I wanted to slap my own forehead. Of all the questions I had, why did that one have to come out of my mouth?

He stroked my hair back from my forehead. It was a riotous mess from tossing and turning all night. "That's not it at all. I'd happily lay you down on that bed and fuck you until you feel like we're meant to be together—if that's what you want. In fact, I can hardly wait to share you with Grady." He held my hand in his bleeding one, slicing my palm open as gently as possible. "But what I really want is for you to get to know me, to learn to want me, and maybe one day, you'll even love me. If we're already breaking the rules, you should have the real experience, Tryst."

I watched the blood well in my palm, and Corrin turned it gently until he was clasping my hand in his, our fingers intertwined. I could feel the warm dampness of our blood combining, the sharp tang of it hanging in the air.

Corrin put his finger under my chin, tilting my face up until I was forced to meet his eyes. "I won't ever be able to thank you enough for this, for giving me Grady back. But I promise I'll be a good mate to you. I will love, honor and protect you, because you're sweet and selfless, and so fucking beautiful. You won't regret this."

I didn't think he'd make me regret it, but it wasn't just Corrin who had the ability to make my life miserable.

Chapter Eight
Tryst

"I'm calling the police. This is against the law. Against protocol!" Agatha gasped, like breaking protocol was worse than murder.

I narrowed my eyes at her. "Go for it. I'm excited to hear how you explain security so lax that an unknown Beta could climb right through my window and into bed with me. Luckily, it was Corrin, and not someone with worse intentions."

The Official's face got so red, I thought she might be stroking. I pushed out some of those fabled Omega pheromones, the ones that soothed troubled Alphas.

"Agatha, I'm sorry. I got caught up in the moment; I promise it won't happen again. The law allows for me to bring in any bondmates I'd made before the Allotment, so how about we all pretend that Corrin is a previous bond, we'll sweep the rest under the rug, call it a computer error, and move on with everything?" I cajoled.

I could see Agatha's brain working overtime, her eyes moving around her office, taking in everyone crowding the room. Grady, Corrin and I stood in front of her desk like naughty children, with RJ over by the door. He was our designated guard for the morning, and I was already happy it wasn't Official Douche-Knuckle who had to oversee this.

Agatha's cold eyes met mine. "Fine, Omega. But you *will* be more cooperative." I bit my tongue to stop myself from snarking back. She wanted to think she had the power here? Fine, I could pretend to be docile.

"Perfectly obedient," I agreed, with only a touch of sarcasm.

Obviously, Agatha was oblivious to sarcasm, because she gave me a triumphant smile. "Good. Now, your *real* new mate should be here soon, so I suggest you go and change into something a little more presentable."

I looked down at my leggings and oversized hoodie. If I hadn't just agreed to be docile, I would have worn this outfit just to spite her. Instead, I gave her a fake smile and hotfooted it out of the office, Grady and Corrin right behind me.

It wasn't until we were all back in my room that I let out the low growl. "I don't want you to get the wrong impression of me and my manners, but that woman is a cunt," I whispered, making a surprised laugh burst from Grady's chest.

Corrin nodded his agreement. "She looked like someone pissed in her Wheaties, that's for sure." He reached out and grabbed me up into his arms, spinning me around.

Corrin was touchy-feely, which made my Omega happy. She enjoyed his constant petting and hugs, without the expectation of it turning into something more.

He put me back on my feet, kissing my head. "I can't believe we pulled it off."

"Me either," RJ grumped from the corner.

He'd pulled a gun I hadn't even known he possessed when he found Corrin in bed with me and Grady this morning. It had taken a whole load of fast talking to get him to not shoot my new bondmate.

"Okay, everybody out. I have to get changed to meet our new Alpha." This whole thing with Corrin had distracted me from the fact that this morning, I would be bonded to a new mate. The nerves rushed back as soon as the guys left the room. I felt sick to my stomach, and my heart was thudding. I could hear RJ on the other side of the door, keeping guard, and I felt a little better with him there, which was ridiculous.

I stripped down quickly and had a shower,

cleaning the scent of my bondmates from my skin, just for a little while. I had heard stories of Alphas and their aggressiveness, as well as the knot they used during sex which kept you locked painfully against them. My body clenched at the thought, and it was disconcerting that my head and my vagina were so out of sync on the idea of an Alpha.

I didn't want to set my new Alpha off. We'd get the bond out of the way, and then maybe I could avoid him. We could be bonded without having to be in each other's pockets all the time, right?

Like right now, I could feel both Corrin and Grady in the other room, their bonds to me faint but enough that I could feel that they were happy. Actually, I thought they might be a little more than happy, since I could feel an echo of lust coursing through our connection.

I dressed in another pretty outfit that had appeared in my closet, this one in black. It had tiny red roses and hugged my body. It was sexy and mysterious, and far less bridal than the one I'd worn for Grady. This was something you'd wear to a funeral.

I did my hair and makeup carefully, wanting to look as put together and confident as possible. I wasn't a weak-willed Omega ready to bend to an Alpha's rule, no matter what Agatha wanted.

A knock on the door told me my time was up.

Grady stuck his head in, and his eyes hooded immediately with lust. "You look like sex on a stick." He moved further into the room. "We can be late, right? Because I want to push that sexy little dress up over your hips, bend you over and make you scream my name."

I grinned, the boost of confidence chasing away my nerves. "Well, I guess it would be one way for our new bondmate to learn who you are." He ran his hands down my back, over the heart-shaped cut-out of the dress, until his palms landed on my ass, gripping it tightly.

Corrin appeared behind him, his eyes wide. "So fucking pretty. Jesus, you look like a wet dream," he groaned, adjusting himself. Well, at least I knew he hadn't been lying about finding me attractive.

A throat clearing at the door had us all turning to look at RJ. "Let's go. Remzi Hart is about five minutes out," he said in a bored tone, looking at Grady with raised brows. "Unless you want to greet him dick-deep in his new Omega?"

Grady looked annoyed, then gave a lopsided grin in my direction. "I kind of do. He's stealing my name from you today. I wanted you to be Tryst Davis for a little longer." He sighed. "But that would probably just cause drama. Let's go, baby girl, before I lose all my common sense."

I shoved my feet into heels, and kissed both Grady and Corrin. This time, when I left my room, I had them at my back. I wasn't alone anymore. Past me, from like two weeks ago, would never have believed I'd be happy to be bonded to two men.

We were back in the small formal living room, and the energy in the crowded space was electric. This was different than with Grady, because Remzi Hart was some celebrity Alpha, not a nobody mechanic from some backwater town. I wouldn't exchange Grady for a hundred millionaire Alphas, though.

Agatha appeared, looking officious and perfectly coiffed, like she was the one meeting her mate today. She eyed me critically, but apparently I passed her appearance test. "Bondmates, please wait in the other room. Your introductions will come later, before the bonding ceremony."

Corrin looked like he was a second away from telling Agatha to stuff it, but I gave him a reassuring look. Grady also looked torn, but his eyes drifted to RJ, and something silent passed between them. RJ gave a barely imperceptible nod, and that seemed to appease Grady.

He strode over to me, giving me a hard kiss on the lips. "Call me if you need me—I don't care what anyone says." He gave Agatha the stink eye as he straightened.

Corrin came over, kissing both of my cheeks and then my lips gently. "It's going to be okay," he soothed, though how he could know that was beyond me.

The sound of a car pulling up in the driveway had my heart racing. My other mates were hustled from the room, and I rubbed my sweat-coated hands on my dress. My skin felt hot and cold, and I could swear I felt my every hair follicle stand on end. My body felt achy, like I had the flu or something; it was hard to describe. Nerves, right? Maybe I was having a panic attack.

I smelled him before I saw him. I knew that sometimes Alphas had a particular scent to Omegas, but normally it served as a warning. It would smell sour, or bad, and then I'd know to run the other way before we crossed paths.

But not Remzi Hart. He smelled like liquid sex appeal, somehow earthy and sweet. Delicious and terrifying. When he stepped into the room, his eyes found me instantly.

His picture didn't do him justice, though that might have been because his presence was like a caress. Or a slap on the ass. He was imposing, his shoulders broad but not overly muscular. His skin was golden and smooth, the kind you wanted to taste on your tongue.

"Mr. Hart, Alpha, it is my pleasure to welcome you

here. Here is the Omega's file, and my card. I've written my personal extension on the back. Please, feel free to call if you have any issues or enquiries," Agatha gushed, but I barely heard her. I was ensnared in his gray eyes, unable to look away.

He strode across the room, ignoring Agatha completely. Reaching down, he pulled me to my feet. He dragged me close and buried his face in the crook of my shoulder, his teeth scraping up the column of my neck, making me shudder.

And then my body cramped, making me bow in half.

"What the fuck is this?" he growled, and I stilled. There was anger in his voice, and my Omega whined. His sudden rejection meant something to the Omega, like a stab in the heart. Suddenly, it was the Omega who was in control of my emotions, of my body, as I whined and curled closer. Remzi didn't push me away, though he wasn't looking at me anymore. His eyes bounced around the room. "I asked a question."

There was that Alpha command they were always talking about.

Agatha stepped forward. "I'm unsure what you mean, Alpha?" she squeaked.

"This Omega is almost in heat. If a weaker Alpha had been chosen, and arrived a day later, she would have been torn apart."

Shock played in the back of my brain. I was going into heat? Normally that didn't happen for a few more years, which was why they held these stupid Allotments so early in our lives.

Agatha stuttered, grabbing a tablet and letting her hands fly across it. "None of her hormone panels came up with anything indicating—"

As if to confirm Remzi's words, there was a stabbing pain in my abdomen. A delicious pain that made my body heavy. I whined again, the logical side of my brain horrified at the noises I was making. I clutched at the Alpha in front of me, and he made a soothing noise in his chest, his eyes still cool despite the soft stroke of his hand up and down my spine.

"Hush, Omega. I will take care of you, after I take care of these *people*."

Suddenly, I didn't really care about that. I felt too hot, and I was starting to sweat.

Remzi growled low in his throat. "She needs a nest. I need to meet her other mate. Formalities can wait."

"Mates," RJ supplied, his eyes bouncing over me worriedly. "She has two other bondmates."

Remzi's gaze snapped to him, sizing him up as a threat. "The file said one."

Agatha cleared her throat, drawing back Remzi's gaze. "Filing error." She looked at one of the other Officials and started snapping orders. "Set up a nest. Hydration—"

I tuned them out. The only things I cared about were Remzi and my bondmates. Was this meant to happen so quickly?

I grabbed hold of the connections between me and the guys, and tugged hard. Part of me heard a shout from the other room, and then Grady was there, Corrin right behind him. Grady only took a second to size up Remzi before dragging me from the Alpha's arms and into his.

I panted, climbing Grady's body until I was wrapped around him, my legs locked behind his back. He looked completely perplexed, but held me tightly to his body. "What happened? Tryst, baby, are you okay?"

All I could do was sob pitifully.

I could feel the Alpha's eyes on my back. "My name is Remzi Hart, your new Alpha bondmate. I believe our Omega is in heat."

Chapter Nine
Tryst

How could this be happening? I buried my face in Grady's neck, his familiar scent easing the burning flood of lust in my body. I guess for a few days I'd been feeling lethargic, but I'd assumed it was the stress of the first Allotment, as well as being cooped up inside for so long. I'd never even contemplated that it might be the beginning of the heat.

I rolled my core against Gradys's stomach, making him groan. Remzi was taking charge, ordering the Officials around like they were underlings and not authorized members of the US government. That was the danger of Alphas—they stole your free will. Yet right at this moment, I couldn't give a fuck. I just wanted him to ease the pain.

"Here, I'll take her for a bit," Corrin murmured to

Grady. One mate passed me to the other, and my body curved around Corrin's like it knew him intimately. I knew his scent, and my Omega liked it. Everything was heightened right now, and I wanted him. I wanted to know more than just his scent—I wanted to know what he felt like inside me.

"Corrin, please," I moaned as another wave of pleasure-pain flowed through my limbs.

With a groan, Corrin walked me to the closest wall, pressing me into it. He was slighter than Grady, but just as strong. "What do you need, Omega? I'll give you anything." His tone seemed as urgent as mine.

I rolled my body over his, knowing what I wanted, but unsure if I could form the words. With a groan, he thrust his hips between my thighs. I shouted at the grind of his body against my clit, and he stilled.

"No, no, don't stop," I said desperately, clawing at his back to make him move again. "Again, *please*." I needed the relief. I needed to be covered in my Pack, needed them to fuck me and chase away the hurt.

Corrin was helpless against my pleas, his hands clutching my ass cheeks as he ground into me again, creating that beautiful friction that tipped the pain into pleasure.

Yes. More, more, more.

Distantly, I heard the hushed whispers of people in the room, and I knew we weren't alone. Remzi appeared beside Corrin, his eyes burning as they took in my wild thrashing. "Come, Omega. We have made you a nest." He looked down at Corrin. "Pass her to me. Anything you have with your scent on it needs to go to her nest. Bedding. Pillows. Anything soft. Her skin probably feels like sandpaper right now." He cleared his throat. "Grab some food while you can. This can be a long, exhausting process."

Corrin looked like he was about to protest giving me up, but eventually he handed me to the Alpha. Remzi's scent wrapped around me and I moaned. This was what I needed.

"I will take care of you now, Omega," he rumbled softly. His face was pulled tight, his eyes morphing into a cool, uninterested gray. The part of my brain that wasn't clouded with lust and pain wondered if this was a chore to him, but the Omega didn't care. She knew what she wanted, and she wanted it right now.

Corrin moved ahead of us, and Remzi carried me like I weighed nothing. He was big, bigger than Grady and Corrin, his shoulders so wide that I could feel the flex of his muscles as he moved.

I needed to touch his skin, to have it pressed against mine. Instinctively, I knew that would make me feel better. I needed his knot more though, and I whined at the thought of him inside me, stretching me, filling me until I thought I'd split apart.

He groaned, his arm clutching me close to stop my grinding. "Be still, Omega." It was the first loss of control I'd seen from him, the first hint of pleasure I'd wrung from him. "Soon we will be out from the watchful eyes of these *people*," he sneered, "and I can make you come over and over on my cock."

I whimpered at his words, and licked his collarbone that I'd somehow managed to expose. Oh, he was now missing some buttons on his crisp, white shirt. My bad.

He walked into my bedroom, and my Omega whined again. This wasn't right. It was too bright. Too open. I frowned, suddenly wanting to cry, my emotions going haywire inside me.

Then Grady was there, moving his bedding into my walk-in robe. It would be tight with all three of my mates in there, and I almost purred at the thought of them all being in reaching distance.

Corrin followed him in with some fluffy throws and laid them on top. His hand stroked down my spine. "Let's get you out of that dress, baby girl."

I nearly purred at the idea of being naked, no longer being restricted by the tight fabric of my pretty dress. Remzi dropped me to my feet, and Corrin made quick work of unzipping the dress, peeling it from my overheated skin. He seemed to hesitate, but then flicked open the clasp of my bra as well. The warm gusts of his breath cooled on my overheated skin, making me pant.

I'd thought being naked would make it better, but somehow it made it worse. I arched back against Corrin, rubbing my ass against his dick.

He groaned, grabbing my hips. "Tryst, sweetheart, I made you a promise." He sounded like he was in pain. "I wanted you to fall for me organically, without all this."

I spun in his hands and gripped his jaw hard, kissing him like I was stealing the oxygen from his lungs. He grunted, kissing me back just as hard, before sliding his hand between us and into my panties, his fingers brushing my needy, overheated folds.

"Yes," I hissed. "Please, Corrin. Please."

Corrin was panting, his pupils blown right out in the low light of the walk-in robe, so there was only the tiniest sliver of brilliant blue. "You're so fucking wet. I knew that Omegas had slick, but fuck—" I kissed him, cutting off his words, and he plunged his fingers inside me.

I let out an inhuman noise as I got my first moment of release. His thumb stroked my clit, and I came, my pussy clenching around his fingers, searching for a knot.

"Oh fuck, oh fuck..." Corrin kissed along the curve of my shoulder. "You are so fucking sexy."

Then new hands were grabbing me, pulling me away from Corrin, and I mewled pathetically as his fingers slid from my pussy. "More!"

It was Remzi who held me now, lowering me into the nest of pillows and blankets, both his scent and his huge body surrounding me. He looked down at my face, his eyes serious. I expected lust, or heat, or something, but there were just those cool gray eyes and a frown.

"You can leave," he said softly, and at first, I thought he was talking to me.

"It has to be witnessed."

I turned my head and saw RJ standing in the door. I reached for him, and the surprise on his face would have been comical if it hadn't coincided with a sharp pain so brutal, it felt like I was being electrocuted. I screamed and writhed, and Remzi hushed me again.

"Shh, sweet Omega. I've got you," he murmured into my hair, and lowered his body to mine. That's when I realized he was naked. I hissed with relief as his hot skin pressed along mine, his wide hips spreading my thighs and the head of his cock sliding through my slick.

"Please, please, please," I chanted under my breath, so close to what I needed, and I rolled my body up, trying to drag him inside. When he gripped my leg and opened me wide, sliding inside me slowly, I gasped.

Grady was well-endowed, but not even he had prepared me for what an Alpha possessed. Remzi stretched me wider than I thought possible, until it was a delicious pain only eased by the fact that I was so wet, it was coating my thighs and his. That slow slide was beautiful torture, and I clawed at his back like we were inside a hurricane, and if I didn't cling to him, I'd float away.

"More," I moaned, and he growled low in his chest, the sound making me gush. Then he slammed himself home, his hips hitting mine as he bottomed out inside me. I felt my eyes widen, and I screeched out something entirely inhuman as he let me settle around him, before dragging himself out again and repeating the whole process. Two more thrusts and I was coming around his cock, but he wasn't done.

He slowly, methodically pumped his hips against mine, until I was writhing for a different reason now. The next orgasm was short and sharp, slapping me in the face with pleasure. But still, Remzi wasn't done.

I wanted to bite him, to make him mine, to ride this wave with him as my mate.

A little voice in my head argued that biting him wouldn't break the skin, because I had blunt human teeth. My Omega didn't give a fuck about that, though. I captured his lips again with mine, sucking his full bottom lip between my teeth and biting down until the coppery taste of his blood spread across my tongue.

He grunted again, his hips picking up pace. He pushed me back down onto my nest, curling his body until he could suck my nipple into this mouth. I writhed and clutched at his back, his mouth moving to the underside of my breast in soft sucking motions. His other hand rubbed my swollen, aching clit, and I came.

"Alpha!"

He bit down on the soft flesh of my boob, making me scream at the pinch of pain and the deluge of pleasure. Our bond snapped together, a strong and fierce thing.

As I came down from the high of my orgasm, I knew I just needed one more thing. The one thing I knew would finish me off, would chase away this torment that had overtaken my body.

I needed his knot, needed that stretch.

"Knot me," I gasped. "Please."

I needed his cum painting my inner walls, needed him to breed with me. He looked down at me with those storm-colored eyes in that beautiful golden face. His slightly curly hair was stuck to his forehead as he looked at me dispassionately.

Then he pulled out of my body, making me whine pitifully. He rolled me over, onto all fours, and I panted with need as I waited for him to fill me back up again.

"What the hell?" Grady shouted, his shocked eyes on the door to my den. When I looked over my shoulder, Remzi Hart was gone. He'd just left me, aching and needy and exposed.

I made a keening noise as the heat pain roared back, coated in rejection. Burying my face in the pillows, I cried.

Chapter Ten
Tryst

I could hear Grady saying something to RJ, and the man in question disappeared from my den, making my Omega cry some more. Two rejections. It was too much.

But Corrin was there, dragging me into his arms and rolling us both onto our sides so he could look at me, nose to nose. "Shh, baby girl, shhh," he said soothingly. "It's okay. I've got you. We don't need him."

I felt Grady's big body behind me, bracketing me between them. "We've got you. Tell us what we can do, what you need."

"More. I need more of everything."

Corrin tilted my head back and kissed me with so much passion, it momentarily chased away the sting of Remzi's rejection. "This isn't how I meant for this to happen, but I'll make it up to you later." He gripped my thigh and curled it upwards, opening me up.

I felt Grady slide his hand down over my ass and then between mine and Corrin's body, grabbing Corrin's cock and lining him up to thrust inside me hard. I let my head fall back against Grady's chest as Corrin filled me, and he kissed my neck and along my shoulder.

This was good. This appeased something in me, though it wasn't the instant relief I knew Remzi's knot could have given me.

Grady stretched my body backwards, so Corrin could take my aching nipples into his mouth. They worked in perfect unison, and the logical, not hormone-addled part of my brain wondered if they'd done this before. Fucked a girl together.

My Omega hissed at the thought of anyone touching what was hers, and I ground against Corrin, riding his dick in time with his thrusts. Grady's hand moved down to play gently with my clit, and I came hard around Corrin's cock, making him grunt like I'd punched him.

"Jesus fuck, she feels too damn good."

But the pressure came right back, building up again, still unsatisfied. "More," I whimpered, making Corrin groan.

"Aw, sweetheart, I'm so sorry. I don't have a knot; I don't have more to give."

Tears returned to my eyes, and I continued to move against him, seeking something else, something more.

Grady suddenly looked across the room. "Is he coming back?"

My heart leapt, but RJ's gruff, "No," shattered what remained of it, until all that was left was a gory mess on the ground.

Corrin stilled. "Fucking selfish asshole."

Grady swore beneath his breath, his hand coming back to play with my clit. "It's okay, Tryst. We've got you. We aren't leaving until you're satisfied."

"Plus, we have a huge stash of electrolyte drinks. I'll fuck this delicious pussy until I'm a dried-out husk if I have to," Corrin added, his smirk making him look mischievously handsome.

"She needs the stretch of a knot. It'll ease the heat," RJ commented from where he was standing, half in, half out of the den.

"No shit, but in case you haven't noticed, neither Corrin nor I have one," Grady snapped. "Official business is over. You can go, RJ."

I wanted to protest, but then Corrin shifted my leg, changing positions and hitting an extra sweet spot. I looked over my shoulder at RJ, saw the heat in his eyes as he watched things he had no right to see. I wanted to reach for him again, to get him to lie down on top of me so I'd be surrounded by warm skin.

He dragged his eyes from mine. "Try double penetration. It might trick her body into thinking it's a knot for long enough to release the heat. At least for a little while." Then, like Remzi, he was gone too.

I let out a low, mournful noise, and Grady stroked a hand down my spine. "It's okay, sweetheart. You won't feel empty for long." He began kissing between my shoulder blades. "Stay still, Corrin. RJ might be right." I felt his cock searching, then he was notching against my already full entrance. "God, she's so coated in slick. You are the best fucking Omega, baby, so fucking good. Corrin and I are both going to take you, and you're going to love it, I promise. Just stay still for a moment." His big dick pushed against me. He grunted as he couldn't get the angle he wanted. "On your back, Corrin."

Corrin wrapped his arms around my back and rolled us over until I was spread against his chest. He kissed me again, slowly plunging his tongue into my mouth to make up for the fact his body wasn't moving at all.

Grady made a sound of satisfaction from behind me, his hands running down my spine. I felt his cock again, butting up against Corrin's, and this time when he pushed, my body stretched to accommodate him.

I hissed out a gasp of pleasure. Yes, this was what I needed. Slowly, he edged his way into me, and I saw Corrin's eyes roll to the back of his head as he breathed hard and fast through his nose.

"God, this is..." He trailed off, but he didn't need to continue. This was everything.

Grady began to move, fucking us both, pushing Corrin against all the good spots in my body as he dragged himself backwards and forwards.

I was trembling, or maybe it was Corrin, who was gritting his teeth so hard I could hear them grinding. Finally, the pain was replaced by ecstasy, the yearning kept at bay by being filled. My body gently shifted between them, and I was so full that each tiny movement sent me higher and higher until I was falling into an orgasm that was like a sucking abyss. It was more than anything I'd ever felt, and my vision darkened at the edges as wave after wave of pleasure-pain washed over me.

Someone shouted, and the hot feel of someone's seed releasing inside my greedy body prolonged my orgasm as I milked them both. Then I came again. And again.

Someone was chanting my name, but the words were almost static-like as I writhed and clenched, sucking everything I could from them until we all collapsed, spent.

Grady gently pulled out, and I felt my eyes grow heavy. After sliding me off a boneless Corrin, he snuggled me down between them, pulling the softest blanket over the top of our naked, sticky bodies.

Then darkness claimed me.

Chapter Eleven
Tryst

We didn't leave the nest for four days. Food, water, and rehydration drinks were delivered to the door of the nest, as well as warm water and wash cloths so the guys could wipe down our sweat—and other stuff—coated bodies.

Remzi never returned. While my inner Omega was nearly inconsolable at the rejection, human me was pissed.

On the fifth day, my heat broke, and we made it out of my nest and into the shower, where the guys washed my body like I was a goddess and they were my acolytes. It was reverent, but there was nothing sexual in it now; my body protested heartily at the very idea of sex.

I stroked my hands over Grady's naked, wet chest. "You guys are..." I was at a loss for words. They'd been amazing. Perfection. They'd stepped up, and as a result, we'd grown close. "Just, thank you. If you'd left like—" I cut myself off from saying his name. "That would have been a miserable fucking week."

Grady kissed me. "You're our Omega. I know this is all new, and we kind of had a trial by fire, but know that I would never, ever have walked away. And neither would Corrin."

The man in question snaked slippery hands around my body from where he stood behind me, sliding them up until they cupped my breasts. Then he honked them, complete with sound effects. I dropped my head back with a laugh, accepting the gentle kiss he placed on my forehead.

"Even if you weren't my Omega, I don't think I'd ever turn down a five-day sex fest," Corrin joked. He kissed my shoulder, his voice turning serious. "That was one of the most amazing, soul-altering experiences of my life, and I thank you for letting me be part of your first heat, Omega."

I wanted to cry again, but I was pretty sure it was just the residual hormones. As if he could sense the shift in my mood, Corrin went back to lathering my body gently. Our bond had been strengthened with all sorts of bodily fluids during our sex haze, including a few bites, so there was a good chance that he actually could sense my moods now.

He sighed heavily. "I was relying on my sex skills to make you love me later. Now I'll have to woo you with my personality."

Grady laughed. "Yeah, I could see how that might be a problem for you."

Corrin punched him in the shoulder, snuggling me back against his body tighter. "Tryst likes my personality, don't you, baby girl?"

I grinned as they joked and played under the steaming hot water, happy they were mine, and pointedly ignoring the ache in my chest where my Alpha bond sat.

I didn't need him. These two were enough.

Grady dried me off with a fluffy towel that fortunately no longer felt like it was trying to slough off my skin, and we all stumbled barely dressed back to Grady's bed. My room smelled like a week-old bordello, and I mentally apologized to whoever had to clean it. I'd still brought in one blanket though, which smelled like all my mates, because it was only the lingering scent of Remzi on there that stopped the ache in my chest from turning into a pounding chest pain right now.

Fucking asshole.

Someone had left food on the small desk in the corner, as well as several cups of coffee. Ugh, that someone needed a raise and my undying devotion. We ate the hoagies and the fruit, and Corrin dragged me to bed so he could hand-feed me the chocolates one by one against the pillows.

"Is it weird that I know how your dick feels, but don't really know anything else about you—other than the fact you're Grady's partner and he loves you a whole lot?" I asked between bites.

Corrin shook his head, looking lovingly at Grady who was surfing the streaming services, looking for something to watch. "Not really. We have decades to get to know one another. There's no written caveat anywhere that says you should know a person inside and out before you have sex with them."

"Well, you've got the inside part down now. Pretty sure you know my insides better than I do," I teased, and he laughed, kissing me softly, then sucking a smudge of chocolate from my lips.

"You aren't wrong. I know you like it when I curl my fingers just so and..." He made a little come-hither motion with his fingers, and boy, did I want to come wherever he wanted me.

I must have made a little sound of want, because Grady's eyes snapped toward us. "Jesus, you two. I'm about to die of exhaustion, and you're still flirting? Lie down and watch the damn movie before you give me a heart attack."

Corrin just laughed, but snuggled down beside me. "What do you want to know, baby girl?"

I frowned. Hmm. "What do you do for work? What are your passions?"

"Other than you two?" he joked, nipping at my lips. "I'm a potter. I run an online business, and make high-end pieces for galleries and decorators. Sometimes, I try my hand at sculpture if I can get Grady to sit for me naked." He sighed, looking at his lover, our bondmate. "That man has a fine physique." His gaze dropped back to me. "Will you sit for me? Oh my god, would you sit for me together? Can you imagine if I could sculpt your bodies, all twined around each other like you're making love?" His eyes were already far away, as if he was picturing something... I just wasn't sure if it was an art piece or me and Grady having sex.

I stroked a hand across his bare shoulders. "Anytime. I'd be honored." His skin was so soft and pale; he was almost like marble, but he had freckles across his shoulders, little sun kisses that made me want to devour them with my tongue. "What about your family? What did they think of your daring plan to make me bond you?"

Corrin frowned, and I realized that it was the first time I'd ever seen the expression. It was jarring on his beautiful face. "My family and I don't really get along. They don't approve of my lifestyle." His eyes flicked to

Grady, and I realized what he was saying. They didn't like that he was bisexual. "Strict Irish Catholics, you know. Didn't matter, I moved to the Midwest, met Grady and his family, and they adopted me immediately. They're my family now." He gave me a quick grin. "Our family."

I wanted what he was offering so bad.

I cleared my throat, chasing away the knot of emotion that had settled there. "Favorite pizza?"

"Anchovy, pineapple and olive."

I screwed up my face. "Well, that's a monstrosity, but I can forgive you for it as long as I never have to ingest such a horror."

He slipped a hand over my hip and squeezed my butt, just for fun. Corrin was handsy, and I loved it. "All the more for me, little Omega."

"Favorite singer?"

"Bowie."

"Least favorite Spice Girl?"

He frowned at me. "Why would you ask me something so heinous? Fine, Sporty Spice, but I'll deny it to my dying day if you tell anyone."

"Cats or dogs?"

He smiled. "I can't choose; I love them both. A dog's love is unconditional, and that's wonderful. A cat's love is laden with conditions, but earning it feels more special, you know? So I say both."

"I'll accept it." I paused. "Before all this, where did you see yourself in ten years?"

Before I'd derailed his life, stolen his one true love, and made him my bondslave.

He rolled over so he was on his back, then grabbed me by my hips, dragging me onto his chest. I pushed myself up on my hands, either side of his shoulders, as he stared up at me.

"Same place I see myself now, Tryst. Living with the man I love, creating art, being happy. But now there's not just one person to love and be loved by me. There are two. And maybe there'll be more. Maybe there'll be tiny kids and goofy dogs and mean cats, all running around and causing mayhem. Maybe there'll be six other bondmates, or maybe it'll just be the three of us. It doesn't matter, because both Grady and I will try our hardest to make sure it's filled with so much love that this whole nightmare will be just that. A distant dream that you had to endure before you got your happily ever after."

I felt Grady's calloused hand run down my back, so different from Corrin's, whose fingers were ridiculously soft, probably from having them in clay all the time. "It's what we both want," Grady murmured, rolling over to kiss me and then Corrin.

I wanted the picture Corrin was painting so bad, it was a physical ache in my chest. "Me too."

Chapter Twelve
Tryst

Despite the fact that I'd just been through my heat, the DoDA didn't want to delay the next draw, which was bullshit. I guess they didn't want anyone to know that they'd fucked up my medicals or whatever. They didn't want the public to know that this Allotment was anything but blissfully normal. But that meant that Remzi was also set to return.

Anger still simmered in my gut about the whole thing. Anger and a whole lot of hurt, though I didn't want to admit to that last part.

I also didn't want to admit that I was scared of the next draw. I'd pulled one amazing bondmate, and one shitty one, and the anxiety of the whole situation was getting to me. This time, I didn't go down to the draw, instead staying up in my room, lying in bed with Grady and Corrin, watching funny romcoms and eating pizza. Corrin had been delighted to get an entire anchovy, pineapple and olive one to himself.

When RJ walked into my room with the new file, his face completely shuttered, I knew I wasn't going to like what was about to unfold. He didn't say anything as he handed it to me, another profile picture staring at me from the front cover of the manila folder. The first word that jumped out at me was Alpha, and I hissed out a breath. Then I took in the rest of the details.

Kacey Boyd. Five years older than me, and covered in tattoos from the neck down, if his profile picture suggested the truth. He had a scar through his eyebrow, and a straight nose that stopped above lips that were too plump for the gruffness of his face. His jaw was sharp, his chin lifted to match the challenge in his eyes. His job wasn't listed, though there was a small footnote that suggested he was financially secure. His eyes were dark, and they burned through the picture. His lip was curled in a slight snarl, giving him a feral expression. He was everything Omegas were warned against.

Grady looked over my shoulder and froze. His eyes shot to my face, and then back to RJ. "Is there no way we can postpone meeting the new mate until Tryst feels better?"

I was exhausted from the heat, my body still lethargic and aching, but Corrin and Grady were equally as exhausted. I just wanted to spend another week cuddled between them, restoring all the fluids we'd lost.

RJ huffed out an annoyed sound. "I tried, but Agatha..."

Was a bitch. Yeah, I got that impression already.

I dropped my gaze back to the profile in front of me. Something about this Alpha made me feel like prey, but more than that, two Alphas would mean dominance problems. We liked to pretend we were all civil and that Alphas didn't jockey for position, but if humans seeked power by stepping on others, then Alphas were twice as bad.

"Is Remzi coming back?"

RJ's face tightened at his name. "He'll be here around the same time as your new mate. We're bringing in extra personnel for the meeting." So I wasn't the only one who saw the potential fireworks between these two.

Corrin tightened his arms around me, and I tucked my head under his chin, allowing him to soothe me. "When will they arrive?"

"Late afternoon. Remzi too."

"I hope he turns around and fucks right back off again," Corrin grumbled, and I huffed out a humorless laugh.

The logical part of me hoped for that too. But this

was why they bonded us so quickly; his distance was an ache in my soul. Not so bad that I couldn't function, but enough that there was a low-grade pain spread along my skin at all hours of the day.

The Omega yearned for her mate, and it annoyed the fuck out of me. I was anxious about seeing him again, but there was nothing I could do about it. My life was out of my control.

"Thanks, RJ." It was a bit of a dismissal, but this man had seen me spread wide and begging for dick, and it was hard to look someone in the eye after that.

He stared at me a little longer, then nodded hard. "Sure. No worries. I'll let you guys..." He trailed off, turning and leaving without another word.

RJ was going to need to go on stress leave after all this. Hell, maybe I would too.

"Is it just me, or does RJ have a really nice ass?" Corrin whispered conspiratorially, and Grady reached across my body to whack him. Then they kissed above my head, my body happily smooshed between them.

I sighed in contentment, no matter how short-lived it was going to be, and pressed play on the TV. "I wish I could just stop at you two. I could be happy with you."

"We're happy with you too," Grady said softly, his lips brushing softly across my cheek. "But things will work out how they're meant to. You'll see."

He pulled my legs over his, and we finished our romcom, my mind whirling with Alphas and Betas and where we would be this time tomorrow night.

I spent the following morning resting, and when it was time to get ready to meet my new Alpha, I found I couldn't summon the energy to complete the whole beautifying ritual. Instead, I pulled on my favorite pair of black jeans, one of Corrin's band t-shirts, and applied the bare minimum of makeup. I'd dressed up for Remzi and he'd left, so what was the damn point?

Agatha pursed her lips when she saw me, and I resisted the urge to flip her the bird. She'd fucked up, and that made us even for the Corrin thing, in my opinion. I'd do what I wanted now.

"You're late, Omega."

I bristled at her tone. "No one came to fetch me. I was just coming down to see if there'd been a delay."

"Your new bondmate has been waiting for five minutes in the reception room," she snapped. "Go through now. You aren't a child who needs to be fetched and dragged around by the hand."

I gritted my teeth to stop myself from telling her to go get fucked. Instead, I stared at her imperiously and strode into the room. Then stopped dead in my tracks as the wave of Alpha pheromones hit me in the face.

He smelled like pizza rolls and bad decisions.

An impossibly tall figure stood at the window, his back to me. I looked him over, from his broad shoulders and the tattoos that ran up the back of his neck into his hairline, right down to the boots on his feet, complete with buckles up the side and scuff marks. Tattoos also coated the back of his hands. I'd bet my life they ran up his arms under his Henley too.

He turned slowly, and I steeled my spine. His eyes ran over my body, starting at my legs and moving up over my breasts, before finally landing on my face. His expression was bored, like he found me wanting.

I wished I'd had the same visceral response; instead my Omega started to pant. I swallowed down the budding attraction.

"You don't want to be here?" I asked.

He raised a single eyebrow. "I doubt there is an Alpha alive who wants to be dragged to the middle of fucking nowhere like a naughty child, and told that they were only allowed to play with one woman for the rest of their life. Especially one who's probably fucking ten other guys?" He snorted. "Fuck that."

I bristled. "I'm not stopping you from leaving."

He strode over, his confident steps eating up the distance between us. "The US government is, though. They made quite a... forceful case that I had to be here."

I noticed the way his bottom lip was swollen, a small, barely healed cut splitting it in two. He also had a scrape along his forehead, like they'd thrown him to the ground.

"They brought you here by force?" Horror stole the strength of my words until they came out a whisper. I resisted the urge to reach up and test the scrapes and bruises on his face with my own fingertips.

He gave a humorless laugh. "I was pretty goddamn content in Boston. I finally had everything I wanted, and this fucking bullshit ripped it all away in a moment." His angry growl was like a whip against my skin. "For what? A chance at weak ass Omega pussy? No offense, Princess, but no fuck is that good."

Seemed to be the theme for all my mates, except Corrin. But not even Corrin was here for me.

"I'm sorry."

He frowned. "Lesson one in life: never be fucking sorry for shit that isn't your fault. Hell, don't be sorry for shit that *is* your fault." His voice was a low growl in his chest, and I couldn't help the visceral reaction it had on my body, my skin tightening and my core clenching needily.

Kacey's eyes widened, his nostrils flaring like he could almost sense my body's response to his Alpha presence. "Let's get this shit over with. I need to go back to Boston."

My heart thundered. Another bondmate was going to leave, and I was already strained by Remzi's absence.

As if I'd summoned the man himself, Remzi pushed into the room. His eyes found mine immediately, but flicked away just as quickly. Another rejection to add to the pile.

Kacey growled low in his chest, a near noiseless sound. Maybe Remzi wouldn't hear it from the other side of the room, but judging by the way his body stiffened, it was a false hope. Kacey stepped in front of me, which I didn't really understand, but the gesture made my Omega preen all the same.

"Come here, Omega," Remzi growled, his Alpha voice tugging at my bond, and I found myself stepping around Kacey with gritted teeth. The fucking asshole had *Alpha'd* me. I couldn't stop my feet from moving toward him, but every step just made me more and more angry. When I stood in front of him, he didn't even look at me, instead staring over my head at Kacey.

So I pulled back my fist and punched him in the balls. His eyes went wide as his breath hissed out between his teeth. He folded in half, staggering away from me.

"How fucking *dare* you?" I made sure he was looking at me now. "Hurts, doesn't it? That pain? I endured that for four days because of you, then you decide to walk into this room and *Alpha* me?" My voice was getting loud, anger raising it an octave. "I will never forgive you for walking away when I needed you, Remzi Hart. I don't give a damn if you turn around and go back to wherever you've been hiding your face for the last week. I don't want you either."

I spun on my heel and strode back to Kacey Boyd, who was openly laughing. "That was fucking hilarious. What did he do?"

"Walked away from me while I was in heat."

All the mirth left Kacey's face in an instant. "He left you to suffer?" I nodded. He sneered in Remzi's direction before looking back at me with a softening expression, essentially dismissing Remzi too. "I take it back, Princess. Judging by that hit, Omega pussy isn't that weak at all. Come on, I'll show you how a real Alpha does this shit, and then we can have a beer."

I left the room with Kacey, and didn't look back at my bondmate, despite the fact I could feel his eyes burning into my back.

Chapter Thirteen
Tryst

RJ followed us into the room, and Kacey narrowed his eyes at him. "Who's the suit?"

I flushed, not meeting RJ's gaze. "Our Official witness." Kacey grunted something derogatory under his breath, pacing around the room. I stepped closer to him, out of RJ's earshot. "You can still climb out the window and escape. You look fast, and they obviously don't give a shit about bringing the Alphas back."

Remzi's absence all week had proven that.

Kacey grinned, and it was all predatory teeth. "Nah, Princess. I admit, you have me intrigued. Besides, my family are all about legacies and heirs, and having heirs with an Omega has a certain prestige."

"Heirs?" I squeaked, the idea of kids making cold fear prickle over my skin.

He threw back his head and laughed. "Not for a while yet, Omega. I'm in no hurry to have you wed and bred, if you know what I'm saying." He paused, letting his eyes rake over my body. "Though I wouldn't mind the practice."

He held out a hand. Despite his rough words, and being the very image of the bad Alpha mothers warned their Omega daughters about, he was giving me a choice. Or at least, the semblance of one. Again.

Apparently, choice was an aphrodisiac to me.

I put my hand in his and let him drag me toward his body. It was hard and lean, like a marble statue. "You ready to see why Alphas and Omegas belong together, Princess?"

He didn't give me time to answer as his face swooped down, capturing my lips with his. I quickly learned he had a tongue piercing as it flicked against my teeth, the sensation almost jarring. The warmth of his chest against mine was intoxicating; he'd been right, the pull of the Alpha and Omega attraction was its own force. Not as bad as when Remzi had triggered my heat, but it was still an ache I felt in my soul.

Kacey's hands roamed along my back, and I curled my fingers into his soft shirt. He slid his hands underneath my own shirt, scrunching it up as his palms traced a trail up my spine. Dragging it up over my head, he inhaled deeply.

"Another man's shirt?" His voice was a low grumble. "You really do like fucking with an Alpha, don't you, Princess?" He laughed softly, almost menacingly. "Don't worry, baby, this Alpha is going to fuck you right back."

He grabbed my ass in his huge hands, lifting and spinning me toward the bed I was beginning to loathe. But instead of moving me in that direction, he stepped toward a small desk that the Officials used in the corner. It was still scattered with paperwork, and Kacey lazily swiped at the surface, scattering half of the items onto the floor. Then he laid me down on top of the rest.

"Let's hope they do that shit in triplicate, hey?" His grin was sexy and mischievous. He grabbed my jeans and panties, and pulled them down my legs roughly, dragging them over my feet and tossing them in the same direction as my shirt. "Fuck," he breathed, choking out the word. He grabbed my knees and spread me wider, his eyes tracing my most intimate areas. "You've got a real pretty pussy, Princess."

I snorted. "Liar. All vaginas look like aliens."

He scoffed. "Yeah, but my mouth doesn't water at the idea of eating an alien." He dropped to his knees in front of the desk, but still had to raise my ass a little so we were mouth to, uh, lips.

I flushed at his hungry perusal. "You don't have to do this for the bond."

He scoffed. "Don't worry, I'm doing this for me, not you." Then he lowered his mouth and attacked my clit with single-minded focus. There was no better description for the way he tormented that tiny bud of nerves with his tongue piercing until I was writhing in his hands.

My Omega was panting, knowing she'd found an Alpha of worth, finally. This one wouldn't leave her aching during her heat. This one made her come, for *his* pleasure.

I was reaching that moment, the one I knew would push me over the edge, and then the bastard stopped. I gave a disbelieving screech. He looked up at me from between my thighs, his smile pure sin.

"Don't worry, baby, I'm not going anywhere. I just want to be inside you the first time I make you come. I want to feel your hot cunt gripping onto me for dear life, begging me for my knot."

As if to make his point, he stood, shedding his clothes inhumanly fast. He pulled me off the desk and put me back on my feet, spinning me around and bending me back over it. He pinned me down with a strong hand between my shoulders, as he kneeled down behind me.

"But first..." There was a sharp sting as his teeth

sank into my left butt cheek, and the beginnings of a bond anchored itself in my chest.

"You bit my ass!"

His answering chuckle puffed between my thighs, cooling my overheated core. Parting my ass cheeks, he buried his face back between my thighs once more and plunged his tongue into my pussy. I felt that studded ball in a whole different way now. He stroked with a practiced rhythm until I was almost there again, my forehead pressed into the stacks of paper so firmly that you could probably read the print off my skin.

Then he halted once more.

"God fucking dammit, Kacey," I swore as I got stuck on the precipice, my body humming. "*Please,* Alpha."

That was what did it, that whispered plea, because in a heartbeat he was behind me, pushing his cock inside me with one hard, stretching stroke. My head thunked back down to the table as I panted and held on, shit falling off the side like we were in an earthquake.

I came on a scream, my body locking down on him until he was dragging himself in and out of me with effort. "Fuck, Omega. You're like a fist around me."

His hands snuck under my hips, tilting my pelvis until he hit a whole new range of spots and my vision got patchy as hell. Every breath was a moan, and I couldn't hear anything over the sound of our bodies slapping together. He pulled out, flipping me over like a doll and sitting me on the desk once more, pulling one thigh high over his hip, and thrusting back in. His arm wrapped around my shoulders, stopping me from falling backwards as all the bones in my body turned to jello.

"I'm going to knot you now, then you're going to bite me and seal the bond. You got it?"

I nodded, but I was more focused on his cock swelling inside me. I stared down at where our bodies were joined, not that I could see anything really. That was all happening inside me. My Omega was almost hysterically giddy at the idea of being knotted for the first time, and the air was beginning to burn in my lungs.

Kacey's tattooed hand gripped my chin, and he tilted my head up until he could see my eyes. "Breathe, Omega," he said, with all that Alpha power, until I was forced to take a big lungful of air. When I breathed out, he slammed inside me, locking his knot behind my pubic bone, and the remaining air burst from my lungs on a scream.

Not in pain, though. In so much fucking pleasure. It hit just the right places inside me, places I hadn't even known existed, and he continued to swell. It got so fucking big, I wasn't sure I'd draw breath anymore, if it wasn't from Kacey's Alpha command.

He began to move in short, sharp strokes, rocking his knot inside me, until I was clinging onto him for dear life. He curled over my body, his neck and shoulder now a mere whisper from my mouth. I knew what he wanted, and I couldn't have agreed with him more at that moment.

I bit down on his shoulder as he rocked against my G-spot in a way that was impossible for regular Beta males, making me explode with an orgasm even as I filled my mouth with the muscle of his shoulder. I screamed around his skin between my teeth, both his blood and his cum flooding inside of me.

I felt a sting on my shoulder, but I didn't even care that he'd bitten me again; I was riding a wave of plea-sure that seemed to encase my every limb.

Locked together still, he pulled away, the brashness gone from his expression, and something softer in its place. "Okay?"

I nodded, but with my energy levels completely depleted, it was more like a doll with a floppy neck. He huffed a soft laugh and scooped me up, careful to hold me in the right place so his knot didn't tug against my pubic bone. I wrapped my legs around his hips, clinging as tightly as I could. He lay down on the bed, that dreaded fucking bed, draping me over top of him and then covering us both in a blanket.

"Sleep, Princess."

I was out before he'd even finished the sentence.

I woke to the sounds of a whispered argument. There was a warm body along my back, and the scent of Kacey was wrapped around me just as tightly as his arm across my hips. Blankets were tucked around my chest, and I was seriously considering just pretending to be asleep until everyone went away.

"You haven't filled out the appropriate paperwork, Mr. Boyd." I would know Agatha's nasally whine anywhere now. "There is also the matter of Alpha Hart."

Okay, pretending to be asleep was off the table now.

"What about him?" Kacey growled.

"He says you are denying his bondmate rights, and that he will challenge you if you don't give her back."

My whole body stiffened, and I could feel Kacey's amusement as a laugh rumbled silently in his chest. "I would relish the chance. But fine, give me your fucking paperwork for us to sign." He pulled back the blankets, but tucked them back around me. "Now, if you don't want an eyeful of my cock, I suggest you leave."

Agatha didn't move for a moment, and my eyes flew open. I glared at the woman who obviously had no problem ogling my Alpha. I didn't realize that I was making an odd growling noise until Kacey laughed openly.

"Lady, that wasn't a fucking offer. Get out before I report you to your superiors for inappropriate conduct."

"Mr. Boyd, I assure—"

"Alpha Boyd," he corrected. "Now leave."

Agatha walked away in a huff. I guess this Allotment wasn't quite as smooth as Agatha's last one, but fuck her. Kacey stood, and his dick swung around his thighs, catching my eyes like a hypnotist's watch.

His gaze was molten, and he hummed a little. "Keep looking at my dick like that, Princess, and I'm going to climb back under those blankets and fuck you until you're covered in my marks."

Slick flooded between my thighs at his words, and his nostrils flared as he caught the scent. His pupils blew wide, and I smiled smugly as he strode back toward the bed.

"I hate to interrupt, but you have the bureaucracy to deal with, as well as meeting Tryst's other bondmates."

I whipped my head to the other side of the room, and there was RJ, standing in the corner, leaning against the wall like this was just another day at the office. Unlike Agatha, my Omega was more than happy with RJ being in the room, and that was worrying in itself. He shifted his focus to me, and his eyes burned. I couldn't tell what emotion was bubbling inside him, but their blue depths were stormy.

When I wrenched my gaze back to Kacey, he wasn't looking at RJ. He was looking at me, his eyes slightly narrowed. What did he see? Was it the flush of my cheeks, like I'd just been caught with my hand in the cookie jar? Or maybe he scented the super inappropriate attraction I had to the government Official whose job description said 'Voyeur.'

Kacey leaned down, claiming my lips in a hard kiss. He may as well have bitten my ass again—that's how claiming it was. He winked at me and then turned away, pulling on his jeans before straightening and glaring at RJ. "Fine. I have plenty of time to make my Omega scream later. Let's get the rest of this shit over with." He kneeled down on the bed, peeling back the sheet from my naked body, despite RJ still being in the room. Had I imagined the emphasis when he said *my* Omega?

He leaned forward, sliding his hands under my knees and back, and hauling me into his arms. Naked. And a little sticky. I was a disgusting, sweaty mess, yet somehow Kacey still smelled divine. He held my body tightly to his as he stared at RJ.

Well, this was a little weird. Whatever macho thing was flying between them, it had the both of them gritting their teeth and left me feeling like I was a juicy bone. I wiggled in Kacey's arms, and RJ finally dropped his eyes.

"I'll go and get Grady and Corrin." He left without looking at me, and I reached up and pinched Kacey's nipple. Hard.

"Ow, Princess! What was that for?"

"You were being mean to RJ, and I don't like being treated like a bush you can pee on and claim."

"You better kiss that better," he growled, and I tilted my head to the side and flicked my tongue over the abused nub. "Your boy needs to learn his place. He isn't one of your bondmates, and he's going to get his ass kicked if he keeps eyeing your body like he has a right to it."

"But—"

"Or one of the other Officials will notice, and he's going to get his ass fired instead."

That made me stop. RJ seemed to like his job, and considering fifty percent of it was basically watching live action porn, I could see why. I didn't want him to lose his job, but also, I was beginning to think of RJ as a friend. Not just a pseudo one.

"My Omega likes him."

Kacey strode toward the bathroom and set me on my feet, pushing me against the cold glass of the shower screen until I was trapped against his muscled warmth. "Your Omega is greedy and my Alpha is a jealous prick. Get clean so we can get this bullshit over with." He stepped away, turning on the shower and fiddling with the taps.

He seemed in a rush, and uncertainty raced through me. Would he be like Remzi? Would he just return to his old life and leave me here?

Giving a small grunt of satisfaction at the water temperature, he turned back to me and frowned. "What's wrong?"

I forced a smile. "Nothing." I refused to be a desperate, weepy Omega. I went to step around him, but he grabbed my arm and dragged me back to his body.

"I asked a question. Don't lie to me, Tryst." He used my name, which probably meant nothing but made my heart leap. He slid his hand up my throat and gripped my chin, forcing me to meet his eyes.

I sighed. "Will you leave?"

His eyes widened, but they never left my face. "Being apart from your Omega causes issues; everyone knows that." I blinked back tears, because I knew it firsthand. Kacey swore under his breath. "I'm going to beat that fucker to a pulp. I hope he challenges me," he grumbled to himself. "No, Omega. I'm not going anywhere until all this is settled. After that, I have a strong argument for returning to Boston, but you'll definitely be coming with me." His hands slid to his jeans and he pushed them back down until he was gloriously naked once more. "Now, get in the shower so I can eat out that delectable pussy and prove to you that there's no place I'd rather be than between your thighs."

He hustled me back into the shower and damn, he was really convincing.

Chapter Fourteen
Tryst

We emerged thirty minutes later to an increasingly irritated Agatha tapping her pen on a clipboard. Kacey held out a hand, and she thrust the clipboard at him. Over the Official's head, he saw my two Beta bondmates.

He raised the clipboard. "Did you read this? Is it legit?"

Grady stared at him like he'd grown a second head. "Uh, yeah? Seemed fine. I'm no lawyer, but the other Alpha signed it too, and he seems like the type to query shit."

Kacey grinned. "Good enough for me." He signed on the line above his name, and then handed it to me. They were all standard—at least, they were according to the DoDA. I wouldn't put it past them to sneak some shit into one of the contracts, though.

When I was finished, Kacey took it back and tossed it at Agatha. "There you go, Aggie. Now, if it's okay with you, I'd like to meet the rest of the people the government has decided I'll spend my life with."

Agatha glared at Kacey, such a contrast to how she'd been panting after Remzi, and I thought it might have been more than her disdain for his tattoos and general thug-like appearance. She spun on her heel and left again, which was a relief.

Well, it was until Remzi appeared in the doorway. His eyes were like brands on my skin, smoldering and possessive.

"Omega." He hesitated. "Tryst. Can we speak?"

I frowned at him. "No." Turning my back to him, I gazed adoringly up at Kacey, who was trying to contain his mirth. Badly.

"Please." Remzi's voice was almost pleading, and I sighed. Kacey captured my face, kissing me possessively.

"Just in case he thinks you belong to him. You don't." He nipped my bottom lip. "You belong to me. And to them." His eyes slid to Grady and Corrin, who were watching the interaction like it was a tennis match. "But most of all, you belong to you. Go get him, Princess."

I gave him a tense smile, but let it drop as I turned toward my first Alpha mate. The one our whole Pack would be named after forevermore, but who was least deserving of the honor.

"You have five minutes before I kick you in the nuts again."

He inclined his head. "I'll take it. After you?" I stepped around him and out of the room. He'd better have a damn good apology.

He led me out onto the patio, and he must have had some sway, because my customary guard was missing. Not even RJ was here to watch that I didn't make a run for it. I guess I had four bonds tying me down now; the DoDA had done its job, and if I absconded with my current mates, they'd pat themselves on the back and still consider it a job well done.

On the table was a selection of fruits and pastries, covered in gauzy white lace to protect it from bugs. Remzi held out a chair, and I flopped into it without any grace whatsoever. If he thought I was going to pretend to be a demure little Omega now, he had a whole other thing coming.

He didn't seem fazed, just sitting across from me and unveiling the food. "Eat, Omega. You must be hungry."

I wanted to tell him to go jump in a shark-infested period pond, but the pastries really did look nice. I was actually starving. Picking up a chocolate croissant, I ate it slowly. "You're down to three minutes, Mr. Hart."

I wouldn't call him Alpha, or Remzi. There was no familiarity between us. We weren't friends. We were tied by the law, and some biological bullshit. That was all.

"I was born from an Omega—did they tell you that?"

Well, that hadn't been where I saw this going. I shook my head. "It wasn't in your profile."

He nodded. "I imagine it wasn't. My mother had six bondmates from one of these lotteries. She hated all but one, my father. No, that makes her sound like the bad guy—they all hated each other. Too many Alphas, and Betas who were bitter at being torn from their lives, who were all tied together by forced bonds and the DoDA. It was a miserable way to live each day, and an even more miserable future to imagine. It was a toxic environment to bring any child into, but they persevered, continuing to have children until my mother committed suicide when I was eight."

I gasped, my hand slapping over my mouth. I wanted to say something, anything, that properly expressed my horror and sadness for any eight-year-old who had to go through life without their mother, but Remzi was continuing.

"The Pack disbanded after that, each bondmate taking their biological child. I didn't see my siblings again until I was an adult. My father was a good man, but he had loved my mother and she had loved him. He was devastated by her death, and he faded slowly every day until he was a pale imitation of the man I knew. When I turned seventeen, he died of a sudden heart attack. I still think it was a broken heart."

I didn't know what to say, and my whispered "I'm sorry," seemed inadequate. He gave me a tight smile, and I was sucked into his gaze once more. Dammit, I felt my resolve weakening. Just because he had a sad backstory, didn't make up for his actions.

"Thank you. It was a long time ago now." He cleared his throat. "When my number got called during the Allotment, I couldn't believe it. The odds that an Omega's child would get drawn are phenomenally slim. It's definitely not something I wanted either. I always expected to marry a Beta and have a monogamous relationship."

He ran a hand through his slightly mussed curls. "I didn't want what my parents had. So when I arrived and you were in your first heat, I just... lost it. Lost it to instincts I thought I had under control. Then it came time to knot you. I don't know what you've learned of Alpha-Omega relations, but if I knot you during your heat, there's a high chance of conception. I'd barely come to terms with being in a Pack, let alone fathering children."

Uh, no. No one had told me that. Fuck, I should ask Grady or Corrin if they knew about that.

Shit, could I be pregnant? We'd fucked... a lot. I mean, at least twenty times during my heat. Maybe more. It was all a blur.

Panic raced through my limbs, but I kept it locked away from the Alpha in front of me. While I understood his reasons, running off and leaving me writhing in agony was still a fucking asshole thing to do.

"So you'll stay, now that I'm no longer in heat?"

The long silence that stretched between us was loaded with misery. "No. I am going to ask the DoDA for a revocation of my bond ties."

It was like he'd hit me. I probably would have reeled less if he'd reached across the table and slapped me. "You can't undo a bondmark."

I'd marked him, and even now, I could see the faint line that ran under his bottom lip, evidence of the fact I'd punctured it with my teeth a week ago. There was a mark on my breast where he'd sealed the bond.

"Why?" I whispered. It was a simple question, but it was fraught with emotional baggage that would probably haunt me forever. Why did he want to break the matebond? Was I not good enough? I mustn't be, because while the Superior Court was capable of revoking the legalities of the bond—basically like a divorce—we were forever tied together through that physical bond.

No one had ever divorced their Omega before, and there'd never been an Omega rejected by her bond-mates after a bond was already created. No one would sign up for the physical repercussions of that decision unless it was really bad.

When he left this time, I would once again feel the dull ache in my chest that yearned for him. He was sentencing me to a lifetime of that feeling. Of a chronic pain that no medicine could dull.

What a fucking asshole.

I stood. "You're a coward, Remzi Hart. I'm glad you're nullifying our agreement, because a real Alpha wouldn't make me suffer forever just because he was scared of his feelings. A real Alpha wouldn't have created a fucking bond when he *knew* he was just going to fuck off. A real Alpha—" I broke off as I realized I was crying over this asshole again. "Your mother would be ashamed of you."

I spun on my heel and stomped back into the house, dodging the Officials in the hallways, my other mates, and hissing at any other human unfortunate enough to stumble into my path.

I hated this. Hated. It.

The way Remzi's rejection kept hurting me so fucking bad, even though I barely knew him. I hated that I'd been forced into this bond with men who didn't even want it, opening myself up to this pain in my chest. What if more didn't want the bond? Kacey only came around right at the end. Grady seemed happy enough now that Corrin was here too, but what if Corrin had moved on with his life and he'd been forced to pine away with only me as a poor substitute?

I wanted to reject all the rest of the applicants. More than that, I wanted to run away, to find a den in the woods like the Omegas of old and live there. Maybe they were onto something, escaping the machinations of the government so they could live in peace without feeling torn in a million different directions.

Chapter Fifteen
Kacey

My lip stung like a bitch where the DoDA dickhead had punched me after my number had been called during the damn Allotment. Sure, I'd probably made it worse kissing Princess like I was trying to suck her soul from her body, but I couldn't help myself.

I thought I'd known what it would be like, fucking an Omega. Using my knot. But I had no idea, not really. It was like the best jerk of my life, while a super-model tongued my balls and I watched Oscar-worthy porn.

No, even that didn't live up to it. I had no idea how that asshole Remzi Hart had managed to leave after having a taste of Tryst, but he was either stupid or a masochist. I watched them disappear onto the balcony, and wondered if I could take him in a fight. As much as it burned like Satan's toasty balls to admit, he was more powerful than me—only just. But I would bet my entire fortune that I fought more. I'd been using my fists as persuaders for as long as I could remember.

"I want to kick that fucker in the balls so hard, he could eat his own dick cheese for breakfast."

I blinked rapidly as I looked at Princess's other mates. Sue me, the nickname had stuck. Watching her march over to an Alpha twice her size and hit him one, man, it had made me so hard I could've cracked glass.

"You're too slow. Our girl has already done that."

"Our girl?" the bigger Beta asked, his tone challenging. I pulled down my shirt and showed him my bondmark.

The blond one, who was super fucking pretty for a dude, rolled his eyes. "I have so many bite marks on my skin, we could connect them together like dot to dot and it would draw out a giant dick and balls." I snorted, and he grinned at me. I liked him. "More importantly, Tryst punched him in the balls? And we let her go out there with him? What if he hurts her back?"

Every hair on my body lifted with the urge to rip the door off its hinges and go out there, grab her up and haul her back to safety, or maybe my bed.

The tall one—fuck, I was going to have to find out their names—shook his head. "We aren't treating her like some simple-minded fucking Omega. She can make her own choices, and we have to respect that." He didn't sound as confident as his words portrayed him to be.

The blond one snorted. "Sure, we can't be overbearing and smothering in our protectiveness, but he can." He lifted his chin at RJ the Official, who was still fucking here like a bad smell.

I gave him props because the guy didn't even stop to ask questions, just moving out to the patio but staying out of sight. He moved silently, and I wondered if he had some kind of military training.

"I should know your names, now that we're like, a Pack and everything," I grunted out, and the blond one rolled his eyes even harder.

"Great, two barely-able-to-hold-a-conversation cavemen. I'm Corrin. I climbed through the window and conspired with Tryst to bond with me, because I was Grady's partner before he got called up for the Allotment. So me and Tryst, we took the power back, even just for a little while."

"So you used her to keep your boyfriend?" Seemed pretty shitty to me.

The big guy stepped forward, a scowl on his face that would have been terrifying if I was just another Beta. "Wait a fucking minute—"

"Grady, no. He's right. It was a shitty spot to put her in. I'd do it again, but I'll feel bad about guilt-tripping her into it until the day I die. I can only prove to her over and over that she made the right choice with us." Corrin smiled. "She makes it so fucking easy to care about her, though. You'll see. She's sweet and kind, but so damn fiery she'll make your dick harder than it's ever been."

The boyfriend—Grady, I guess—glared at me like he was still considering taking a swing, but then sucked in a deep breath through his nose. Look at him, making good choices. I'd always sucked at backing down from a fight, even one I knew I couldn't win.

He stared at me right in the eye, and I resisted the urge to smirk at him. Ballsy. I liked that too.

"We may have been a couple before this, but I don't want you to think we aren't one hundred percent on Team Tryst. I don't give a fuck about you, or any of the mates that come after you, Alpha or not. You hurt her, and I will beat the shit out of you until I can't hold up my arm anymore." Bloodthirsty. Another point in his favor. "She deserves more than what the world has handed to her, so much more than the scraps of affection thrown to her by her parents, the mistreatment that was labeled protection by these assholes"—he waved a hand around, indicating the DoDA in general, I assumed—"and the heartbreak dished out by Remzi fucking Hart. Corrin and I, we'll fight for her, and you're either on board like that or you can fuck off. She doesn't need an Alpha pushing her around, taking advantage. She's had enough of that her entire life."

"I'm not going to Alpha her into anything she doesn't one hundred percent want. Manipulating those weaker than me isn't my thing." I lowered my voice to dangerous levels, and I saw Corrin twitch. "If I want to make someone submit, I have more creative ways."

Corrin cupped his chin in his palm, making moon eyes at me. "No, please. Tell us more."

I chuckled, and even Grady shook his head. "Sorry, man, I don't play that way. Happy to share, you know— having our Omega spread out between us is going to be so fucking fun. But you gotta keep your meat stick to yourself."

He actually pouted. "I knew hoping you were bisexual would be too much to ask. Fine. Orgies it is."

I laughed easily, surprising myself. When I'd been crash-tackled by fucking Federal agents outside my apartment yesterday, this had felt like a life sentence. Shit, I almost would have rather gone to jail than be tied to an Omega for the rest of my life. But Tryst, and now these guys, were a pleasant surprise.

"I'm Kacey Boyd." I held out my hand, first to Grady, who shook it firmly, and then to Corrin. He grabbed it like he was going to shake it, but then turned it over and stared at my tattoos.

"So, I gotta know—do these tattoos go everywhere?"

I opened my mouth to tell him he'd have to wait and find out for himself, when RJ slipped back into the room, his face pale. Only seconds behind him was Princess, but she didn't head back to the sitting room to us. No, she power-walked down the hallway, like the hounds of Hell were on her tail.

"What the fuck happened?" I snapped at RJ, and he looked at me, shaking his head.

"Alpha Hart is going to ask the courts to annul their bond."

I sucked in a breath. The fuck? I mean, I admit, I'd been pretty fucking cut up about coming here, but ten minutes with Tryst—and another forty or so between her thighs—had basically sealed the deal for me. I might hate the DoDA for making me be here, but I would never make her suffer because of it.

Grady was shaking his head like it didn't make any sense. "But what about the pain? Corrin and I have made a concerted effort to be touching her at all times over the last fucking week, because it's the only thing that eases the proximity ache of being separated from a bondmate."

Corrin shook his head. "Not that we care; I'll fucking tie her to my side forever if it helps. But surely he wouldn't do that to her on purpose, right?

Knowing it hurts her like that? It would be fucking cruel."

Grady punched the wall. "I'm going to speak to fucking Agatha. He can't do this." He stormed out of the room, and I watched him go. He really did care about her; it wasn't lip service at all.

RJ just stared at us, his mouth opening and closing aimlessly. He had no answers either, that much was obvious. Only one person had answers, and I intended to beat them out of him. I would take a pound of flesh for Tryst, and I'd do it with a smile on my fucking face.

Corrin narrowed his eyes at me. "I don't trust that look. What are you going to do?"

I smirked, cracking my knuckles because I liked the drama of it. "I'm going to share the pain."

Corrin pursed his lips. "Fine. I'll go and make sure Tryst is okay; you go and kick his ass. Get a good hit in for me."

I saluted and strode out of the room, past RJ who made no move to stop me, even though I was about to break several fucking rules. I pushed onto the patio, and it was like Remzi Hart had been expecting me. He uncurled himself until he was standing at his full height.

"Remzi Hart, I'd challenge you to the right to be the primary Alpha of this Pack, but honestly, I'm pretty sure you'd just hand it over. So I'm going to fucking kick your ass instead, and you can either take it, or run away like the little bitch you are."

Remzi just stood there, attempting to stare me down. I'd fought men more bloodthirsty than him, more powerful, more ruthless. He didn't scare me at all.

"You can try."

I grinned. Fuck yeah, I liked a challenge and I didn't play by the rules.

I grabbed the plate of food and threw it at his head, and the shock on his face at the move would have been comical if I wasn't launching myself at his gut and shoulder-charging him off the patio.

He was going to regret the day that he fucked with what was mine.

Chapter Sixteen
Tryst

I wasn't sure how long I lay on my bed, staring unseeingly at the ceiling, when the door opened. Corrin ducked his head around the doorjamb, an empathetic expression creasing the lines around his eyes. "Can I come in?"

I nodded, and he was climbing onto the bed beside me and hauling me into his arms in an instant. I sucked in the familiar scent of him. He smelled sweet and clean, with just a touch of Grady, which was a strangely addictive scent. Like fresh laundry and marshmallows. I pressed my face hard into his chest, like that scent could chase away all the shitty things in my life.

"We heard what Remzi plans to do."

I looked up into his face, and his soft, under-standing expression made me want to cry. Maybe it was allergies. Maybe I was allergic to empathy. "You and Grady might be able to cruise through on his unbinding proceedings. They might just declare me faulty and let you all escape."

Corrin frowned. "What?" He grabbed my waist and hauled me up until we were nose to nose. "What are you talking about? Baby girl, it might have been a rough start, but I'm happy here. More than happy. I get the man of my dreams, a beautiful, soft Omega who I know I will love, and my entire life is paid for. I won the jackpot. Neither Grady nor I have any grievances about how things turned out."

I snorted. "Rough start. That's one way to put it. I stole Grady from your life."

Corrin pushed my hair back from my forehead. "All good relationships have rough patches. Best to get it out of the way early. You know how I met Grady?"

I shook my head, feeling like shit that I knew so little about their lives. It had been two weeks of sex and that was about it.

"I hit him with my car." I gasped, and he let out a small laugh. "I was pulling into his garage, didn't see him, and hit him with my bumper. Broke his leg in three places. I brought him dinner every day for a month and by the time his leg healed, we were totally in love." He leaned down and kissed my nose. "Grady and me, we aren't going anywhere, I promise. Besides, I like your new Alpha. He's not nearly as stuffy as Remzi, and that ass?" He did a chef's kiss gesture with his fingers. "Are those tattoos all over?"

A laugh chased away my blues, and that was the power of Corrin. If I'd been able to choose my own Pack, I would have chosen him regardless. He was sunshine and light, and he made me laugh. That was worth more to me than being a billionaire, or even being breathtakingly handsome, though Corrin definitely had the latter in abundance. He'd healed my heart, and I would cherish him everyday.

"Where is everyone else?"

"Grady is arguing with the Officials, and Kacey is kicking Remzi's ass in the backyard. He challenged him. I wonder who'll win?"

I bolted upright, accidentally digging my elbow into Corrin's gut. "*What?!*"

He coughed a little, then grinned, like the chaos lover he really was. "My money is on Kacey. He looks like he's split his knuckles a time or two, and he seemed real angry on your behalf."

I scrambled off the bed, rushing out of the room. As soon as I hit the hall, I could hear the shouts and the sound of shit breaking outside.

Oh no.

. . .

They'd managed to direct the battling Alphas out into the front yard, yet somehow the two men had still managed to leave a path of destruction.

Along with their compulsive leadership qualities, Alphas were physically superior to Betas. It was like every single one of them was Olympic-level at all the things; they were just stronger, faster, more resilient. Which was amazing, except when two Alphas were fighting. Then it was a bloodbath.

The sound of a crunching bone made me shudder. They were still human, though. They still took damage like any other person.

Blood dripped down Remzi's dress shirt, and at some point Kacey had lost his tee. His tattoos undulated under the waning sun, and I could see his lip was split open again, making blood drip onto his chest.

I went to rush into the fray, break it the hell up, but RJ was suddenly there, wrapping an arm around my waist and pulling me back. "Better not get between them, Omega. They've got their blood up and they aren't thinking straight."

"Why aren't you guys doing anything?" I growled, trying to ignore the hard flex of his body as he pressed me tightly to his front.

"Pack matter. Besides, no one wants to get between two Alphas. One of those hits would put me in the

ICU." He seemed disgruntled by the fact that he was as helpless as I was.

As if to make RJ's point, Kacey punched Remzi in the face, making his head snap back in a daze, and the sound that echoed around the crowd was painful. That would have been enough to render any of them unconscious, but Remzi just shook it off, charging at Kacey and laying a shoulder into his gut, taking them both to the ground.

Once they were down, it was hard to track the hits and jabs, but the sound of fists meeting flesh told me that this brawl was pretty evenly matched. I felt the echo of every hit, every grunt of pain, and I hated it.

Didn't they realize they were both bonded to me now? I could *feel* their damn pain.

"Stop!"

They couldn't hear me over whatever things they were muttering at each other in close combat. They probably couldn't hear me over the jeers of the surrounding people either, the violence reverting us all back to a schoolyard mob.

I stepped out of RJ's arms, fury overcoming me as they grunted with each hit that landed. "*STOP!*"

My scream reverberated around the clearing, and both Alphas stilled, their heads turning in unison. Their faces were swollen and bloody, but I couldn't tell whose blood was whose.

I looked at Remzi, his eye black and a cut on his cheek. I hated him, but still, I wanted to go to him and clean his wounds, make sure they were bandaged properly, because I was his goddamn Omega.

It just made me angrier. I glared at him with all the pain I felt. "Just go."

His eyes burned with bloodlust, but he lifted himself off of Kacey. He tugged at his shirt, straightening it even though it had lost most of its buttons. I watched him slide into a car that probably cost more than my parents had ever made. He shot me one last loaded look, then peeled out of the driveway.

I watched his taillights until they were long gone. Kacey still lay in the dirt, and my Omega desperately wanted to go to him, to bundle him up and make him better.

Agatha got there first, and she looked like she was resisting the urge to grind the heel of her sensible shoes into his balls. "In all my years as an Official, I have never seen such a display of... of outright hostility. I should call the police and have you charged with assault."

Kacey just let his head thump back down to the dirt and laughed, his teeth bloody. "I'd like to see you try, Aggie."

The enraged Official stormed off, snapping at the other DoDA workers just standing around. I waited until they'd left, all except RJ, and then walked over to my Alpha. I kneeled in the blood-soaked dirt beside him, the sticky mess coating my knees.

"What were you doing, Kacey?"

He grinned. "Defending your honor, Princess."

I brushed my thumb against his split lip, pressing a little too hard on the swollen gash there. He hissed, but his eyes were fiery and filled with lust. Did Kacey like a little pain? "Well, stop it."

He lifted himself up into a sitting position with a groan. "No can do. I'm your Alpha; it's my job to protect you, even against your other bondmates."

"You don't even know me."

"I know how you feel from the inside."

Well. I couldn't argue with that.

Grady and Corrin appeared beside me. "Stubborn idiot," Grady muttered, but there was a note of respect there. He reached down and pulled the larger man to his feet. "But I'm not mad you smacked the arrogant fuck around a little. You beat me to it, and I'm man enough to admit I would've gotten my ass kicked. Worth it though, just so he got a small taste of Tryst's pain."

Grady was more furious than I'd ever seen him, even after the last time Remzi left. I guess he'd assumed Remzi would come back, not apply to prolong the pain forever.

Corrin laughed. "Come on, Bruiser. We'll patch you up and get a beer." He wrapped an arm around my waist and guided me inside first. "We should all get to know each other more. It's just been me, Tryst and Grady for a little while now." He dropped his voice until his lips were just beside my ear. "And I, for one, have a massive hard-on for your new Alpha."

Grady rolled his eyes. "We can hear you, you know."

Corrin winked over his shoulder at them. "I know."

He kissed my cheek hard and led me to the upstairs sitting room that we'd taken over as ours. But I didn't miss the sound of the deadbolts being thrown. They weren't going to let us escape again.

It turned out Grady knew his way around a first aid box pretty well, and he insisted it was because he was a mechanic and not because he liked brawling or anything. Working with four-thousand-pound boxes of metal every day equaled a few injuries.

"So what do you do for work, Kacey?" Grady asked, making small talk as he cleaned the broken skin on Kacey's knuckles.

"This and that."

"What kind of answer is that?" I felt Corrin's voice through his chest. His fingertips were tracing circles on my thighs as he held me on his lap. The action wasn't sexual, more like he just enjoyed touching me. I kind of liked it too.

"An untruthful one," Grady said, meeting Kacey's eyes. "Better to get this shit out in the open now. We only have room for one dramatic Alpha, and you're too slow to get the role."

Kacey sighed, pulling his hand away. "Fine, but don't fucking freak out. I work for the family business."

Well, that wasn't so bad. "Why would we freak out about that?"

Kacey met my eyes and held them. "My father is Patrick Mullens." Nope, no idea. "Of the Boston Mullens."

I was missing something, but Corrin's body was rigid beneath me. "You're the fucking Irish Mob?"

Holy shit. Holy shit, holy shit. Okay, so I was definitely freaking out.

"Why weren't you excluded from the Allotment?" Grady asked, his eyes as comically wide as mine probably were. Anyone with a criminal history got bumped. Couldn't have thugs copulating with the babymakers, breeding more thugs with no respect for the iron fist of authority.

"Guess they don't do their homework that great. I've got my mother's name, and let's face it, Patrick Mullens is not out there declaring all his illegitimate bastards now, is he? His name isn't even on my birth certificate." Something flashed in Kacey's eyes, but was gone just as quickly. "He has his publicly declared successor—my half-brother, Doughal. He even has a spare, Adam. I am just somewhere down the line." He winked at me. "Plus, I never get caught. No criminal record, no automatic exclusion."

A little of his bravado dropped as he searched my face. He kept opening and closing his mouth like he wanted to say something else, or make a joke, but then changed his mind. It was kind of interesting to see the cocky Alpha suddenly off-kilter. Endearing even, as long as I forgot he was a criminal.

I mean, he was in the mob—maybe he was even a murderer.

"Have you ever killed anyone?"

He winced. "Yes. But he deserved it. Beat his kids and ran a sex ring out of his garden shed." He paused again, searching my face once more. "What are you thinking?"

Fuck, I didn't know.

"I really don't..." I sighed. "On one hand, I feel kind of betrayed, or duped, or something. You should have told me before we bonded. I really hate that people keep waiting until after I'm tied to them for life to drop these bombs." They all looked kind of guilty, even Grady, who had been the most honest so far. "On the other hand, you've been kinda nice. You've been attentive, you haven't growled at me or treated me like I was less than you, and you get on well with my other bondmates. If you'd never told me about your family, I would have continued to think you were the perfect Alpha. Not that I wanted you to lie to me for any longer," I added quickly. "What I'm trying to say is that I'll judge you for who you are and how you treat our Pack, rather than who your family is. Remzi is the pinnacle of society, and he broke my heart into a million pieces. A man is more than his reputation, right?"

I wasn't sure who I was trying to convince, but Corrin squeezed me tighter against his body. "The world doesn't deserve your soft and forgiving heart, Tryst O'Sullivan." He looked at Kacey. "I'm cool with it. My folks would have a heart attack, but that just makes it even better. Besides, I like that we have an Alpha with some sort of power to protect our Omega. As long as your family is cool with all this? They aren't going to track us down and take you back, right?"

Kacey snorted, finally relaxing back onto the bed. "They couldn't be more excited about the doors this bondship will open." He gave a humorless laugh. "I'm finally worth more to them than as a grunt with loyalty literally flowing through his veins."

Unease flowed through me, but I pushed it down. I

had enough of my own problems right now, without borrowing what-ifs from the future.

I climbed off Corrin's lap, squeezing his thigh appreciatively, and walked over to Kacey. I kissed his split lip softly once more, then lay down beside him. Someone flicked on the television, and the other guys slouched down on the floor together.

Then there were four.

Chapter Seventeen
Tryst

T he collapse of US society in the years after the War to end all Wars was almost whole-sale, except for the judicial system. Law and order was maintained, barely, which meant the court system was the first thing to get back up and running, so it had remained essentially the same as *before*. Which meant when I was delivered separation papers by a court official, everyone tensely watched as the man handed me an envelope and then hightailed it out of there.

Agatha held out a hand, as if she was my parent and I was an unruly child who'd had a letter sent home by the principal. I stared her down, clutching the envelope to my chest and stomping out of the room. She wasn't the only one who could do dramatic exits.

I ended up back in our sitting room, blindly looking at the packet of papers. None of it made sense, just pages of indecipherable legal jargon.

I huffed, glaring at my bondmates as they entered the room. "Why does this have to be so damn complicated? There's like, fifty pages here? It's an overcomplicated novella considering he just wants to have our bondship annulled."

Grady came over and slid his body behind mine, pulling me back against his chest and wrapping his arms around my waist so his whole body surrounded me. It was like the world's best weighted blanket.

Kacey eyed me warily, looking at the sheaf of papers. "Can I take a look?"

I thrust the stack of pages at him. Blinking back those stupid tears that only Remzi Hart seemed able to elicit, I rubbed my chest, where his bond sat. I channeled my sadness down the connection and hoped it hit him square in the place where his heart should be.

Kacey sat down on the armchair, crossing one leg over the other and resting the papers there. He frowned as he read silently, and I realized he was going to read the whole thing before he told me what it said.

I sighed and tilted my head back against Grady's chest. My steadfast first bondmate. "I'm sorry this is so much drama. I'm sure it's not what you signed up for."

He kissed the top of my head. "I didn't really sign

up for anything, so in a way, this is exactly what I signed up for."

I screwed my nose up at that backwards logic, but he was saved by Corrin appearing with coffee. I took it from him gratefully, breathing in that sweet nectar. Corrin managed to get it perfect every time, and it was just another reason I was glad I'd made him mine. Or he'd made me his. The logistics were sketchy with that one.

We talked the last few days about the normal stuff: hopes, dreams, our families. Corrin was a potter, and he just wanted to make a living out of his art. He didn't want to do big showings, or sell millions of pieces. "I just want someone to pick up a vase at a yard sale in fifty years' time, and make like a thousand dollars on it because it is a genuine Corrin Sanderson." I made a mental note to ensure our future home had a studio space with good light, just for him.

Grady was happy with whatever life handed him. He'd like another workshop, but he was happy if he just spent his time refurbishing pre-War cars. It was completely possible now, and besides, those pre-War muscle cars went for an absolute mint.

Everything we needed to start our new life would be paid for by the DoDA, as long as I was a proper little Omega breeding machine.

Whoops, that reminded me. "Uh, actually guys, I

should tell you that Remzi insinuated that I was more... uh, fertile during the heat. There's a chance—though not high, because I'm on contraception—that I could be pregnant. I'm so sorry. But he did say it was worse if I was knotted by an Alpha, so I think we should be fine," I said quickly.

Corrin blinked at me. "Oh. Well, I knew you were on contraceptives, which was why I—I mean *we*, you know..."

"Came inside her like she was a cream bun and you were a patisserie chef?" Kacey provided without looking up from the papers in his hand.

"Something like that. Though you liked it better when we spread it across your skin, so we pulled out a lot." Corrin grinned with absolutely zero shame, and Kacey raised a brow at us all. I flushed so red, my cheeks were probably going to explode like stigmata from all the blood pooling there.

Grady was still frowning, though. "Are you... Do you want a baby?"

I looked at him like he'd grown a third eye. "God no. I mean, maybe one day, but not now. I haven't even met half my Pack. What if they're awful? Nothing is secure. I don't have a home or a nest." Even the idea was making me feel panicked. Oh god, why hadn't I thought of that?

He rubbed my arms. "Don't stress. We'll see what happens and then make plans." I tilted my head back and kissed my calm voice of reason.

Kacey distracted me by dropping the stack of papers on the coffee table. "Well, either way, you're going to be rich as hell. Hart is giving you a tidy sum of money to break the bond agreement and probably put a bandaid on his damn guilt. Unfortunately, because it has to go to the Superior Court to create a precedent for this craziness, you're going to need a lawyer."

Great. Just fantastic. "Does anyone know a lawyer?" I didn't want to rely on one given to me by the DoDA.

Kacey grinned, his smile sharkish. "I happen to know just the person. You're going to love her." He grabbed his phone and made the call.

Over the next hour, I learned the lawyer's name was Keisha, and in a roundabout way, I also learned that she'd once slept with Kacey. I wasn't sure how I felt about that.

Logically, I knew that all my bondmates would probably have had sex before our bond. I mean, Corrin and Grady definitely had, obviously. Humanity doesn't survive a near die-out without doing its darndest to repopulate, in the best way possible. It was only because I was Omega, and therefore the very embodiment of entrapment, that I'd still been a virgin before Grady.

Still, it kind of burned that a smart, successful woman had once slept with my Alpha. I locked that thought down, even as Kacey messaged Keisha copies of all the documents, putting her on retainer immediately. Keisha seemed excited by the prospect of a precedent-setting case, and said she'd drop all her other cases. She sounded nice, and extremely capable, which should've reassured me, not made me jealous.

Tomorrow was another Allotment day, and I had other things to worry about. I was so fucking tired. I didn't need more drama or more mates. I was happy enough with these three. But the DoDA didn't care what I wanted.

That became very clear the next day.

I was awoken by banging at my door. I was curled around Kacey, my nose pressed against his spine, and I buried my face deeper under the blankets, hoping they'd just go away. Grady and Corrin had gone back to their own beds in the early hours of the morning, long after I'd fallen into an exhausted sleep. My fingers were curled against Kacey's abs, and he held my hand protectively against him, even in his sleep.

Apparently, I'd gotten the good and the not-so-good when it came to Alphas, but I didn't fool myself. Remzi might have broken my heart a little, but he was by no means the worst Alpha I could have had. There were horror stories whispered in the Omega world, about abusive Alphas who wanted submissive Omegas, and who beat their Betas. Who took what they thought belonged to them, regardless of anyone else's wishes, including the Omegas'. So no, while I was pissed at Remzi, it could have been worse.

The banging at the door continued and Kacey swore under his breath. He rolled over, dragging me up and along his body. I flushed, because since our bonding, we hadn't had sex again. Actually, they'd all been treading carefully around me, like they were afraid I was one wrong move away from a full emotional breakdown.

They weren't wrong.

But they'd all been very touchy-feely, especially Corrin, who seemed to default to touching me somewhere whenever he was close by, even if it was just twining our fingers, or stroking my hair.

Kacey was the same, but we hadn't known each other long enough for it to not be sexual. Every touch set my nerve endings on fire. Being pressed chest to chest with him made me want to bite down on his pec and then dry hump him to completion.

Another loud knock. "Omega! Official Danvers

would like to speak to you." There was a pause. "She seems impatient." It was one of the guards, not RJ, so I sighed.

"Coming," I shouted, and Kacey curled up and licked my throat.

"Not yet, but it can be arranged."

I legitimately giggled and slapped his chest. Holy shit, had I turned into a caricature of an Omega?

He gripped my hips and thrust up, his morning wood sliding against my night shorts and making me hiss out a moan. One hand slid up my back to palm the back of my head to pull me down into a soft kiss. "Would you like that, my Omega?"

"Yes," I breathed, and he sucked my bottom lip between his teeth.

His nostrils flared as he scented just how much I wanted him, then he groaned. "Later, Omega. Tonight, you're mine."

I wanted to argue, because he'd forgotten that it was Allotment day, but instead, I leaned close so my lips brushed his. "Yes, Alpha."

The noise he made was pained, and he rolled me back onto the bed. "You're dangerous, Tryst O'Sulli-van. Get dressed and see what that old hag wants. I'm going to have a cold fucking shower."

I watched his ass as he strode toward my ensuite,

those tattoos that ran across his whole back completely mesmerizing. Finally, I rolled out of bed and slipped on some sweats. Time to face the dragon.

Chapter Eighteen
Tryst

"Two at once? Has that even been done before?"

Agatha's lips were pressed so tightly together, it was a wonder they didn't explode. "No, and I doubt it will ever be done again. This whole Allotment has been"—she paused, schooling her features back to neutrality—"an exception to the rules. The quicker it is over, the better for society as a whole."

I wanted to rage at the stupid woman that it wasn't my fault. If it was anyone's fault, it was the Department's, with their dumb, antiquated system. Instead, I held my tongue. I wanted this over and done with just as much as she did, so I'd keep my mouth shut.

"Both Allotment numbers were drawn last night, and will arrive here within the hour. I suggest you start looking at the housing portfolios and packing your bags. Your *divorce case*"—she sneered the words at me, like it was my fault Remzi had decided to break the bond, like he'd found me wanting somehow—"has dragged up some extraneous issues that the DoDA will need to prepare for, so the usual Allotment procedures have had to be expedited and kept from the public. From your psychological testing before the Allotment, we concluded that five was the preferred number of bondmates, so with your unexpected Pack member— and despite Alpha Hart's cold feet—you will have the pre-approved amount. That is all that matters. The rest is just for show, to keep the masses appeased that the due process is happening."

Her lip curled, like regular people were below her. I decided I really, *really* hated Agatha Danvers.

My whole body was thrumming with anger. "You didn't think I had the right to know? To be prepared for the fact that I was going to have two brand new mates at once?"

She gave me a cold look. "Miss O'Sullivan, you will find that you have no rights when it comes to your future or your pairings. The sooner you come to terms with the fact that you are the property of the US government, the happier you will be."

I stared at this woman, this person who controlled my life, with horror and hate. "Fuck you."

She sneered. "It's you who will be fucked, Omega."

I jumped to my feet, launching myself across the desk between us. "You fucking bitch!"

Arms quickly wrapped around my waist. RJ was there, pulling me to his chest and spinning me toward the door. "Calm, Omega. You don't want to do that," he whispered in my ear. He looked over the top of my head. "Official, I will be putting your words in my report."

She had the gumption to snort. "You'll find my report of your behavior equally damning, *Official Hicks*." There was no missing the threat, and I struggled to get out of RJ's arms so I could smack the bitch.

RJ tightened his grasp around my waist. "So be it." He marched me out of the room and hefted me up the stairs until we were back in my sitting room. I hadn't realized how bad it looked until Kacey was on his feet, his hands clenched around RJ's collar. Fuck, he was fast.

"Get your fucking hands off of my Omega," he growled.

To RJ's credit, he let go of me immediately. Kacey lifted him up and tossed him against the wall. I was simultaneously turned on by Kacey's strength and scared for RJ's wellbeing. That couldn't be healthy, right?

Grady got in between them, holding Kacey across the chest and herding him back. Grady was a solid guy, but he wasn't as strong as an Alpha, so whatever he was muttering to him, it was obviously having an effect.

"Chill out, Alpha. RJ was just stopping me from doing something that would've gotten us all in trouble. No matter how satisfying it would have been."

Kacey growled low in his throat, and I swear, it flicked my clit like someone with a light switch in a pitch-black room.

"I wanted to punch Agatha," I explained softly, dragging my mind back out of my pants. Kacey glared at RJ once more, then turned his back on him. Ouch.

"What did Aggie want?" Corrin asked softly, obviously trying to lower the testosterone in the room back down to non-suffocating levels. We'd all adopted Kacey's mocking nickname for the Head Official.

"Apparently, because we are such a fuckup as a group, they are rushing the Allotment draw. They drew the last two in secret yesterday. They'll arrive in forty-five minutes."

They all just gaped at me. "That's... against the rules." Corrin looked pale.

I slumped down on the couch. I should be getting ready, trying to make a good impression, but honestly, I was kind of glad they'd drawn them together and that this uncertainty would be over. It would be a relief to get on with the rest of our lives.

After the court case with Remzi, at least.

"Breaking your matebond is against the rules too, but apparently they're pissy and the person bearing the brunt of that is Tryst," Grady growled. "Did they at least give you their profiles?"

I shook my head. We all turned to look at RJ, who hadn't left yet. Maybe he had a death wish, given the way Kacey was glaring at him.

RJ shrugged. "It came from higher up. I don't know any details either."

I doubted that was true, but I didn't push. There was something going on with RJ, but it really wasn't my business. He wasn't my mate, no matter how much my Omega liked him. In a week, we'd be booted out of this house, let loose into the real world, and I'd probably never see him again.

The sadness I felt at the thought of never seeing him again was unexpected. He was not my mate. He was just an Official. My Omega had to get that through her thick head.

RJ's phone flashed, and he looked down at it. "I have to go."

Well, there went our inside source. The other guys looked varying levels of angry and worried. I understood the feeling. We were barely treading water as it was, and it was like the DoDA wanted to push us under, hoping we'd drown.

I couldn't help thinking about Remzi's mother, and

her story. But unlike his Omega mother, I was happy with these guys. I knew in my soul that they wanted what was best for me, and given time, we would come to love each other. I already cared about them, even Kacey.

I straightened my shoulders, pushing down my anxiety. I would dress like a proper little Omega. I would make a good impression, and I'd get to know my new bondmates before tying myself to them—if the DoDA didn't like that, they could kiss my fucking ass.

"Get dressed. If they want to mix things up, so can we. We'll meet these strangers as a united front, and we'll decide if we want them in the group. I have three of you; I've done my fucking duty to the country. Just because they think there should be five—or six—of you, shouldn't mean I'm obligated to do it, right?"

"Right," Grady said, giving me a reassuring expression.

"You know what would have been good? An orgy," Kacey mused, running his knuckles along his jaw. "Nothing says 'united front' like the scent of combined bodily fluids."

I... what? But the thought of what he was suggesting filtered into my brain and refused to leave. Kacey's tattooed hands on my body, while Corrin ate me out and Grady fucked him at the same time.

Holy shit.

"Forty-five minutes isn't long enough for that, right?"

The heavy lust in Corrin's eyes ensnared me and refused to let me go. "No, baby girl. If we want to do it properly, even four hours won't be enough." He sauntered over to me, his lithe body doing crazy things to my brain. "When we have our first Pack orgy, you're going to be hoarse from all the screaming we'll make you do. You won't know your own name—all you'll know is the taste of us on your tongue." He smacked my ass. "Now, you better go change. We've got less than an hour before you meet the rest of your destiny."

Chapter Nineteen
Tryst

The guys sat around me protectively, though you wouldn't know it. Their positioning seemed casual, but that would be a lie.

Kacey slouched with feigned insouciance in an armchair facing the door, almost like a prince. Corrin had one ankle crossed over his knee at the end of the sectional couch, but he was within reaching distance of my fingers, which he stroked with his thumb periodically. Grady wasn't subtle at all. He sat pressed right against me, and if I sneezed, I'd probably land on his lap.

Grady seemed to be taking this sudden change in procedure the hardest, grumbling about how the rules could change, but only for the government. The rest of us just had to do what we were told. He'd reeled it in by the time we'd reached the sitting room, but now, as he sat beside me, his arm ran along the back of the couch behind my shoulders in a move that was possessive and protective, and made me so fucking happy.

When was the last time someone was ever worried about my feelings? Or felt protective over me as a person, and not as a commodity? These guys were an unexpected blessing.

I held my breath as I heard footsteps in the hall, and then the door was opening, Agatha's fake-smiling face taking us all in. Her eyes narrowed, but I had to give her props, her pleasant mask didn't drop. "Ah, Alpha Bell, it seems like you get to meet the whole Pack at once."

My skin prickled. How did I get another Alpha? Three Alphas drawn during the Allotment should be a statistical improbability.

My eyes were pulled to the man in front of me, who was well over six feet tall, so I had to crane my neck back to look at him, even from a distance. He had warm skin and almond eyes that spoke of some type of Asian heritage, though I wouldn't even try to guess where specifically. His hair was dark and straight, though slightly messy, like he'd been running his fingers through it all day.

I stood, smoothing down the skirt of my dress with sweaty hands. He gave me a warm smile that exhibited perfect teeth and slight creases around his eyes. His jaw was straight and square, and he was so fucking handsome it hurt. Did the DoDA vet them with an attractiveness test no one told me about? I guess it would make sense, considering that reproduction was the end goal for the government here.

He bowed at the waist. "Omega."

"Alpha Bell," I choked out.

The man stepped further into the room, looking over his shoulder at whoever was still in the hall. He lifted his chin, waving the other person into the room. And when they entered? My jaw fell to the floor like an old school cartoon.

My Omega brain and my human brain were at war. Because the second man in the room was the doppelganger of the first, so close in likeness that they had to be twins. Twins were even rarer than Omegas these days.

My Omega was confused, because only one of them was Alpha. The new guy didn't feel like an Alpha, but not quite like a Beta either. He was altogether different, and his eyes swept around the room. His mouth was turned down in a frown as he looked at my bondmates, with none of that automatic warmth I'd gotten from the first man.

"Well fuck me, you're twins." That was from Kacey, who was bristling slightly at another Alpha being in the room. Yeah, a bit of heads up about that would have been handy.

The second guy's eyes met mine, and his face softened. "Omega." He bowed at the waist like his twin. His voice was raspy, and the way he said the word was almost like a caress.

Oh boy.

The non-Alpha twin traced my face with his eyes, and I couldn't help but feel like he was cataloging every imperfection. He seemed intense. "I'm Jak. This is my brother, Akio." We stood around, being awkward, while half a dozen Officials and all my bondmates watched on.

"Well, no guesses as to why we suddenly have two new bondmates instead of one." Grady stood and walked over, holding out his hand. "I'm Grady."

Akio stepped around his brother to shake the peace offering Grady was giving them. Jak shook his hand as well, mumbling pleasantries as Corrin stood and repeated the gesture, his other hand firmly on my lower back. The dark eyes of both men took in the stance, but no one said anything about the possessive move from a Beta.

Finally, Kacey stood and swaggered toward us. Akio stood taller, meeting Kacey's eyes, and his twin stepped up beside him. A united front. Or maybe two parts of the same front.

"Kacey Boyd," my Alpha grunted, holding Akio's gaze, neither of them wanting to drop their stare first.

Jak rolled his eyes and stepped between them. "We could do this fucking posturing bullshit all day but I'm tired as hell, and I'd like to get this shit over with. I'm Jak. I'm not an Alpha, even though we're twins. Don't know why I didn't get the gene, but let's forget it, okay?"

"Fair enough. I like your ink," Kacey said, his tone amused.

I noticed that Jak had a hand tattoo under his long-sleeved white button up. Did he have other tattoos too?

"Thanks," he murmured, then stepped from between the two Alphas. Akio put his hand out first, and they shook.

"Alpha," Akio greeted, and Kacey shrugged.

"Call me Kacey. Calling people by their designation is fucked up." He looked over his shoulder at me. "Except in the bedroom, Princess."

I hadn't missed how much harder he fucked me when I called him Alpha.

"We were taught that acknowledging and showing deference to an Omega was the respectful thing to do by our grandparents, but generally, we agree. It's always been a bit of a thing with us."

Something relaxed in my chest. They were respectful. Nice. I could work with this.

"Good to know." Kacey looked over at the Head Official. "It's also good to know that the DoDA can pick and choose who wins the fucking Allotment too."

Aggie gave him a haughty expression. "I assure you, *Mr.* Boyd, that the Allotment was conducted completely legally and follows the strict protocol set out in legislation."

Kacey looked at the older woman like she was stupid. "You're going to jerk my dick and tell me that you randomly selected twins? Please." The look he gave her would melt a lesser person's face like acid. "Either you're stupid or you think I am, because it would be statistically impossible. More likely that the government wants a little selective multiple-birth breeding, am I right?"

We all looked at the Official, whose face was turning a worrying shade of puce. "That is none of your goddamn business. Just do what you do best and *fuck*, and leave the more complicated matters of humanity to the US government, Mr. Boyd."

She slammed out of the room, and the twins looked at the door with confusion. I was kind of used to her hissy fits now. There were still a bunch of Officials in the room with us, and they all looked vaguely uncomfortable at Aggie's outburst.

Though there was no RJ. Surely he wouldn't let

some other Official witness the bonding? I wasn't sure why the idea upset me so much.

"Sorry about that. Apparently, my Allotment has been a little stressful for Official Danvers." I looked around the room, but none of the other Officials would meet my eye. I shook my head at their cowardice, before smiling at my new potential mates. "We should sit. I, uh, have had some problems so far, and I think it would be nice to know you guys a little better before we get to the bonding part of the evening."

There was no polite way to say that my first Alpha was so disgusted with me that he'd decided it'd be better to be in constant pain and part with a whole chunk of guilt money, than to be committed to me any longer.

Akio gave me a sympathetic look. "We were informed that one of your mates is seeking to annul the bond."

Jak snorted. "They made it sound like it was your fault. Like you, we should prepare ourselves to consider you defective." He put on a voice that sounded a lot like Aggie. "But gosh, the government would awfully appreciate it if we could overlook her flaws and bond with her anyway and create a bunch of babies."

Rage and embarrassment fought inside me for supremacy. Akio looked panicked, and he shot his brother a scathing look. "We don't agree, of course. You seem perfectly nice."

"Hot as fuck," Jak added.

"Wait until you're inside her. It's like an other-worldly experience. That might be thanks to the extra set of hands where her labia should be," Corrin teased, and I whipped my head toward him, my mouth hanging open. He was literally doing jazz hands, reen-acting my mythical hand labia.

I was going to murder him.

The Bell twins looked horrified, until Corrin started laughing, followed by Grady. My lips twitched even as I death-glared at Corrin. "Not funny, asshole." I looked back at my potential new bondmates. "They're joking. There are no extra things." I frowned. "I don't think I'm defective?"

Kacey grabbed me up and sat back down on the couch, settling me on his lap in a definite power move. "Of course there isn't, Princess. If anyone's defective, it's fucking Remzi Hart."

"Or the system," Grady added.

Definitely the system.

"Holy shit, your other Alpha is Remzi Hart?" Akio gasped. "Like CEO and founder of HartWire Tech, Remzi Hart?"

Sometimes I forgot that Remzi was mega-mega-rich and kind of famous. No wonder he could just decide he didn't want to play anymore, while everyone else had to deal with the consequences.

I gave a curt nod while Kacey squeezed my thigh reassuringly. I pasted on a self-deprecating smile. "That's the one. I'd offer to introduce you, but he never wants to see my face again..." Shrugging, I tried to swallow down the rejection once more.

Akio shook his head, frowning like it just didn't make sense. "His loss, Tryst. Can I call you Tryst?"

I smiled, because that was kind of sweet. "Considering we'll probably be having sex at some point today, I'm going to have to insist on it."

Akio's olive-toned cheeks flared bright red, and a laugh burst from Jak. "Yeah, definitely his loss."

Chapter Twenty
Akio

S he wasn't what I was expecting. Granted, I hadn't really met an Omega before, so any preconceived notions I had about what an Omega would be like were based on old family stories and Hollywood movies.

Sure, she definitely hit some of those expectations; she was graceful as well as beautiful, and she called to the Alpha inside me like a siren. The loyalty she inspired in those around her was expected too. Well, except for Remzi Hart.

I still couldn't believe it. I'd always admired Remzi —he'd taken the world and molded it to his satisfaction. We were both in similar industries, though I was a business consultant for companies that had never worked in a global economy. I was humble enough to admit that my job wouldn't be necessary if it wasn't for

HartWire and their technological advancements. We'd still be sifting around in the technological Dark Ages without him.

Apparently, Remzi Hart was smart about technology, but blind about treasures right in front of his face. I couldn't imagine giving up the opportunity to really satisfy my Alpha, to appease that base desire that was always simmering there below the surface.

What a fool.

But I'd only known Tryst for less than thirty minutes, so we'd see. She might have met some expectations in some ways, but she'd also surprised me in others, and honestly, that was even more exciting. Like the fiery way she'd glared at Official Danvers, or the protective way she stood in front of Corrin and Grady, who were so obviously a couple you'd have to be dumb not to see it. I wasn't sure Tryst was even aware of the way she stood between them and our judgment, like it was innate inside her to protect them.

But also the way she didn't take herself so seriously, the way she playfully laughed off Corrin's jokes. I'd always believed that Omegas were emotional, dependent on those around them to keep them safe and happy. But five minutes with Tryst and her Pack had told me that while she relied on them, she'd also fight for their happiness.

I liked that. I looked at Jak, who was completely

smitten. I could tell. He hated the idea of being called up, of being paraded in front of an Omega like we were just a piece of meat she could choose.

He'd been grouchy as hell the whole way here, but I think he'd been scared. His whole life, he'd been an add-on to me. I'd exited the womb first, and he'd come out after, a complete surprise to both my parents and the doctors. The bonus baby.

When I'd presented as an Alpha, everyone had waited for him to present as one too. He never had; he'd remained a Beta, and that had burned him because everyone automatically dismissed him again. Like I was somehow more special.

So I was pretty sure that until the very moment he walked into the room and met Tryst, he'd been scared that someone would change their mind and tell him that he wasn't wanted or needed. That we'd be split up for the first time in our lives. Because as much as we craved independence, it was never from each other.

We were two halves to a whole, and we always would be. I'd been scared too, that our Omega would demand he leave.

But looking at Tryst, I didn't think that would happen. She obviously didn't care about the tattoos or the rough demeanor, judging by her new Alpha. She didn't care about his sharp tongue or the way he was sarcastic at least 90% of the time, if Kacey was an example to go by.

No, Tryst wasn't what I imagined an Omega would be. She was better.

"Alpha Akio, I have to say, you're a pleasant surprise. A welcome one at that."

"Oh?" I said, refocusing on the conversations going on around me. "Please, call me Akio." The Alpha honorific always hurt Jak's feelings—a shining example, to him at least, of how he'd never measure up.

"Most of my mates didn't want to be here. They actually had to beat Kacey into submission to get him here."

The other Alpha turned from where he was talking to Jak to give her a hot look. "I don't submit to anyone, Princess."

She grinned, and I could see the affection so clearly on her face. It was beautiful. She was beautiful. I wanted her to look at me like that one day, like she was remembering all the ways I'd made love to her in vivid detail.

I cleared my throat, partly because my dick was now harder than iron in my pants, and partly because I wanted those pretty blue eyes back on me. "I am happy to be here. So is Jak, though I think he wouldn't let himself be hopeful until he met you."

She smiled understandingly. Gah, so pretty. "RJ

told me that there would be people out there honored to be my bondmate, but I have to admit, I was beginning to think it was all pretty lies."

I frowned. "RJ?"

Her cheeks flushed pink. Interesting. "The DoDA Official who has been my handler, of sorts, since this whole thing started. I like to think he's a friend." I looked around at the Officials in the room, but none of them seemed particularly friendly in their observations. More like they were watching a nature documentary in progress.

"I was fortunate enough to still know my great-grandparents. They'd been teens when the War to end all Wars was fought and lost. They remembered the emergence of Omegas, and the original Mud Maidens, but they didn't call them that. They said it was offensive. They insisted that Omegas were the blessed children of the gods, the saviors of humanity, and that they should be treated that way."

Tryst actually snorted, and it was adorable as hell. She slapped a hand over her mouth. "I'm sorry, I don't mean to be offensive. It's just hard to think of myself as blessed by anything other than Satan sometimes. Do you believe those things?"

I shook my head. No, I'd loved hearing my grandparents' stories about the goddesses coming down to bestow kisses on the wombs of chosen women, and feeding magic seeds to chosen men to make Alphas and Omegas, but I knew that wasn't true.

"No. I know it was just a side effect of nuclear warfare and some unlucky DNA. They'd been through so much trauma that they had to cling to the idea that it was for a purpose, right? That all that suffering and the dark years afterwards were *for* something. But their lessons on how an Omega should be treated have stuck with both of us for the rest of our lives, including what an honor it would be to be chosen by an Omega." I frowned. "I'm not sure they would have appreciated what a sham the Allotment has become, though. They were from the school of thought that these proceedings were really for the protection of Omegas. They'd be so disappointed to find out that it was just to subjugate you."

She gave me a sad smile. "I would have liked to have met them. They sound like good people."

"They were. They died when we were five, but their stories stayed with us. They were reinforced by my own grandparents, who are happily still alive, and then my own parents."

Her eyes lit up. "So much family." Small lines appeared between her eyes. Was it weird to find them adorable? "I didn't get a profile on you, so I'm sorry, but where are you guys from? The accent sounds like the West Coast."

I grinned, loving the way her cheeks flushed and her eyes widened. She wasn't unaffected by me, and that was a plus. "California. Our family owns a fast food chain out there."

"Sounds warm. And you? Do you work in the family business?"

I shook my head. "No, I'm a global business consultant. Jak works in construction. He's always been a master craftsman with his hands."

Her eyes lit up at that, and I might have been slightly jealous of my brother's occupation for a split second. "I wanted to be an architect."

"Not anymore?"

Her smile dimmed a little. "The DoDA wouldn't let me enroll in anything they thought might compromise my safety or standing. Apparently, architecture and engineering is considered too much of a man's world. I studied Literature, which I enjoyed..."

I didn't need to be psychic to know that it wasn't what she was passionate about.

"You and Jak would work well together. You could design and he could create. The DoDA won't matter soon enough, and you can do what you want. Jak will be there to support you in that 'man's world,'" I said derisively, doing the quotation marks because it was so fucking stupid. They wouldn't stop a Beta woman from pursuing architecture.

We were too quick to pigeonhole Omegas as weak creatures and men into something base and animalistic, like we didn't have complete control. I'd sat in this room for awhile now, talked to this Omega, and I hadn't turned into a horny shark unable to control myself.

It was an excuse. An excuse to keep Omegas under the DoDA's thumb. I might have been happy to be chosen for the Allotment, but it didn't mean I was blind to its faults.

The door opened, and another Official slipped inside. By the way the tension left Tryst's shoulders, I assumed this was the infamous RJ. Behind him, people began to arrive with food.

I watched a more relaxed Tryst settle into a conversation with Jak about his building jobs and flipping houses, about what he liked to create, and the Alpha inside of me let out a relieved breath. This was what it was supposed to be like. It was rushed and artificial, but I felt in my soul it could be good.

The Alpha roared to make her mine now, before someone else stole her. But she deserved time to get to know us, and I'd give that to her, the DoDA be damned.

Chapter Twenty-One
Tryst

The conversation had lulled a little as we snacked on a fruit platter brought in by one of the kitchen staff. The Officials around us were looking impatient, or maybe just bored out of their minds, and it wasn't until RJ slipped into the room that I realized I'd been waiting for him. He met my eyes as he stood near the door, but he looked preoccupied.

Or pained to see that we still haven't consummated our new bond, my brain provided, unbidden.

My eyes drifted to the Official at the desk, who looked like she was about to fall asleep as she gazed out the window longingly. I didn't blame her really.

I looked at Jak. "Are you sure you want the mate-bond? No hard feelings if you say no."

"Well, not on our behalf, anyway. I have it on good

authority that the DoDA gets a little upset if you say no to them." Kacey pointed to the almost healed bruise on his face. "But if fucking Remzi Hart proves anything, it's that if you have enough fucking balls, you can shit on laws and tradition as much as you want with no consequences."

I eyed Kacey warily. He leaned over and kissed my temple. "I wouldn't do it now, Princess. I've kinda grown attached to how you feel on my dick."

Corrin snorted. "Who said romance is dead?" He stood, adjusting his jeans as he looked meaningfully at Kacey. "On that note, we should, uh, go and let you guys get on with the fireworks portion of the day." He came over and kissed me softly, his eyes bright. "No pressure, babe. Do what feels right." His voice dropped lower as he moved his lips to my ear. "But two words. Twin. Sandwich."

My face flushed, and Kacey whacked him in the back of the head, but Corrin's eyes continued to sparkle with mischief. It would be a lie to say I hadn't thought about what it would be like to be kissed by two sets of the same lips, touched by the same hands, and honestly, I kind of wondered if their dicks were identical too.

Sue me. You'd wonder too.

Grady stroked a hand over my hair and gave me a wink. "Be good."

I rolled my eyes and waited for Kacey to loosen his arms around my waist, but if anything, he held me tighter. I turned slightly so I could look at him, but his eyes were burning into Akio's. "Hurt her and I'll gut you."

Akio didn't power play this time, dropping his eyes immediately. "The only thing we want for Tryst is happiness. We wouldn't dishonor her or our family in any way."

Kacey grunted, but grabbed my chin and kissed me hard. It was definitely a claiming kiss. He didn't want to leave, and I had a feeling he'd enjoyed being my only Alpha. I kissed him back and hoped it was reassuring. He wouldn't be replaced.

Finally, he shifted me gently to my feet, and strode out of the room. I watched him leave, his shoulders bunched, though he didn't slam the door. Instead, he closed it with a soft snick that still managed to reverberate around the room.

All the comfort fled with him, only to be replaced by awkwardness. I looked everywhere but at the two men in front of me. My gaze stopped on RJ, and he gave me a comforting smile, even if it didn't really reach his eyes.

The other Official in the room stood, handing us all our paperwork. I knew what it said almost word for word now, but still, I read every single letter. I didn't trust the DoDA not to screw me after Remzi's little departure. But it seemed pretty much the same so I signed it and the duplicate one behind it. Two forms. Two mates.

"Uh, do you want to complete the matebond separately or..." I pushed down the thoughts of being stuffed like a jelly donut. These guys had probably had to do everything together since they were young. Maybe they hated the idea of completing their matebonds together?

Jak signed his name with a flourish and shoved it at the Official before sauntering over to me. He lifted a hand and touched my cheek. "What do you want, Omega?" He looked at me with impenetrable eyes, so dark they almost sucked me down. "Akio and I, we were always meant to be two halves to a whole, but that doesn't mean we aren't more than capable of giving you so many orgasms separately that you won't remember your own name."

Akio finished dotting his i's, and didn't even bother handing back the clipboard, just letting it fall onto the couch. He stepped up to my back, the tips of his fingers brushing down my spine.

"Or, we can take you together, touch you in places that will make you scream with pleasure. With our hands." He skimmed his hands down my sides. "And mouths." His lips brushed down my neck and along my shoulder. "And our cocks."

I shivered, pleasure already spreading through me at his filthy words. I heard, rather than saw the other Official leave like her tail was on fire. Nothing like overheard dirty talk to suck the politeness right out of the room.

Jak lifted my hand and brought it to his lips, kissing my knuckles softly. "But the choice is yours, Tryst. Always yours." He spread my hand out, bringing the tips of my fingers to his lips before nipping the tip of my index finger. I moaned softly as he sucked it into his mouth. They'd fogged my brain with their words and their hands.

I decided that if Akio's grandparents were right, and there was a goddess bestowing blessings, she had definitely blessed me in the mate department. Well, mostly.

"So what do you want, Omega?" There was Alpha power in Akio's words, compelling me to lay my desires bare before them.

"Both," I whispered. "Please."

The words brought Jak to his knees in front of me. Akio held me tightly as Jak gently removed my soft flats, then placed my bare foot against his chest. His fingers roamed up and down my calves, and he kissed the inside of my knee.

"Jak and me, we're going to worship every inch of you," Akio whispered in my ear as Jak's mouth moved up higher to the inside of my thigh, holding it in his strong hand as he placed my leg over his shoulder.

"Fuck, I've been thinking about this since I walked into the room and saw you," Jak groaned as he nipped my flesh. Akio ran his hand down my stomach, scrunching up the folds of my skirt until he could see what Jak was doing between my thighs. I tipped my head back against Akio's chest, my eyes closing of their own accord.

I didn't see who tore off my underwear, but it didn't matter, because someone was rubbing my clit and there was a sudden cool gust of breath against my slit.

"So wet for us already, Tryst. So fucking pretty, and your scent..." Akio groaned in my ear, his twin lifting my other leg until I was propped completely over his shoulders and he could bury his face in my pussy. They held me easily between them, and I had to admit, there was something heady about only being connected to the earth by the hands of the men worshiping me.

Akio's clever fingers worked my clit in synchronization with Jak's tongue, the sensations they drew from me so intense that I was climaxing already. Jesus, did this guy play video games on expert mode or something?

I was panting as my body shook with the aftermath of an orgasm that had hit me like a gut punch. "Please," I begged, though I didn't know what I was begging for.

There was the slide of a tongue along my inner thigh, and then a sharp bite against the fleshiest part, piercing the skin there. I hissed, the pain edging out the pleasure momentarily, but then Jak's lips wrapped around my clit, sucking hard and sending me spiraling into another, stacked orgasm.

Holy freaking suction, Batman.

I was still coming down from my release when Akio pulled me off Jak's shoulders, and I took a moment to gaze down at him reverently. His face was shiny, and his grin was smug. It was a sexy as hell picture that I was committing to my mental spank bank forever.

Akio spun me, capturing my lips with a hard kiss. "You ready to take my knot and become ours forever, Omega?"

I'd never been more ready for anything.

He picked me up and walked me back to the bed, falling down onto it until he was on his back and my knees were either side of his slim hips. I didn't know when he'd gotten naked, but his well-endowed cock was pressing right where I wanted him. I shifted myself up and down his shaft, running the head through my wet folds, making us both groan.

"Tryst," he groaned. "You feel fucking amazing."

I grinned, and for the first time, with this Alpha on his back looking up at me like *I* was the gift, I felt powerful. Maybe even for the first time in my life.

I slipped a hand between us and notched him against my entrance, before sliding slowly down. I was officially a bona fide sex addict. This first stretch, the first moment of being filled was unlike anything else. It was perfection.

Akio's hands spread wide across my hips, his head tilted back in pleasure, just watching me through his lashes as I began to move. I tilted my hips backwards and rolled, sighing happily when he hit all the right places inside of me.

Strong, tattooed hands wrapped around my body, coming up to cup my breasts. I turned to kiss Jak, never slowing my rolling pace. The pleasure building inside me was frantic and consuming, and I knew deep down in my soul, that it was going to be something intense.

Akio moved my hips faster, grinding me down onto his body, and the heat of the moment ratcheted up to ten. Jak's fingers slipped down to my clit, and that was all I needed to come.

And come hard.

My thighs bunched, my body clenching at Akio's

cock, trying to cajole him into filling it with his knot. Not that he needed much persuasion.

"Yes, Tryst," he grunted, holding my hips tight to his as I rode out my orgasm, his cock perfectly placed for his knot to swell and lock me.

I felt so much more full from this position, and I collapsed forward onto Akio's chest. He wrapped his arms around my shoulders, holding me tightly as he thrust hard, shifting his knot inside me gently, but the effect was the same. I squeaked out a high-pitched moan, his knot rubbing against my G-spot until I was coming again and he was right there with me.

I pressed my teeth to his chest and bit down hard, creating a bite so perfect, if I was ever murdered, they could use it as dental records.

Akio moaned, lifting my arm to bite the underside, just below my elbow. This time, the splash of pain had no chance of breaking through the overwhelming waves of pleasure. I was cognizant enough to sit up, gasping through the electrifying sensations making all my limbs tingle, until I reached for Jak.

"Come here," I slurred, orgasm-drunk. He stepped forward, his hand stroking his cock. I frowned, because I wanted to do that, but when I reached for it, he sidestepped.

"This is your moment, Omega. You can handle my cock any time you want, but right now, I want you so blind with lust that you can't breathe, let alone suck my dick."

I wanted to argue, to take it as a challenge. I reached out, and he stepped forward. I grabbed his dick, stroking it roughly, but he was right. My whole body was shaking as release after release hit me. I gripped Jak's ass until his body was pressed close to me, and then I leaned over and bit just inside his hip, right at the top of the V of his obliques. He hissed, and I stroked his cock a little faster, until the sound of pain turned into a moan of pleasure.

I could multitask. They'd learn. I mightn't be able to summon the necessary coordination to suck cock at this very moment, but I could stroke it just fine.

I didn't need to bite Jak, because he was a Beta, but it felt right. I wanted them all marked up, my bite warning off anyone who thought they could take them from me. A logical, not sexed-up part of me wondered why I'd taken to these two so quickly, why I felt so possessive over the twins, but the Omega shut her down. She didn't care, especially when one was giving her amazing orgasms that kept coming in waves, and the other was painting my breasts with his seed. Jak's cock twitched in my hand, his balls pulled up tight as he sprayed hot ropes of his release on my skin.

"Omega," he gasped.

I lifted my hand and rubbed him into my skin.

Yeah, that shit was 100% Omega. I wasn't arguing with her for once, though. It was hot as hell.

The effect it had on the guys was nearly instantaneous, their groans almost synchronized. Akio had filled me to the brim until he was leaking out around the knot, and I found I really liked that too. I collapsed onto his chest, completely boneless and uncaring that I was smearing his brother's cum between us.

I didn't care about anything right now, and it was an entirely blissful feeling.

A strangled noise had me turning toward the door, catching just a glimpse of RJ before he left. At least this would be the last time he'd have to witness me being pounded like a chicken breast.

This was the last time I'd have to bond anyone on someone else's orders.

My Pack was complete.

Chapter Twenty-Two
Tryst

As much as I wanted to laze around in bed between Jak and Akio, I really wanted to be out of this room, and away from this particular bed. If I never saw it again, I'd be happy. To be honest, I really wanted to set it—and everything it represented—on fire. Still, it was really hard to drag myself out from between the warm bodies of my new mates.

They seemed enamored, and I breathed a sigh of relief. Jak, who was by far the most prickly, was tracing soft circles on my bare shoulders, not breaking the silence.

Despite being the Alpha, Akio was definitely the most nervous. Maybe it was because he was the Alpha. He kept lifting his hand, like he wanted to pet me, but then dropping it again. All that sex-fuelled charisma had disappeared, but left him endearingly cute.

Deciding to put him out of his misery, I rested my head on his chest, hooking my legs through Jak's. "This is weird, right?"

Akio let out a relieved breath. "Thank god it's not just me. This is... I'm not going to pretend that I haven't gone out to a club and had sex with a person I just met—"

"Dude, we have to work on your game," Jak scoffed, shaking his head. "You don't say you're a manwhore to your new Omega mate."

Akio reached over me and punched Jak in the shoulder. "Fuck off. I wasn't a manwhore." He looked at me imploringly. "I swear."

I couldn't help but giggle at his earnest expression. "I understand we can't all be virgins. I don't blame you for not saving yourself for the one-in-a-million chance you'd be picked in the draw." I looked between the two of them. "What would you have done if they'd only drawn one of you?"

I had my suspicions that's what had happened, but the DoDA had decided to double their odds. Or more likely, they hadn't even bothered with the draw.

Akio looked past me to his brother. "If they were adamant that I couldn't bring Jak with me? We would have run, probably to Canada. No offense, Omega, we're honored to be here. But I couldn't live without my twin."

I tried to imagine being able to rely on anyone the way these two could with each other, and it was impossible. I had brothers, but they were older than me, and my Omega status had basically cut any fledgling sibling bond we'd had.

I'd never even had a close friend. The best I had were these men, mates, who I'd had less than a month. How fucking sad was that?

Jak must have been able to feel my dejectedness through the bond. He dragged me closer to his body, wrapping me in toned, muscular arms and placing a kiss on my nape. "It's all just what-ifs. Now we have you, and you have my loyalty just as much as Akio. You're my *mate*. That means something to me. I hope —" He cleared his throat. "I hope eventually you might even grow to love us, as friends, if not as more. We are extremely aware that the choice in partners wasn't your own, and if it were, we mightn't have been your first choice. But I promise, we have your back."

I tilted my head back, rubbing my cheek against his. "Same. I'm glad you didn't run," I whispered, in case the DoDA had this room bugged and tried to steal them from me for something stupid like treason. Or conspiracy or whatever else they could concoct to stomp on my tentative happiness.

I sat up, clutching the sheet to my chest, though modesty was probably so far behind me, I could no longer see it in the rearview mirror. "Let's get out of here. We should head back up and get to know each other with our clothes on."

Akio pouted, and it was cute as fuck. I couldn't help but lean forward and kiss him. He kissed like a dream, and it was impossible to resist. But we'd been locked away in this room for hours now, and I could feel the restlessness of my other mates deep in my chest.

Swallowing down any residual embarrassment, I rolled over Jak. His hands ran down my sides with a salacious grin, but he didn't stop me as I stood. After spending a few seconds searching for my clothes, I picked up my dress and my torn underwear, which I waved accusingly at them.

"One of you owes me new underwear," I tutted, despite the fact my body clenched at the memory. Let's face it, it had been hot as fuck.

Akio grinned at me again, swinging his legs over the edge of the bed and uncurling to his feet. It was mesmerizing. Or dickmerizing, because I was still looking at his cock when he snatched my torn panties out of my hand and tossed them to his brother.

"We'll keep them as a memento." Jak smirked. "Bite marks and torn panties. Definitely a day to remember." He jumped up, shimmying his pants back on while I watched with blatant hunger.

Geez, I needed my libido to take a chill pill, otherwise I'd wear out my vagina. Besides, I now had five mates, and we'd have to talk about how this would all work. I had more important things to do with my life than fuck all day, every day. I just couldn't remember what they were right at this moment, as I watched Akio lazily pull on his crisp black pants over his naked ass. Commando.

Okay, maybe we needed to work it out so I didn't die of dehydration, because even the sight of that muscular ass made me wet again.

I cleared my throat, pushed down the need and slipped my feet into my flats. Akio padded up behind me to wrap his arm around my shoulders, giving me a quick kiss on the temple. "I can sense your panic, Tryst. I promise, we'll all get on fine. There are a lot of decisions to make, which are far more important."

I knew he was right; we'd had a great afternoon before the bonding. But Alphas needed a pecking order. It was stupid and animalistic, but inevitable, otherwise they'd never be content. I just hoped my newfound happiness survived too.

. . .

"There's no way I can live in LA. My whole family is in Boston. My *life* is in Boston. No offense, Princess."

I raised an eyebrow at him. "Why would I be offended? I'm not a state capital."

Corrin was wrapped around me like a cat, and I sunk into his warmth. "I don't know. I wouldn't mind spilling the tea in your party, if you know what I mean."

Grady snorted. "No one knows what you mean, because that made zero sense." He'd been mostly silent, sitting on the floor with his head resting between my thighs. It was a subtle claim, which was fine. Grady was the first, and I worried that he thought he was being replaced over and over. Luckily, Corrin picked up my slack.

How did Omegas with straight, vagina-loving mates cope? It would be like juggling sharp knives with grumpy attitudes all the time.

I stroked my hand through Grady's hair, and he closed his eyes. The Alphas in the room looked at the gesture like they wanted to be in his position. It might have calmed Kacey, but I wasn't going to move Grady to appease my volatile Alpha. He'd just have to deal like a grown up.

"I understand that you want to go back to Boston, Kacey, but we have to at least come to some kind of compromise."

Akio laughed. "I vote anywhere but the Midwest." He grimaced at Grady. "Sorry, man. It's just a long way from LA, you know, and not just distance-wise."

I frowned at the other Alpha. "Corrin and Grady get to weigh into this decision too. Just because they aren't from a city, doesn't mean they automatically don't get a choice. They were torn from their lives just as much as the rest of us."

"Yet they get to be the ones between your thighs, being soothed," Kacey grumbled.

Ugh. Lord save me from whiny ass men.

Grady heaved a sigh. "I don't mind where we live. I can do my job from anywhere. As long as Tryst is happy."

Corrin snuggled into my back. "Same." He sounded smug as fuck.

Kacey flipped them the finger. "Kiss-ass." His grin softened his words.

They really were friends, I think. They'd bonded over this week and their shared dislike of Remzi Hart, who I was purposefully not thinking about at all. Not even a little bit. Or the fact he lived in NYC.

"What is it you do, anyway?" Jak asked.

"Kill people," Kacey deadpanned, and Jak laughed it off.

"Cool." He shook his head at the joke. "But really."

When no one else laughed, his eyes got wide. "Seriously?"

Corrin nodded. "Irish Mob."

I frowned, because that was a real point. "Kacey..."

The man in question threw up his hands. "Obviously I won't be anymore, but I'll still be in the 'company'"—he did little air quotes—"even if it is something a little more legitimate. They're my family, Tryst. I can't just wipe them because I got bootlegged into this."

"We can't raise a family if you're out there being a gangster and making enemies that threaten Tryst's safety, either," Akio ground out, losing his good humor. "You might not have had a choice, but you have a duty to your Omega now."

"I don't see Tryst as an *obligation*," Kacey growled. "You don't even know her, so I'm going to let this pass, but she's not a fucking child who doesn't have a clue what she wants or how to survive. She's smart, with her own fucking thoughts in her head, so you should get that 'duty' shit out of *your* head right now."

Well, that was actually kind of sweet. "Look guys, we don't have to decide right now—"

"Actually, you do." The sound of Agatha's smarmy voice made my jaw tighten. "Pack your belongings. Your holiday here is done."

Akio stood, a pleasant smile on his face that didn't reach his eyes. "Ms. Danvers, we've only just arrived and bonded with our Omega. You can't expect that we'll have decided on a Pack home yet?"

Ah, that fabled Alpha charm. I could already see Aggie softening.

Well, she was until Kacey snorted. She narrowed her eyes on Akio. "You're heading to New York for the *trial,*" she sneered at me, glaring, like it was my fault. "You'll be put in a hotel there, at the Department's expense, until the culmination of the trial. Then we can reassess your relocation." Her tone insinuated she'd like us to relocate straight to Hell. Or Salt Lake City. "You have an hour."

With one last smug smirk, she slammed the door shut, leaving us all gaping behind her.

Chapter Twenty-Three
Tryst

Everyone disappeared to pack their stuff, and the twins went to rustle up some food, since none of us had eaten since brunch. I stood in the doorway of my closet, the one where I'd had my first heat and all that bullshit with Remzi. I had mixed feelings about it, really. I'd bonded with Grady and Corrin here, truly became a Pack with my two Betas, but it also held memories of pain and rejection.

I didn't want to pack any of the dresses, so I decided to leave them all hanging in here. Let Agatha clean them out, the heinous cow. I didn't want to start my new life with reminders of the DoDA.

A throat cleared behind me, but I knew who it was. His scent was as familiar to me as my own Pack's now. I looked over my shoulder at RJ, who stood in the middle of my room, his face oddly expressionless.

"Do you need help?"

I shook my head, stuffing one last pair of yoga pants into the bag and zipping it closed. Wheeling it out, I shut the door on the closet forever. Sadness swamped me, and it was something I wasn't prepared for. "I guess this is it?"

RJ rubbed a hand down his face. "I've been called as a witness in Hart's trial, so it's not forever."

But it was forever. He wasn't part of my Pack. Grady had said that bonding with an Omega who'd been in his charge was considered a gross misuse of power by the DoDA and would result in immediate dismissal from the Department, and all government positions. Apparently, he and RJ had had that conversation, but I didn't read too much into it.

Besides, I didn't want to bond with RJ. I was just sad I was losing a friend. Yeah, that was it.

"Tryst..." RJ started, stepping toward me until he was within touching distance. And I *wanted* to touch— I could admit that much.

But I'd wanted men before and resisted. I could do that for RJ too.

"RJ..." I sang back, pasting a teasing smile on my face. "I'm sorry that you saw my vagina more than you probably wanted."

He choked on a laugh. "It's been the greatest honor of my career, Omega."

I winced. "I find that hard to believe, but thank you." My smile fell a little. "You made a shitty situation a little more bearable, and I'll always owe you a debt for that." I put out my hand to shake and he gripped it in his large, warm palm.

"You owe me nothing. You don't owe anyone a single damn thing. Look at me, Tryst." I realized I'd been staring at his chest, because it was easier to deal with the roiling feelings inside me if I didn't have to look into his bright blue eyes. I dragged my gaze up to his, and sucked in a breath at his expression. He looked like he was in pain. "In another life, Tryst O'Sullivan, I would have tried my fucking hardest to make you love me. I would have made it my life's mission to ensure you'd never have known a single day of this turmoil."

My heart thudded in my chest, and I shook my head. Not in denial, but like my ears were broken and I wasn't sure I'd heard him right.

I was still staring at him, my lips parted in a surprised O, when he leaned in and kissed me. It was a soft touch, barely there, but I felt it all the way to my toes. It was a myth that a kiss could tie you to an Omega, but suddenly, I wished that was true.

"Goodbye, Omega." He dropped my hand and was gone before my brain had caught up to his words.

I wanted to cry, but I sucked it down. This was

expected. This was how it always had to be. Crying about it would change nothing.

But my traitorous heart didn't listen to reason.

Kacey appeared seconds later, a frown on his face and his fists clenched at his sides like he was about to throw hands. "You okay?"

Well, fuck. So much for sucking the emotion back down, because I immediately burst into tears. I couldn't even appreciate the look of panic on Kacey's face.

He strode across the room, his eyes bouncing from side to side like he was still looking for the source of my heartache. He didn't realize that I was the cause of my own pain right now. There was no one to beat down, because it was my own stupid emotions betraying me.

He wrapped me in his arms, and I clung to his shoulders as I sobbed. Kacey didn't give me soothing platitudes. He didn't stroke my back or kiss my head. No, he held me tightly, fiercely, like he would fight for me. He was like a mountain in a storm. He didn't roll with the torrential wind; he stood firm against it and told it to go fuck its incorporeal self.

"Who do I have to knock out?" His voice took on a thick Boston accent, and I looked up at him.

"My stupid fucking Omega emotions would be a start."

"No can do, Princess." He looked pained. "I could tongue fuck your pussy into submission, if that'd help?"

I let out a noise that was somewhere between a snort-laugh and a sob, then choked on it. "Raincheck?"

He kissed my head. "Anytime. Look, the cavalry has arrived." The rest of the guys had appeared in the room, apparently called by my pain.

Maybe having a Pack wouldn't be so bad.

It took five hours to get to the hotel in New York, and Kacey had blown up when he discovered there was only a single two-room apartment for all six of us. Only two double beds. We were definitely being punished.

Akio had smoothed it over, managing to cajole hotel management into finding us a couple of rolling beds, and I could see how the two Alphas could work together so well, if they didn't keep giving each other the stink eye.

They'd fallen into the good cop/bad cop routine so naturally. The DoDA agents had dropped us and run, no longer caring if we took off, I guess. I was legally obligated to be at those stupid divorce proceedings, so I was kind of stuck here, but I got the distinct impression the DoDA would be happy if we disappeared forever and they could wash their hands of us completely.

Part of me enjoyed being a pain in their ass.

"Food?" Akio asked, his hands brushing softly over my arm to get my attention. I felt sorry for him and Jak. They'd been dropped straight into this shit without any time to get to know me, to get to know *us*.

"Sure. What does everyone feel like?"

"I wouldn't be opposed to Kacey's suggested orgy?" Corrin yelled from the other room, and Akio made a choking sound.

Fucking Corrin. I couldn't keep the grin off my face, as I gently patted Akio on the back like that would help him breathe. "He's kidding." But not really. "I meant for dinner," I yelled back.

Grady strolled out of their shared room. "We're easy. You don't get much by way of takeout where we're from, so trying new things is good."

"Are you from the same town?" Jak asked, reclining on the only couch, his legs spread so wide I had to resist the urge to crawl between them.

Oh shit, we hadn't explained this part?

Kacey stepped out of the bathroom. "Let's get sushi and beers, then these guys can tell you that they were a couple before the Allotment, and Princess can tell you that she hijacked Corrin into the Pack as a giant fuck you to the government."

I narrowed my eyes at Kacey, but he grinned unapologetically. Well, it was probably a conversation we should've had earlier. I moved toward my first two mates.

"Both Grady and Corrin are bisexual, and they're also a couple. Grady was my first Bond, but uh... we kind of conspired to bring Corrin in too, behind the Department's back."

Jak grunted in surprise. "Ballsy."

Kacey sat down beside him. "Our girl has big brass ones." He smirked at me with heat in his eyes, and I swallowed down the raw lust that threatened to possess my body like the Ghost of Orgies Past.

"Uh, yeah. So basically, the DoDA sucked it up rather than admit any failure on their part. Grady got to keep the love of his life, and I got these two, and honestly, it was the best decision I ever made." I paused and looked toward Akio and Jak. They seemed more traditional than Kacey, who just wanted to fuck the world and let it burn. "I hope their sexuality isn't a problem." My tone let it be known that we'd have a problem if it was. "I am happy to keep all our relationships separate as much as possible so you don't have to worry about being, uh, in any position that makes you uncomfortable. But I don't want you to think you can treat—"

Akio held up two hands. "Slow down, Tryst. We have no problem with Grady and Corrin's relationship. This is a brave new world and still stressing over that bullshit is dumb. Do I want to cross swords with them? No. Will them kissing or fucking bother me? Not even a little. This isn't an issue," Akio said softly, throwing a quick, reassuring smile at Grady and Corrin.

I let out a relieved breath. "And Jak?"

"Same. Though I'm not going to freak out about a little sword-touching," he said with a wink, and I felt my face flush.

Corrin groaned behind me. "Fuck, am I about to swoon?"

Chapter Twenty-Four
Corrin

The first day of us all jammed into close quarters was tough. Despite us assuming the DoDA had dumped us and left, we'd soon found out differently when we tried to leave for the day and three Federal Marshals had informed us that we were to stay put in our hotel.

It had taken some seriously fast talking to ensure that Kacey didn't get himself put down like an unruly pitbull at that. Tryst, that goddess-sent angel, had managed to tame her wild Alpha, and I got to see that fabled Omega mojo up close. It was like she stroked his back, whispered something in his ear, and he was putty. A purring kitten, who moments ago had been a rabid lion.

Honestly, it was hot as hell.

So inside the hotel room we stayed. We binge-watched television, ate as much takeout as we could just so the DoDA had to foot the bill. Still, by the evening of day three, we'd all had enough. Even worse was the fact that the twins were basically strangers. I mean, we were all basically strangers, but they'd been thrust right into the thick of it. They didn't even have time to roll with the punches; it was sink or swim.

So we were basically stuck under one roof, and no one was having sex because it was just awkward, or seeing the sun, or doing anything that would expend any of the insane amount of pent-up energy flowing through the hotel room.

Even Tryst's good humor had disappeared.

It was time to take things into my own hands. Kacey was pacing around the room, and Tryst was watching him warily. Akio was napping, and Jak was doing push-ups. We were a tinderbox, waiting to explode. Maybe that's why they'd locked us in here. They were waiting for us to sort ourselves out in a rather permanent fashion.

I looked over at Grady, the great fucking love of my life. God, he was handsome. But he was holding Tryst in his lap, and the two of them together stole my breath. It was pretty soft of me, but I felt like we were always meant to be together, the three of us. Watching them together did something to me. Well, it did several things to me, but the most important one was making my chest feel so full of emotion, I thought I might explode in a hail of glitter and rainbow jizz.

I loved her. She was easy to love.

Grady and I had talked about what we would do when we had a complete Pack. Actually, we'd talked about it *a lot*. I wasn't going to let any stupid, caveman misunderstandings ruin our happiness.

We were a couple once, but not anymore. Now we were two facets in a Pack of six. We would all be together forever, and if we kept our love secular, remained a couple within a Pack, then nothing would ever be cohesive. We had to embrace polyamory properly for our lives to be smooth sailing.

'Teamwork makes the dream work' had never been more apt than when there was only one female in the Pack.

So Grady and I, we'd come to the conclusion that we'd throw jealousy right out the window. Sex would be as inclusive as it needed to be, and we wouldn't get hurt feelings if the sex was open within the Pack. It didn't diminish my love for Grady any less, and it'd strengthen the Pack for Tryst.

It really didn't hurt that they were all so fucking hot, though.

I looked over at Grady. "It's time."

Tryst eyed me suspiciously. "Time for what?"

Grady just grinned, gathering her up in his arms a

little more. "Pack-building exercise." He kissed her, his tongue slowly sliding against her bottom lip.

Could I come from watching two people kiss?

I crawled over the couch and stroked my hand up her spine, under one of Kacey's t-shirts. It smelled like him, and it seemed to make her happy to be surrounded by her Alpha's scent. I'd seen her pilfering one of Akio's too.

Grady pulled away so I could drag the t-shirt off her body, leaving her bare. No bra. God, I definitely loved her.

She looked at me, her cheeks flushing prettily already. "Oh?"

I gripped her chin and leaned forward to kiss her too, plunging my tongue in her mouth with none of Grady's gentleness. I was never going to be the most dominant of her mates, but I was a good watcher, and I knew what she liked. I was going to be the one who gave her the most orgasms, the most pleasure.

I pulled away so she could suck in a deep breath. "Uh-huh. Grady and I are going to make you come, right here on the couch, and we're going to time how long it takes for everyone to join in." I looked around at the men who'd already stopped what they were doing to watch. I gave her a smug grin. "I give it three minutes until they all fold like a house of cards."

"I say until the first time you come on my cock. No

one can resist the way you look when you come," Grady argued. He turned her face back to his, kissing her.

I kicked the coffee table out of the way and laid down the throw blanket we'd stolen from the Allotment house, the one that kind of still smelled like the heat. She'd left it behind, but I'd seen her hesitate over it, fighting with her Omega.

I'd also seen her relief when I dragged it from my bag here. She wasn't completely at ease with her Omega urges, but I guess they'd been the very cause of all her pain for as long as she could remember. I just had to show her that they could be the catalyst for all her pleasure too.

I lay down on my back, my arms spread wide. "Tryst O'Sullivan, I'm going to need you to get that sweet, sweet ass down here and sit on my face."

She gave a surprised gasp, and someone laughed. Grady nudged her from his lap, and she kneeled beside me hesitantly.

"Babe, I want you to imagine this is an alien planet, and the only thing that can save me from the Zorgs is your slick all over my face." I grabbed her thigh and dragged her toward me. "Don't let me be probed, Obi-Wan Kenobi—you're my only hope."

"That's a fucking travesty to every Star Wars fan in history," Jak said, lying on his side, having given up on push-ups. The tent in his pants gave away why he wasn't lying on his stomach.

"You're right. I'd totally be down for probing," I said with a wink. Jak was at least curious, and I was happy to let that tattooed hottie explore any part of me he wanted. "Enough chit-chat. Ride my face, my beautiful Omega."

She looked aroused, but also kind of hesitant. "Safe word?" Grady prompted.

I rolled my eyes. "Corn."

Both of her brows raised. "Corn?"

"Yeah. No one is going to yell 'Fuck me with your corn cob' outside of Iowa. Totally a good safeword." She shook her head like I was insane, and I made grabby-grabby hands. "Hurry. I can hear the Zorgs. I'm too young to die."

Grady picked her up and dropped her on my face. She held herself stiff over me until I gripped her thighs and licked her from taint to clit. Yeah, that had her grinding right down onto my face. I gave her a happy little hum against her clit, then moved into my three-pronged attack plan.

One, Grady moved in behind her, his hands coming up to massage her breasts, his body pressed tight against her ass, helping her move and adding force to the grind. Breathing was for losers.

Two, I tongue fucked her into submission.

Honestly, if she could still hold up her body after this, I'd have done my job wrong.

Three, hopefully one of these other fuckers would pull their weight and make us a sexy ass triangle with her in the middle. The noises she was making as her clit bumped my nose were impossible to resist. Build it, and they'll come. Literally.

I saw feet from my peripheral vision, and I grinned against Tryst's pussy. Hell yeah. Was that three minutes or what? I gripped her hips and pushed her back a little, sucking in some much-needed air but also looking to see who'd caved first.

I was one hundred percent surprised to see it was Akio. He was naked, with his fingers under Tryst's chin, staring down at her with the kind of intensity wet dreams were made of.

Then he fed her his dick, and I felt like I was about to explode.

"I can see your balls wiggle from down here," I teased, because I just couldn't help myself. He gave me a shocked look, which kind of told me everything I needed to know about his level of kinkiness in the bedroom, but hey, we were young and there was a lot of fucking in our futures. I'd find this vanilla Alpha's buttons and we'd press them until we found the one that made him go sploosh.

I pulled Tryst back down on my face and worked

overtime until she was screaming around Akio's cock, and he was coming down her throat with a grunt. I was gasping for oxygen and making peace with my maker when she was plucked off my face. Sucking in a deep breath, I was surprised to see Grady on his knees in front of Jak. I checked myself for jealousy, but all I found was pleasure shooting to my achingly hard dick.

I looked up to see Kacey holding our girl, lifting her easily and sliding her down on his dick, right there where he was standing. This was the best angle ever. With a grin, I pillowed one hand behind my head and used the other to grip my cock.

I guess I'd just solved our entertainment problem.

Chapter Twenty-Five
Tryst

After six days in that damn hotel room, unable to leave, we were stir-crazy. I would have happily walked through the dump like it was Central Park, as long as I got to get out of those four walls. Don't get me wrong, the sex was great. But me and my vagina needed a rest.

I was actually looking forward to the court hearing. I knew I was going to hate it on a soul-deep level, but at least it wasn't in the damn hotel.

But no one had prepared me for what I would see outside the courthouse. Maybe the DoDA had sheltered me from this, but I hadn't expected the crowd of people that ran down the Superior Court's steps, right out onto the street until they were in danger of getting hit by the cars crawling past.

The mass of people jostled each other until they

were one huge organism, ebbing and flowing like it was drawing deep breaths. There were reporters and television crews, obvious by the huge cameras on their shoulders and the presenters in their fine suits. Another faction held signs like *Omega Rights are Human Rights* and *Omegas are People, not Property*.

But right opposite them was a group so coiled with hatred, it threatened to overflow into violence. Their signs scared me. *Designations For Death. Die Fucking Omega Sluts. Omegas caused the Apocalypse,* which made me want to laugh humorlessly, because that was giving us way too much credit.

"What the hell is all this?" Grady growled, making my skin prickle. Sometimes I forgot he wasn't an Alpha.

The DoDA Official whose job it was to ferry us to and from the courthouse shrugged. "Word got out about the case and now every weirdo has come out of the woodwork. The news channels have been camped out the front since six a.m.," he grumbled. "This looks so bad for the Department."

"Fuck the Department. That guy right there is directly threatening Tryst," Kacey shouted, and the Official gave him a droll look. That took some serious balls.

"It doesn't mention Miss O'Sullivan directly, and free speech is still a right we have. We're keeping an eye on the more unsavory element." He pulled up to the base of the stairs, people scattering all around the car. I noticed the odd *I Love You Alpha* sign, and I wondered if they meant Remzi or Alphas in general? "Our lawyers are waiting for you inside the foyer," the Official said, lifting his chin at the door, indicating we should step out into the roiling mass.

"You're sending her out into that?" Jak snapped. "Are you fucking *insane?*"

The guy narrowed his eyes at Jak, a disdainful look contorting his face. Was it because Jak was a Beta? Or because he was of Japanese descent? We'd come so far on some things, but often all it took was one small thing to set off all the old hatreds again. "The NYPD are out there doing crowd control. If you can't keep *your* Omega safe..." He let the sentence hang, but his meaning was clear enough.

Fucking asshole.

Kacey looked absolutely murderous. Grady shoved him toward the door before he could do something stupid like launch himself between the seats. "Concentrate, Alpha," Grady snapped. "How do we do this?" He looked between Kacey and Akio.

Did we need to have a primary Alpha? Was that how this shit worked?

"So stabbing people until they move is off the table?" Kacey asked seriously.

Jak barked a laugh. "I'm with the gangster on this one."

Akio rolled his eyes at both of them. "Kacey out front. Feel free to throw elbows. Grady and Jak to her left and right. Corrin, I want you attached to her side like a fucking barnacle on her ass. Do not lose her. I'll bring up the rear and watch our backs."

"Killjoy," Jak teased.

But that was the last of the levity as Kacey slid from the car and started yelling at people to back the fuck up. Lightbulbs flashed, people shouting "OMEGA!" until it was one continuous roar. Kacey grabbed some guy's phone and threw it back into the crowd, and then another, until people were stepping back just to protect their equipment.

Grady slid out, followed by Jak, and they created a small wall of defense so I could move out of the car. The screaming got louder, and the noise grated against my brain, making my Omega whimper.

Corrin's hand gripped mine, his body pressed tightly to my side until I was molded to him. "It's okay, Omega. I've got you," he murmured into my ear, squeezing my hand. "Concentrate on the feel of my hand, and keep your eyes on the doors. We'll take care of the rest."

We stepped forward, and I felt Akio's hand on my spine, giving me a little nudge. "Let's go," he shouted, and then Kacey did what Kacey did best. Cracked skulls.

He threw out that barely contained violence until people scattered from his sneer and the murder in his eyes. If they didn't, he walked over the top of them, sending out more than a few front kicks into people's knees when they didn't move fast enough. It was probably assault, but in a crowd this wild, who would know?

After the longest thirty seconds of my life, we pushed inside the courthouse, and the sheriffs kept out the crowds. I was panting, and suddenly realized that high-pitched sound was me. My Omega was beating against the confines of my mind, hating the feel of strangers' hands on my body, the screams and the cursing, and the blinding flashes of light.

Jak wrapped his arms around me, and partially around Corrin who was still glued to my side, and hummed something low and soothing into my ear as he rubbed patterns on my back. It was like my whole body went limp in his, my heart rate dropping until I was zen as hell.

Corrin openly gaped at him. "What the hell was that sorcery? Honestly, I think I just got wet, and I don't even have a vagina."

I could feel more than hear Jak's chuckle. "We can't all rely on Alpha mojo, so I did some research. It's almost like reiki, but focuses on the bond and channeling our connection." His hands stilled, but I didn't want to drag myself away from his warmth just yet. It felt so damn nice, pressed against his chest, my cheek against his heart, and Corrin's solid warmth at my back.

Unfortunately, reality always had a way of forcing itself into my happiness. "Omega Hart?"

I gritted my teeth at the name. "For now," I said, straightening from Jak's arms. I looked at the two people standing in front of me in high-end tailored suits. The man who'd just spoken had a thick mustache that seemed out of place with the rest of his clean-cut look.

Next to him was a woman who glared in his direction, before turning a softer expression to me. "Tryst. It's lovely to meet you."

Keisha Kelly looked like a model who wanted to be a superhero. She was tall, her tawny skin making her vibrant green eyes mesmerizing. Her frame was strong, and her expression was fierce. She was easily six feet in heels, and she stared at the DoDA lawyer like she imagined punching her hand through his chest and feasting on his heart.

I briefly questioned my sexuality. Could you be Keisha-sexual?

A little dazzled, I shook her hand. Kacey rolled his

eyes, dragging me to his side. "Good to see you, Keish. Thanks for coming to help. Stop eye fucking my mate."

Keisha grinned, even as I flushed bright red. If a woman could be an Alpha, it would be Keisha Kelly. "If she ended up with your dumb ass, she needs all the help she can get."

Kacey gave her the finger, making Keisha's grin widen.

The other lawyer cleared his throat, and all casualness left Keisha's expression. "Let's go to the private conference room. We can discuss what will happen today, as well as the case the Department of Designation Associations wants to put forward." She added the last part disdainfully, and I could've sworn I saw the other lawyer's mustache twitch.

We followed the lawyers down several hallways filled with people in power suits, all walking with a single-minded focus. We arrived at a large meeting room, though I hesitated outside the door. The room had no windows, and looked like a tomb, but it was stupid not to want to go in. I was an Omega; I was meant to like enclosed spaces.

I could feel eyes on my face, and I knew who it would be before my eyes even made contact with his stormy gray ones.

Remzi Hart.

He looked determined and guilty in equal parts.

Beside him was a beautiful blonde woman, her pantsuit perfectly tailored to her curves. She was frowning as she said something to him, her hand on his arm.

I wanted to walk over there and rip her fingers from his body. I wanted to claim him as mine to everyone who would listen. I hated seeing him with this female who was more beautiful than me. Smarter. Not such a fucking hot mess.

Remzi was right—we weren't suited at all. He belonged with someone like her; someone who could match him in age and life experience. His early forties may as well be an entire century away with as much as we'd have in common.

"Princess," Kacey murmured in a rough voice, and I dragged my eyes from Remzi's. I turned back to my Pack, each of them watching me out of the corner of their eye. They could feel everything, so I didn't lie and say I was fine.

Instead, I stepped into the room and shut the door between me and Remzi Hart.

Chapter Twenty-Six
Tryst

If this had been a regular divorce, we would have gone our separate ways and after a year or so, we could have been done and dusted with the whole thing. I didn't want anything from Remzi, except for all this to be over.

My Omega whined at the obvious lie. She wanted something from her Alpha, but wanting someone who didn't want you in return was an exercise in heartache, especially when we had so many amazing mates.

Still, she'd felt the bond in my chest, that ache that said for just a moment, he'd wanted us too. That was the hardest part. He'd bitten me, bonded me, fucked me during my first heat. That had meant something, and it made this whole circus twice as hard.

I sat up at a table beside Keisha, my guys in the row behind me. Remzi was on the other side of the courtroom, studiously staring at the Superior Court's coat of arms like it was going to come to life and chew him out for being such an idiot.

We weren't regular divorcés. What we had wasn't made to be separated by the law or by anything in nature.

The lawyers argued, using concepts that I didn't really understand, in convoluted jargon that was part English and part Latin, but was basically deciding not only my future with Remzi Hart, but the future of all Omegas.

That was what Keisha Kelly wasn't telling her DoDA counterpart, but had whispered to me in secret. She'd met with Remzi Hart's lawyers before the trial, and one thing they'd agreed on was that if we came out of this trial with more rights for Omegas, the results for their individual clients would be an added bonus.

Which made me feel a little bad for wanting to bite Remzi's lawyer's fingers off. So as they talked about constitutional transgressions and fundamental rights in a courtroom packed to the rafters with people, I couldn't stop my gaze from drifting to Remzi.

He looked rough.

Don't get me wrong, he was still breathtakingly handsome, but his face was drawn and there were dark circles under his eyes. His back was ramrod straight, and his jaw was flexed so tight that I hoped he had a good dentist on the books.

I'd been practicing discerning whose bonds were whose in my chest. I mean, I logically knew there wasn't a golden cord attached from my heart to each of them or anything like that, but the emotional connections sat heavily in my chest. Grady's was steady and sure, while Corrin's was a little wild. I'd had theirs the longest, so they were the easiest to feel.

The Alpha bonds were a little stronger. Kacey's bond was almost like a heady darkness, filled with coiled violence and the promise of pleasure. He was like being strapped to bed, blindfolded, and feeling a paddle brush against your ass.

Not that I knew what that felt like, but it was the only way to describe it.

The twins were the newest, so I was better at grabbing hold of Akio's and Jak's bonds, and they were easy enough to tell apart. Akio was like a thick blanket on a cold night, warm and encompassing. Jak felt kind of similar, but there was also something a little darker about it, the same way as Kacey. More like black silk sheets than flannel.

By the process of elimination, the bond that smoldered like the desert sun was Remzi Hart. It made sense. I poked at it a little, and I saw him jerk in his seat. Good. He could avoid looking at me as much as he liked, but he would know I was here.

As much as I hated the fact he was putting us through this, part of me—the non-Omega part—understood. Now that a few weeks had passed since my heat, and my hormones weren't wild, with that writhing ache a distant memory, I could empathize with his position.

Seeing him looking so... pained, it hurt me too. So despite the fact that I'd promised myself I would hate Remzi Hart forever, I sent a reassuring brush of warmth down the bond. Not forgiveness, but something close.

His face whipped toward me, the storm in his eyes swirling like the feel of his bond. I gave him a crooked smile, and regret washed over his face. My smile faltered, and I sucked in a deep breath through my nose.

I'd thought maybe we could do this without being antagonists, but maybe I was wrong. Maybe it would hurt too much, like poking at a wound so that it never heals. I dropped my eyes to the desk in front of me, feeling the smooth wood beneath my fingertips. I scratched at it with my nails, trying to push my emotions back down into that safe little box.

It was my turn to jump when a warm feeling forced its way into my chest, spreading through my limbs. I knew the feel of it, and I smiled softly as Remzi lit up my bond with confident reassurance. I didn't look up, but the smile stayed for the rest of the hearing.

I was almost dozing off by the time the court adjourned for the day. The judge had closed out the proceedings by raising furious hands at the lawyers, his voice echoing over the courtroom. "The Constitutional Rights of Designated Individuals is not what the court is here to rule on, Counselors."

Keisha gave him a polite but neutral expression. "With all due respect, Your Honor, you can't rule on one without ruling on the other."

The judge gave her a flat expression, and banged his gavel. "Court adjourned until tomorrow at ten a.m."

I stood, stretching, and walked over to my guys. Kacey looked like he'd been napping, his eyes hooded and, if I was honest, sexy as fuck. Grady reached for me first, and I stepped into his arms. "Doing okay? We felt you reaching out to him in the bond."

I felt my eyes widen. "You can feel that?" I looked between the guys, my eyes snagging on Jak.

He shrugged. "Kind of. We're all connected through you, so I guess, if one of these guys was in trouble, we'd all feel the unease. It's hard to explain. We don't feel it as strongly as you do, though. Except maybe me and Akio, because we have the twin bond as well and it strengthens things."

That all sounded completely woo-woo, yet somehow legit. Nothing about the matebond system made sense on a scientific level.

I nodded, wondering what they felt when we were all having sex. I made a note to ask Corrin, because I was fairly sure he would tell me in graphic detail and not leave anything out. That was just the kind of guy he was. He was looking sexy as hell right now in tailored gray pants that cupped his ass just the way I wanted to, and a white shirt that stretched across his broad shoulders. He was like a marble statue, but better hung. No offense, David.

The crowd in the courtroom dispersed, and the walk through the halls was quiet now that most of the cases had wound down for the day. However, the silence amplified the sound of the crowd outside.

Word must have spread that this wasn't just a sensationalist celebrity divorce case, but that the lawyers were pushing for Omega freedoms, because when we emerged, the hateful protestors had quadrupled in numbers. Hundreds of them stood outside now with placards. I froze momentarily behind Kacey, as the wave of the noise hit me.

If the signs were hateful, then the chants were terrifying.

"Beta purity!" a man screamed beside my face, his spit coating my cheek, before he was wrestled away by courthouse security. The guys closed in around me until Corrin was basically carrying me down the stairs, his face uncharacteristically solemn.

We were rushed by reporters, each sticking a camera in my face and shouting questions that I had no idea how to answer. Kacey shoved someone, and they shoved him back, the anti-designation crowd now baying for blood as they surged past the NYPD barricade.

That was the moment things turned.

I screamed as we were swamped by an angry mob, the guys throwing punches as they closed in around me. Hands were grabbing at me, yanking me further into the crowd and away from my mates, their nails pinching and scraping my skin roughly.

I was dragged away from Corrin, who was yelling my name. Strange hands pushed me further into the crowd, my body getting battered and something sharp piercing my hip. I cried out, flailing around, desperate to get the hands off me. I was screaming, my throat aching, but no one could hear me as I was carried away.

Then Remzi Hart was there. He scooped me up

into his arms and boomed, "MOVE!" until people scattered, the urge to get the fuck out of the way almost visceral. He looked feral, growling at anyone who dared to step in front of him until he was at our Department-provided SUV.

The formerly nonchalant driver looked shocked at the mayhem as he raced around and opened the back door for me. Remzi pushed me in and went to shut the door, but I put my hand out. "The guys?" I shouted, as his eyes kept me pinned to the seat.

"They're coming. Lock the doors, Omega," he growled, and I had no choice but to move my hand as he slammed the door shut. I watched him melt back into the crowd, and they still parted for him like they could sense he was barely hanging onto the beast.

With my hands pressed against the heavily tinted window, I watched the undulating crowd, the fists flying and blood spattering, looking for any sign of my mates. I pulsed my safety down the bonds, so they knew to stop looking for me and make their way back to the car.

Finally, Akio and Corrin emerged, the latter with a huge scrape on his face like he'd been shoved into the pavement. Akio had a black eye and his shirt was torn, but other than that, he seemed fine.

By the time they made it to the car, the other three appeared, Jak and Grady dragging a beat-to-hell Kacey between them. I gasped, wanting to unlock the doors but the Alpha command stopped me from doing so.

"Unlock the doors—let them in!" I yelled at the driver, who didn't argue.

Corrin climbed in first, straight into my arms. "Fuck, Tryst. Fuck!" he murmured, holding me so tight I could barely breathe. "I let go. I didn't mean—" His whole body shook.

Akio squeezed his shoulder. "Not your fault, man. We all lost her." My eyes shot to him, and I noticed that he looked as shaken as I felt, his cheeks pale and his jaw pulsing with tension.

Finally, Jak and Grady made it to the car, faces bloodied and bruised, but Kacey looked the worst. Grady climbed into the front passenger seat and turned to the driver. "Get us the fuck out of here, *now!*"

Chapter Twenty-Seven
Tryst

According to Grady, the mob had swamped them, converging on Kacey, and once they got him on the ground, they'd kicked the shit out of him. Grady and Jak had done their best to keep them back but the protestors still managed to cause a serious amount of damage to my Alpha.

We'd taken him straight to the hospital, and discovered that he had two cracked ribs and some serious bruising. He'd fractured his cheekbone, but his head scans showed there was no scarier damage done. If he'd been a Beta, he'd have been laid up for a few days—or worse, dead.

Alphas were tougher, stronger, and healed quicker. Still, I hated the scent of his blood, the swollen lump of his cheek, and the way he winced when he shifted in the hospital bed. I wanted to scream. Kacey, for all his injuries, was the same bad-mannered, snarky flirt that he normally was.

I stayed plastered to his side, even going with him to get a CT scan, and they assumed I was there to keep him calm. In truth, his warm, tattooed hand in mine was the only thing keeping me from a full mental breakdown.

By the time they signed his discharge papers, everyone was watching me warily, like I was about to snap. My bondmates drifted to my side, each giving me comfort, but I wanted to scream and scream and scream.

They'd all been injured to varying degrees, mostly bruised, split knuckles and face lacerations. The nurses had cleaned them up while we waited with Kacey, though my mates had grumbled about it.

They made Kacey sit in a wheelchair, and he pulled me down onto his lap. I didn't fight it, despite the slightly disapproving expression of the head nurse. I laid my head on his shoulder, propping my leg over the side of the chair. I tried not to put too much weight on his torso though, extremely aware of his ribs.

"I've had worse, Princess. Stop freaking out."

I raised an eyebrow at him. "Was that meant to make me freak out less? Because it doesn't, not even a little."

Akio pushed us, which made Kacey huff and Akio's eyes sparkle with laughter. There was something heavy hiding behind his happy expression though, and I felt like my uninjured Alpha was affected by what happened at the courthouse too—he was just hiding it better. I felt guilty, but one of us had to hold it together right now, and it wasn't me.

Even the DoDA Official had seemed a little shaken, so I wasn't surprised to see a different DoDA vehicle collecting us. Though I *was* surprised when RJ climbed out of the driver's seat to come around and open the rear door.

I gasped, leaping off Kacey's lap and running to him. There was nothing in my brain about appropriateness or his job or even my Pack. I just ran at him until he was forced to catch me. He wrapped his arms tightly around me, and even though his body was stiff, I felt his deep inhale as he breathed me in. I did the same to him, my face buried in his chest.

God, I'd missed him more than I had any right to do. It had only been a little over a week, but before that, I'd seen him almost every day for months.

"I missed you too, Tryst," he whispered in my ear before releasing me. He stepped back, giving me a warm smile that didn't reach his eyes. He bowed his head respectfully at Kacey and Akio, and then the others. "Alphas, bondmates. It's good to see you, though I wish it was under better circumstances." He looked at Kacey, his jaw tightening.

Kacey waved a hand. "Like I said to Princess, I've had worse. So whose dick did you have to suck to get stuck being a glorified chauffeur?"

RJ's lips twitched. Kacey and RJ always had a kind of adversarial relationship, which I thought was ridiculous, but maybe Kacey had always known something I didn't want to acknowledge.

"They decided after the courthouse scenes that you may need an Official escort with a little more combat training—for *our* safety, of course, not yours." He frowned, seemingly in disgust. "They've decided to distance themselves from your upkeep, given the contentiousness of your mating. So they were more than happy to let me volunteer, seeing how I'm in their shitbooks already. They'd probably be happy if I died on the job."

Akio growled, before swallowing it down. "Come, Omega. I'd be happier if we weren't out here in the open for much longer. We'll go back to the hotel."

Kacey grunted. "Fuck that. There's nowhere safer for Princess than Boston." Everyone went to protest, and he just raised a hand. "Doesn't have to be for-fucking-ever. Just until this bullshit is over, and then we'll *negotiate* locations. But I have a fucking penthouse apartment that's locked down so tight, it'd take a small army to get in there, and the bottom three levels are all family." I didn't think he meant actual blood-related family. "She'll be safe there."

There was a tense silence as the two Alphas stared each other down. Grady rolled his eyes so hard, it was amazing he didn't permanently strain an eye muscle.

I mouthed, "You okay?" I hadn't checked on him yet, but every time I closed my eyes, I saw his blood-spattered face.

He winked at me and flashed a smile. I needed to spend more time with him and Corrin. I used them like a security blanket, and they were more than that. I also needed more time with Akio and Jak, who'd been thrown right into all this bullshit, so they'd only seen the worst of Pack life.

Would it always be like this? Feeling like I was being pulled in a million different directions?

Jak huffed. "You guys can measure dicks in the car. You're stressing Tryst out and she's already had a shitty day." He picked me up and looked over at Corrin and Grady. "I think she needs a Beta snuggle in the back seat. I'll rock-paper-scissors you for it."

He herded me into the back seat, and I heard Corrin crow with delight. "In your fucking faces." He dived over the seats and landed beside me, cuddling me into his side. Jak was right—being in Corrin's arms did make me feel better, but I think it had less to do with him being a Beta and more to do with him being the man he was. He clung just as tightly to me, like he was scared to let me go again.

"Are you all right?"

"No, baby girl. Not even a little. But I will be, especially if I get to hold you like this." He kissed my temple, then rested his cheek on the top of my head, curving me into his side. "I never want to feel like that again. I love you, Tryst O'Sullivan, and I'm not too macho to admit that losing you in that crowd almost killed me. I promise to never let you go again, ever."

He couldn't know that for sure, but I hoped to hell that he kept his promise.

In the end, protectiveness won out over Alpha posturing, and RJ drove us to Boston. I could see Kacey's shoulders visibly relax the closer we got to his old stomping grounds. We'd all been blindsided by the violence of that mob, and I guess it was better the devil you know.

He directed RJ through the busy Boston streets to an apartment building on the waterfront. It was about eight floors high, a big square cube covered in windows that overlooked the bay.

"It has its own parking," Kacey grunted, indicating the mouth of an underground parking lot. We pulled up to a booth, and a guy with a scar through his eyebrow and a cigarette hanging out of his mouth looked at RJ with a bored expression.

"Private parking. Fuck off."

Kacey leaned over. "You kiss your mother with that mouth, fuckface?"

The guy's eyes went comically wide. "Holy Jesus, is that you, Kace? The fuck happened to your ugly mug? And who's the suit? Smells like a fucking Fed."

"Tommy, I've had a long as hell day. Let's skip the goddamn inquisition, hey?"

Tommy grinned, showing perfectly white teeth. "Sure thing, Boss. Is your new Omega in there too, or are you just traveling in the Oscar Meyer Weiner Mobile?"

"Keep ya eyeballs to yourself. Grab Lupo and come upstairs to the penthouse in an hour. We need to talk about security. Why are you on fucking gate duty anyway?"

The guy shrugged, and I noticed the ash on his cigarette was precariously long. "John's missus went into labor, so I told him I'd cover him. Man's gotta be there at the birth of his first child."

Kacey snorted. "First legitimate one anyway. The man has bastards all over downtown. Send him a bottle of whiskey and Darla a fruit basket or a fucking cheese of the month subscription or something." He looked at RJ. "Let's go."

RJ just raised an eyebrow at him, like he was going to make him say please, but he didn't cause a scene in front of the gate guy. He drove forward, up to the spot right beside the elevator.

I climbed out and stretched my legs, smelling the brine of the ocean on the bay breeze. It was kind of nice. I was a little worried the elevator wouldn't hold us all, but no one else seemed particularly stressed, despite the tight squeeze.

Kacey waved a card over a reader, and I leaned back against Akio. He rested his hand on my hip, squeezing softly once but keeping his touch light. Supportive but not crowding. I was going to send Akio and Jak's grandparents flowers, just to show my appreciation for the way they'd taught them how Omegas liked to be treated.

The doors opened on a small foyer, with several tiny cameras flashing in the corners of the ceiling. It was completely mirrored on one side, making it appear bigger than it was, and while it was lavish, it was basically a coatroom.

"For security," Kacey grunted, swiping his card and opening the door to the penthouse. He ushered me in first, and I sucked in a breath.

I wasn't sure what I'd expected Kacey's home to look like, but it wasn't this. The man himself was dark and broody, but his home was light and airy, with minimal furniture and crisp lines. Everything was decorated in neutral colors, except for the bar, which was a warm mahogany with brass rails.

It oozed luxury.

"I thought you said you weren't an heir?" I gasped.

Kacey shrugged, throwing his leather jacket over a chair. "I'm still his son. I might never be in power, but I still get some of the perks. My own crew. This fancy as fuck apartment. A family." He tilted his head to a hall that led off the living room. "Come on, I'll show you where to put your shit. I've only got three spare rooms, so you'll have to bunk together. Princess can have her own." He looked over his shoulder, pointing to double doors at the end of the hall. "That's mine. You're welcome there anytime," he told me with a wink.

His eyes were tight with pain, and I frowned, hooking my arm through his. He leaned into me, like it was the most natural thing in the world. "I'll take you up on that right now, Alpha. You need rest. We can get the grand tour later."

He looked at me with interest in his eyes, but five minutes later, he was tucked under his blankets with a pout on his face and me curled around his back fully dressed. Within seconds, he was sound asleep, and I climbed out from behind him. I needed to see the rest of my Pack settled before I could rest too.

Chapter Twenty-Eight
Tryst

Kacey was still sleeping when there was a knock at the door. We all looked at it, and logically, I knew that it was probably the guy from the gatehouse. Still, it felt weird opening Kacey's front door without him.

We hesitated so long that the door opened by itself. The guy from the gate—Tommy, I think was his name—stuck his head around the doorjamb, covering his eyes with a large, tattooed hand. "It's just us. We have a key, but wanted to give you a bit of warning in case you were having an orgy or something."

A laugh burst from my mouth like a bullet. "You can look. No orgy."

Tommy lowered his hand slowly, as if I might be lying. Then his mouth fell open. "Holy fuck, you're hot. Kacey is a lucky bastard. To think he put up such a bloody fight about it."

He stepped into the room, followed by another guy, and my eyes widened. Tommy was attractive in a rough kind of way, the same kind of way as Kacey, but this second guy was classically attractive. He had blond hair coiffed high on his head, and a body that looked like it spent a lot of time at the gym, or he was a social media model or something.

He slapped Tommy on the back of the head, and then turned to me, lowering his eyes respectfully. "Omega. It's nice to meet you."

Tommy cleared his throat, a flush spreading across his cheeks. "Uh, shit. Sorry, Omega. Good to meet you." His eyes flicked up over my shoulder, and I felt Grady's warm hand on my back. On my other side was Akio, his face more serious than I'd ever seen it. He looked scary.

The blond guy raised his hands. "Tommy meant no offense, Alpha. He's just got a big mouth and not enough brain cells to knock together. Kace has given us a skewed idea of what Alphas are like."

As if I'd tugged on the bond, the man himself appeared. He still looked sleepy, but the swelling on his face had gone down a little. "Most Alphas would gut you for ogling their Omegas, Tommy. Probably something you should remember. Not all of them are gonna be as attached to you as I am." He stretched, and I knew he needed another ten hours of sleep. He'd been out for barely more than forty minutes, but I didn't want to say anything to him in front of his friends. "Tommy and Lupo are my best friends and my seconds-in-command. I trust them with my life, and yours. Probably not with your wallet, though."

Tommy grinned, like it was a compliment. "Thanks, brother. We honestly didn't expect you back for a couple more months, though. Have you called the old man?"

Kacey waved a hand. "I messaged him on the way here. He said we need to come to dinner tomorrow."

I sucked in a breath as panic hit my bloodstream. He wanted me to meet his family? Shit, what if they hated me? What if they'd wanted someone else for Kacey and blamed me for dragging him away? What if they didn't like my guys?

Grady held me closer, kissing my temple lightly. "Easy, Tryst. No one's going to make you do anything you don't want to do. Isn't that right, Kacey?"

Lupo's eyes bounced from where Grady's hand was splayed across my stomach, to where his lips were touching my face, and then across to Kacey.

Kacey shrugged. "It's pretty non-optional, but I'll make an excuse if you really don't want to go."

Tommy snorted a laugh. "Holy shit, look at you.

Did the Omega give you a set of brass balls for a mating gift? I wouldn't want to piss off the old man, no matter how much I admired my Omega." Somehow, he made the word 'admire' sound almost pornographic.

Lupo whacked him again, and Tommy hit him back, and then they were brawling on the floor. Kacey handed me a dram of whiskey, waving a hand at the bar to the rest of our Pack. "Help yourselves. What's mine is yours now." He said it flippantly, but I got the impression he meant it more than he let on.

The two men were still trading kidney punches on the floor like wrestling toddlers, and I looked over at him. "Should we stop that? Are they actually fighting?"

Kacey rolled his eyes. "Fuck no, they aren't. Closer than brothers and thicker than thieves. Though if they don't cut it the fuck out and stop embarrassing me, I'm going to give them Granny duty for the next month."

They stopped immediately, as if someone had hit the pause button. Honestly, neither of them so much as twitched. "Come on, Kace. You wouldn't do that," Tommy whined, but he didn't seem confident in his words. Kacey raised an eyebrow, and they both flopped onto their backs. I was pretty certain their wrestling mat was actually a genuine Persian rug.

I must have looked confused because Lupo came to my rescue. "Kace's granny is wild as hell, and likes to pretend she's senile so she can grab your dick in the middle of Macy's."

"Or convince the old man that it was your idea to bet a hundred K on the ponies, while getting drunk on top-shelf whisky until you both get ejected because she keeps flashing her tits at the jockeys as they cross the finish line."

"The woman is ninety and her nipples line up with her navel," Lupo added with a shiver, like if she had perky tits, then a ninety-year-old exposing herself in public would be entirely okay.

Corrin laughed so hard, I thought he might wet himself. "She sounds like a fucking riot."

Kacey's lips twitched, and I could tell he liked his grandmother. "She'd love you. Remind me to never let you two meet."

"Too late, Tryst is going to take us to dinner with your family. Isn't that right, baby girl?"

Well, now I kind of had to meet Granny Boyd.

I nodded. "No time like the present." I chewed my lip. "They'll like me, right?"

Kacey wrapped an arm around my shoulders. "Of course, Princess. We'll bring Tommy and Lupo as backup, just in case." His grin was straight up evil.

Tommy groaned and flopped back to the ground. "For feck's sake, not again."

"Get up, you lazy ass. I need to up the security

around here, so *this* doesn't happen again." He waved at his face, and the men on the floor went from playful to soldiers in a second.

We slept away most of the following day, oddly secure in Kacey's little fortress. For the first time, I was mad at myself for not packing some of the wardrobe the DoDA had provided for the Allotment, because now I had nothing appropriate to meet Kacey's family.

Kacey didn't seem to think it was a problem though. "Wear anything."

I pinched the bridge of my nose. "Alpha, I *cannot* meet your family in yoga pants and an oversized hoodie. It just isn't happening."

Kacey looked like he was in more pain today, and I pushed back his hair from his face. "Fine, but I'm coming shopping with you," he sighed, grimacing as he folded into a sitting position. I pushed him back down to the bed with firm but gentle hands, before leaning forward and consoling him with a kiss.

"You need to rest so your bones heal properly. I'll take some of the others. We're a Pack, remember? You can share the burden." I gave him a lopsided grin, and it probably looked self-deprecating. Hell, it definitely was.

Kacey grabbed my hips, pulling me to his body

with a grunt. "Princess, you aren't a burden to anyone. If you don't stop talking that way, I'm going to spank you until you get it." He sagged back into the bed, and I went with him, holding myself up so I didn't hurt his ribs. "Take Tommy and Lupo with you. They won't get in the way, but I'll be happy if there's someone with a gun there watching your backs."

I wanted to argue that it was unnecessary, but I still had bruises and claw marks, as well as a big gash on my hip. Logically, I knew it was extremely necessary. So I just dipped my nose against his throat. "Okay."

"Mmm, good girl." He slapped my ass, then pushed me off the bed. I yelped as I fell to the floor, and he laughed. "You better hustle; we have to leave in two hours. Take Akio."

I looked at the clock on the bedside table. Fuck, we were going to be late. "You give a lot of orders for a bedridden man."

"I'll show you just how I like to be ridden in bed if you don't get out of here right now," he growled, and it went straight to my core.

I grinned, darting in for a quick kiss before racing out into the living room. "Akio! I need to go shopping."

Akio groaned, and Tommy laughed as he cleaned his gun at the breakfast bar. Such a casual exhibition of potential violence.

"Don't get ahead of yourself, Chuckles. Kacey said you and Lupo had to come."

His laugh turned into a pained look. "I hate shopping."

Grady eyed them both. "I'll come too."

Pleasure burst through my chest. I hadn't spent enough time with Grady lately, so this would be fun.

Chapter Twenty-Nine
Tryst

Tommy and Lupo argued about where to take me shopping, finally settling on a small mall with high-end shops. Lupo insisted that while they weren't stuck up, Kacey's family had been rich as hell for long enough that they prided themselves on being the best dressed people in the room. Kacey didn't give a shit, of course, given his entire wardrobe consisted of band t-shirts and torn jeans.

I looked at the dresses on the hanger in the dressing room, which cost way more than I could afford. Although the sales assistants had initially turned up their nose at me, apparently the appeal of Akio—who was dressed like he was going to be a centerfold spread in GQ—had changed their minds. Did GQ even have a centerfold?

"Do they have, like, a Walmart or something

around here?" I yelled outside the dressing room curtain, and someone hissed a horrified breath. Whoops, guess the assistant had been out there too.

Grady stuck his head in the curtain. "Tryst, just try on something that makes you feel like a badass and stop worrying about the money. You're certifiably loaded in your own right after fucking Remzi gets his head out of his ass, no matter which way it goes."

He slipped into the cubicle with me. Grabbing the bottom of my hoodie, he dragged both it and my shirt over my head until I was just in my bra and yoga pants. It was slightly difficult since Grady filled up the cubicle with his huge shoulders, but he made it work.

"Should have brought Corrin. He's better at this shit," he muttered, flicking through the dresses before selecting one in emerald green lace. "This one."

I grabbed it and tilted my head up for a kiss. He obliged, his lips brushing over mine, but I grabbed the back of his head and pulled him deeper.

"Fuck, I've been aching to touch you for hours," he whispered against my lips.

"Then touch me, Grady," I breathed, and he ran his hands down my sides until they slid into the waistband of my yoga pants. He tugged them down to my knees, then ran his hand back up between my thighs, until he was cupping my sex.

I rubbed against him, seeking the friction I needed.

Grady pressed me against the dressing room wall, sliding his thigh between mine so I was pinned tightly between the wall and his clever fingers. He rubbed them against my clit, stroking in soft, quick motions, before he slid them down and inside me. One. Then two.

Then he leaned in harder, thrusting against my body so his palm bumped my clit deliciously even as his fingers curled inside me. I ground against him, fucking him back with my tongue in his mouth. I moaned, and he pulled back.

"Shh, don't want to scandalize the shop assistants. They might shit out the stick that's lodged up their asses." A laugh-moan burst from my lips, and I lifted my hand to muffle it.

Grady curled his fingers, his hips grinding into me faster until my moans were barely held back by my palm and I was coming on his hand. He grinned smugly at me, slipping his fingers out from my underwear and sucking them into his mouth.

Why was that so fucking hot?

He handed me the green lace dress. "This is the one. Come on, we better hurry. Wouldn't want to be late to meet the in-laws." He kissed me hard with lips that tasted like my own release, and strode out of the dressing room.

Fuck. I definitely loved him.

. . .

Kacey's family home in Boston was... insane. It was like we'd gone from the bustling city to the middle of nowhere in the blink of an eye, with nothing but rolling green hills, manicured gardens, and a mansion overlooking it all. We drove in a bulletproof SUV sent by Patrick Mullens, and RJ had elected to stay behind. This was no place for a Federal Official.

Further down the road, back toward the city, most of the houses were owned by the family, according to Kacey. It was a way to keep them close and also for them to become the last line of defense before the big house.

And the big house was no euphemism. The place was palatial, perched on top of a hill with 360-degree views.

Corrin looked at it with wide eyes. "Who else lives here? Surely it isn't just your father?"

Kacey shook his head. "No. My father and his wife, as well as Granny, live here. Plus my uncle Dermid and his wife, Luella, and their three sons too. My youngest half-brother, who's third in line, splits his time between here and the city. So just family."

"Did you live here?"

Kacey shook his head. "No. I lived over in Roxbury with my mom."

The bastard son of the patriarch. Blood, but not really family. I wonder what tiny Kacey had thought about that, or whether he'd been too young to understand why his father lived in a palace and he lived in a lower socioeconomic area of the city with his single mother.

There was more to this, but now wasn't the time to delve into the dark past of Kacey Boyd. Hell, the time had probably been two weeks ago when I first met him, but everything had been so busy, so stressful.

The door was opened by a housekeeper, her small white apron the only indication she was staff. The rest of her outfit was beautiful, and her hair was perfect. Imagine getting up every day and having to do your hair like that to go to someone else's house and work.

Kacey grinned wide, stepping into the foyer. He wrapped his arms around the woman. "Hey, Mom. Meet my Omega, Tryst."

Every drop of blood rushed up toward my cheeks. Had I just assumed his mother was the hired help? Fuck, I hoped she couldn't read my mind. "It's a pleasure to meet you," I said, putting out a hand for her to shake. She took it softly and appraised me. Her expression wasn't mean, nor overtly disdainful. Nope, I was being weighed and measured.

"It's lovely to meet you too, Omega." Her voice was deep and soft, and when she stared at me like that, there was no doubting she was Kacey's mother. He had her face shape and coloring. "Come in. They are waiting for you in the sitting room."

We followed behind her, and Kacey wrapped his arm around my waist, holding me tightly to his side. She opened the sitting room doors, then stepped to the side, out of the way.

"The guests of honor have arrived," she announced.

"Thank you, Mirabelle," a woman I couldn't see answered, the dismissal obvious.

Kacey's mom, Mirabelle, didn't seem upset by it though. "I better get back to preparations. Come for dinner on Sunday if you're still in town."

Kacey kissed her cheek. "We'll try."

With one more polite nod at me, Mirabelle disappeared into the cavernous home. Kacey stepped into the room that already held at least ten people. Added to our huge group, it was basically a party.

There was no doubt that the room centered around a shortish man with silver hair and a grin on his face. But his eyes were hard and assessing, even as he laughed at whatever the man beside him was saying.

Catching Kacey's eye, he beckoned us over. "Kacey, my boy. Come in. Introduce us to your new Omega."

There were at least three Alphas in this room other

than Kacey and Akio. Maybe four. That was a lot of fucking Alphas in one room, and it was making my skin prickle. I was going to kick Kacey's ass for not telling me. Sensing my unease, his arm tightened around me.

"Dad, this is Tryst O'Sullivan, our Omega." Okay, I'd go a little easy on him, considering he'd just gently inserted the entire Pack into the conversation.

"Pleasure to meet you, Omega. Or would you rather Tryst?"

"Of course she'd bloody well prefer Tryst. No one wants to go around being referred to as their designation," a strong but elderly voice called from a wingback beside the bar. "Come here, girl, let me look at you."

Kacey pushed me toward the tough old woman. She had tightly curled white hair and a glint in her eye that meant mischief, but a smile appled both of her cheeks.

"Ah, but you are beautiful. Too good for that scoundrel for sure," she teased with a wink.

"Thanks for the vote of confidence, Granny," Kacey said, from where he was pouring out whiskey at the bar. "Need a refill?"

"What kind of question is that, boyo? Of course." She thrust a glass at him and turned her focus back to me. I swear I shrunk an entire foot under her gaze. "You got a backbone under that pretty exterior?"

"I hope so." My voice wasn't nearly as strong as I'd

have liked. "I don't take shit lying down, but it's hard to be prepared for the curveballs life throws at you."

She nodded. "True that." She took the glass, now topped up with a smoky amber liquid, and raised it at me. "You'll do just fine. I get a feeling about these things in my waters." She took a deep swallow before smacking her lips. "Now, what do you know about horse racing?"

Several people groaned around the room, and I decided that I *really* liked Kacey's grandmother.

Chapter Thirty
Tryst

At dinner, I was placed between Kacey and his oldest brother Doughal, just down from the head of the table. Doughal was 100% one of the Alphas in the room, his strength surpassing that of both his father and Kacey, though I imagined that would probably irritate the hell out of my mate.

I was tense, my body stiff at being so close to an Alpha who wasn't my own. It was a learned behavior—logically, I knew that, but it didn't ease the reaction. Kacey had his hand on my thigh, squeezing it reassuringly, even as he spoke to his uncle in the next seat down.

Doughal leaned closer. "Relax, Omega. I can scent your distress. You're among family here. No harm will come to you—I swear it on my life."

My eyes whipped up to his. Kacey had gotten the

family's golden eye color, despite the rest of his features being Mirabelle's. I tried to look for deception, though that was probably dumb. This guy was the heir to a massive crime family. You didn't just go around with your heart on your sleeve. Despite that, I could see the tiredness pulling around his eyes, and his earnest honesty melted into me.

I shook my head. "No offense intended, Alpha. It's just... second nature, I guess."

"Please, call me Doughal. I completely understand. You gotta know, our family has never been one for the Allotment. Raffling off Omegas like they're Christmas turkeys is a fucking ridiculous concept. We were more than a little worried when Kacey got called up." He looked over at his half-brother, and although I expected jealousy—or something more insidious, considering Kacey's existence obviously meant Doughal's dad had cheated on his mom with Mirabelle—there was nothing but love there.

"He doesn't back down from a challenge, and when your first Alpha was Remzi Hart... We thought we might have to step in." He gave me a sympathetic look as someone passed him the mashed potatoes. "Potatoes?" I nodded. "But that situation took care of itself, and I have to say, Kace looks almost happy. Which surprises me, because for as long as I've known him, even when he was a baby, he was furious and wild." He spooned a heaping of potatoes on my plate with a laugh. "As a little kid, he'd go so red in the face when he was angry that I used to worry he'd pass out."

"Why was he so angry?"

Doughal sighed, passing on the potatoes to Kacey and accepting the beans. He lifted the tongs and dropped some on my plate at my assent. "I think some of it was the nature of how he came to be. The first few years were... rough for us all. Even as a baby, they say you take that shit in. Me and Adam, we tried to shield him from it as best we could, but I was ten and Adam was eight. There wasn't much we could do in the affairs of adults," he said, his voice pitch so low that I knew he was being discreet.

"Are you trying to steal my Omega, Brother?" Kace teased, but there was a dangerous glint in his eye.

I patted his hand where it rested on my thigh. "He's just telling me all the embarrassing stories about when you were a kid." I looked around at the rest of the table. "He said you were wild."

Patrick Mullens, the Old Man as they called him, let out a booming laugh. "Well, no lies were told there. I had to pay off more police to keep him without a juvenile record then all my other boys combined. Got your Granny's penchant for mischief, didn't you, boy?"

Kacey shrugged. "Sure. *Granny's* penchant for mischief." He raised his eyebrows at his father, who laughed again. "At least I got it all out of the way early."

Doughal rolled his eyes. "I'll believe that when I see it."

I hadn't paid much attention to Lenore Mullens, who sat to Patrick's left, across from me. "O'Sullivan is an Irish name. Any relations we'd know?"

"Not that I'm aware of, ma'am. I don't talk to my family much."

Lenore chewed her food thoughtfully, her eyes shrewd. "Family is important."

I shrugged. "My family handed my care over to the Feds pretty early on. I think family is what you make it, and doesn't necessarily mean blood." I cleared my throat. "Though most of my bondmates have strong ties with their families, and I look forward to meeting them all."

That was a bit of a lie; the idea of having to recreate this awkwardness at least twice more made me want to puke.

Lenore nodded. "Indeed, it would be a terrible thing to have an Omega daughter. I am glad my sons have escaped the Allotment so far. I'm hopeful they'll both marry soon and be exempt. Though, I guess getting an Omega would be a massive social power boost without much effort being needed."

The subtle inference that Kacey wasn't her son,

laid out there on the table for the consumption of perfect strangers, made a small kernel of anger flare to life in my chest. The idea that Kacey was coasting to success on the back of the Allotment and not his own hard work just fanned the flame.

Apparently, I was broadcasting my anger a little too loudly down my bonds, because Kacey began to rub my leg soothingly.

Adam, who was sitting beside his mother, let out a theatrical groan that drew her gaze. It was almost a practiced gesture, and I wondered how often they'd had to avert their mother's focus from Kacey. "Don't look at me. I'm not getting tied down anytime soon, but I'm with you about the Allotment. I mean, the Alpha in me would be honored to have an Omega, but having her sold off to me like a prized cow isn't the way I'd go about it." Doughal cleared his throat loudly, and Adam blushed. "No offense."

Granny scoffed loudly. "Why would she be offended, lad, when you just called her a fancy bovine?" She shook her head from the other end of the table. "Back in Ireland, they treat Omegas with the reverence they deserve; they'd do well to pick up those habits here too. She makes her own choices, lives her own life. Not any of this government bollocks." She muttered some more, then downed the last of her whiskey.

The rest of the conversation started back up, and Adam mouthed "Sorry!" across the table with a disarming grin. I smiled back at him, but not before catching his mother's eye. She scowled at me, nothing but disapproval in her expression. Okay, so Mrs. Mullens didn't like me, and I got the impression she didn't much like Kacey either.

She could go fuck herself.

Doughal grimaced down at me as Kacey started talking to one of his cousins, explaining what had happened at the courthouse. "We saw it on the news. It looked rough," he murmured to me quietly.

I swallowed hard. "It was scary. It was like they were rabid or something, all pulling and pushing." The panic rushed back. "RJ, our DoDA Official, said I could do the rest of the case by teleconference. Alpha Hart insisted on it."

I didn't really know how I felt about that. The fear in Remzi's eyes when he'd pulled me out of that crowd, the way he looked at me when he shoved me in that car, it had felt like it meant something. I knew Remzi meant me no real harm, despite the fact that what he was proposing would mean a residual pain forever. It wasn't too bad when we were close by. The pain in my chest was a low hum right now, two hundred miles away, but when we were in the same city, it was basically bearable.

I realized Doughal was speaking. "As much as my brother will hate it, this life isn't one for an Omega either. We have enemies, and Jesus knows that Kacey collects them faster than anyone other than the old man. With the extra Federal attention on you, this is no longer a life for him. He'll rail against his fate, but he has other, more legitimate responsibilities now. Eventually, we'll talk about transitioning him into one of our more..."—he waved a hand—"socially acceptable and not easily traceable branches of the business." His voice was soft again, and I wondered why he was telling me this, and not Kacey.

"We'll talk to him about it tomorrow, but I thought perhaps you'd want a heads up. He's going to be angry, but we do it because we love him, not because we don't want him in the family business." Doughal shook his head. "He never really believed that we loved him at all. He's always felt separate. And some of that was our fault." His eyes drifted to his mother. "But I've only ever wanted what was best for him, and between you and me, I was glad when he was called up for the Allotment. He was on a one-way path to a bullet between the eyes. No matter what he thinks, he isn't a disposable grunt. At least, not to me and Adam."

I felt like I was meant to read more into that statement. Did it mean he was disposable to his father?

I gave a tight nod. "I understand. I'll make sure he's okay."

The relief on Doughal's face was quickly concealed. "So, tell me about Remzi Hart. Want me to send someone to kill him?"

His mother gasped. "Doughal! Not at the dinner table."

But Patrick Mullens was roaring with laughter at the idea of assassinating a man just because he didn't want me, and honestly, I finally got what the heir to the Mullens crime family was saying. This was no place for me, and I wasn't too ashamed to admit it.

Chapter Thirty-One
Kacey

T'd left Tryst asleep in my bed as I drove back to the big house with Lupo and Tommy the next morning. We'd all been called here, and I was pretty sure that the old man wanted to find out more about the perks of being chosen in the Allotment, and maybe catch me up on business.

If I was honest, I'd rather be back home, buried between Tryst's thighs.

She'd put me on a sex ban while I healed, but I was fairly sure I could get Grady or Corrin to help convince her that I'd be fine. Hell, she could be on top and ride me, and I would stay real still and think about the Red Sox, not the way her tits bounced as she rode me.

"You sure there's nothing big going down I need to

know about?" I asked the guys, trying to distract myself from the thought of Tryst on my dick.

Tommy shook his head. "Nah, man. Without you here pissing off the other players and fucking their girlfriends, it's actually been pretty smooth sailing. Aurelio tried to screw us over on a shipment, but we cleared up that misunderstanding real quick. Other than that, I haven't had a good brawl since you left." He grinned. "Maybe we should take your girl to a club. I'm sure someone will say something stupid, and then I'd have an excuse to beat down some ugly fuck and feel like a hero all at once."

Lupo slid him a look. "There's something fucking wrong with you. I think your Ma dropped you on your head one too many times."

I sunk back against the leather seats, happy to be with my two best friends, even if I hated being away from Tryst. I felt her in my chest, a happy thrum that made me feel more pure just from its presence.

Fuck, I was turning into a sappy bastard.

What the rest of my Pack hadn't noticed last night were the half-dozen men my father kept as guards positioned around the house, ready to protect my father with blood at all times. Either the blood of their enemies or their own.

I waved at my father's second-in-command as he pulled in at the same time as us. Lewis was old now, ready to retire, but I still remembered him when he was young, covered in the blood of a man who'd betrayed us. Some things made lasting impressions.

"Kacey, boy, didn't expect to see you here again so soon. Thought the Feds would either have you locked up for trying to do a runner, or your Omega would have you leashed to her side."

I raised a shoulder, and bit my tongue so I didn't tell him not to talk about Tryst that way. I'd once seen him chop the ear off a man for not listening. He might be old and he might be a Beta, but Lewis wasn't someone you pissed off.

"Well, when the old man calls."

Lewis gave a sharp nod. "Time he hands it over to Doughal and enjoys his retirement. I wanna enjoy my grandbabies before I'm too fucking old to push them on the damn swing. Preferably without bullets flying in our direction too."

I tried to imagine Tryst and our babies in this life. My father had four brothers, but only one still lived. The rest had been gunned down when I was a kid, martyrs in a turf war. No one had been safe then, not even the kids. I found myself rebelling against the idea of her being scared for her life, ever.

I slapped Lewis on the back. "You'll have to talk to him, Lew. You know he doesn't listen to anyone but you."

"Like talkin' to a brick wall, but not half as pretty."

It was Mom's day off, so one of the maids let us in. I'd seen Tryst's surprise to see my mother as the hired help yesterday, and while it was something I was used to, it was still something I hated.

It was Lenore's provision, of course. If my mom wanted me to have anything to do with my father or step-brothers, she had to continue doing her job as a housekeeper. You see, my mom had worked for the Mullens for a couple of years before my father seduced her in his office, which was when I'd been conceived.

Why Lenore would want to keep the very real evidence of her husband's infidelity right there for everyone to see, I'd never know. But she was a wily old cow and she would have had a reason.

It was probably a test for him, or maybe a taunt for me. My father had never touched my mom again, though they were passably friendly with each other. He was like a fucking stud bull. He never went back for seconds.

No, I think she was punishing me for being born, just by showing me exactly how different I was from the legitimate children. She didn't take into account how *good* Doughal and Adam were, but I was fairly sure that their natures had more to do with the way Granny raised them than anything Lenore had ever contributed.

I walked into the old man's office, and wasn't surprised to see Doughal there. Though Adam was a surprise. Normally, he was busy in the city, running the illegal poker ring and underground fights. Gambling of the illegal variety was his baby.

My second oldest brother stood up and hugged me, giving me a slap on the back. "I'd say that mated life suits you, but you look like beaten-up dogshit, brother."

I gave him the finger, and he just slumped back onto the chair with a laugh. Adam always seemed like the nicer one, until he wasn't. By the time you'd worked that out though, you were dead.

"I like your Omega. She's sweet and shrewd. A good match," Doughal said, handing me a drink and slapping me on the back.

"A fine-looking thing too," my father added, and I gritted my back teeth.

I just raised my glass in a toast to that. "Indeed. A beauty that I left warming my bed. So I don't want to rush you, but..." I grinned to soften my words.

"Can't argue with that, son. Sit down, boys," he told Lupo and Tommy. All the familial warmth left his face, and all that was left was the man who was the head of the biggest Irish crime family on the East Coast. "Kacey, I'm relieving you of your current duties. You've got an Omega now, and way too many Federal eyes on you. We'll let shit cool down for a bit, and then we'll transition you into any of the legitimate businesses you want. Maybe start a club, or something. Stay out of trouble, and out of Boston."

I reeled backwards like he'd backhanded me. "You're kicking me from the family?"

Doughal answered, though. I should have known it was his idea. "No, Kacey, that isn't it at all. You'll always be part of the family. But now, you have opportunities to advance our cause, connections to make while you're rubbing shoulders with rich dumb assholes who attend shit with Remzi Hart." He stared at me, his face neutral but his eyes imploring me to understand. "An Omega is a point of pride. The ability to have children—as many as you fucking want, heirs with Mullens blood in their veins—is something to be proud of. She has too much heat to put her in a position where someone takes her out to get back at us, and then we'd have the entire Department of Designation Associations and the FBI on our ass."

The burn that was churning in my gut was tempered a little by the idea that my father's enemies, that *my* enemies, would use her or our kids to get back at us. I wouldn't let that happen, but I'd seen it time and again. Lewis's son had been taken from school and had his little finger cut off by an opposing family.

Kid had never been the same. He haunted the fucking streets of Boston now, like a fucked up vigilante, killing people who he decided deserved it. Problem was that they did, so the family didn't do anything about it, even though we should've. He was cleaning up the filth, plus there was a lot of guilt around what had happened to him.

Doughal looked at Tommy and Lupo. "You boys have a choice—stay in the turf you have now, oversee it in Kacey's stead. Or go with him and watch his back."

I frowned, because he was giving them a choice. You didn't *get* a choice in the Mullens family; you were either a lifelong soldier or you were dead. They must feel pretty fucking guilty, if they were offering Tommy and Lupo an out as well. Well, if Doughal was offering. I doubted it was my father's idea.

Tommy and Lupo looked at each other for a moment, but that was it. A split second was all they needed to decide. "We'll go with Kacey. We left him alone for five minutes and look at how fucked up he got. Not saying we're the reason the fucker is still breathing, but evidence would suggest..." Tommy's shit-eating grin made the others laugh. They liked Tommy; he was a stereotypical good old boy psycho.

Lupo nodded his agreement. "We work better as a team, anyway."

Doughal nodded. "So be it. When Kacey comes back, you can come back too." He looked back at the old man, who was smoking his cigar, watching Doughal take the lead with pride. I'd always thought having him look at me like that would be the best thing that ever happened to me, but now I realized it was bullshit.

Having Tryst look at me with love, like she gave a fuck if I lived or died—that was the best thing ever. The rest of this? It meant nothing without her.

Chapter Thirty-Two
Tryst

Despite being forced to watch the country's most boring daytime television every single day, with me in a starring role, the lawyers had insisted that I be in court for the verdict on the final day. I was nervous as we all drove back to NYC, but the lawyers were certain I'd be able to safely enter and exit the courthouse.

Well, at least that's what they said.

RJ had been called back earlier in the week, needing to testify about the consummation of my mating with Remzi. Seeing him sitting there on the stand, swearing under oath about my sex life, well, it'd been a little weird. I was even more glad I wasn't there for that one. Remzi had looked horrified, which was a nice change from his normal blankness.

We arrived to see the crowd outside the courthouse

hadn't dispersed at all. If anything, it had swelled until it spilled out onto the street. Just seeing it made anxiety fill my chest until I wasn't sure I could breathe.

"Jesus fucking wept, what the fuck is wrong with these people?" Tommy grumbled from behind the wheel. The Mullens family had given us an armored vehicle and Tommy and Lupo as bodyguards. Actually, they'd basically gifted the two men to Kacey as a 'sorry we're kicking you from the family business but here, keep your best friends as pets' gift. Tommy had seemed slightly disgruntled, but if I read Lupo correctly, he just looked relieved.

This was an out from the violence that they never would have gotten if it wasn't for our situation. You didn't leave the Mullens family unless you died or fled the country; Kacey had told me that himself. Even when you were old and gray, you were still a Mullens.

Even now, they were still Mullenses. They were just stuck looking after Kacey's disgruntled ass, and me. Probably seemed easy when you were used to running drugs and guns, and dropping bodies into the harbor.

"Drive straight through and take the next left. If you run over some of them, good," my grumpy Alpha growled. Yeah, Kacey was still in a shit mood about it, though.

We pulled up to a service entrance, and while

there were a few people loitering around, none of the masses of people were there. Just a few hopeful members of the press waiting to see if I'd show up for verdict day.

The six or so people surged on the car, and Lupo slid from the passenger seat, grabbing the first guy's phone and tossing it in a beautiful arch, right into a dumpster.

The reporter stared at the dumpster and then back at Lupo's menacing grin. "You asshole, you broke my phone!"

Lupo gave him an affronted look. "Nah. It's not trash day yet, so the dumpster is still full. Pretty sure it's as safe in there as a babe in the cradle. Just got to go fish it out." He looked at the other guys, still snapping pictures. "Your shit is about to get tossed too, or worse, so I suggest you fuck off before I smash it all into a thousand pieces."

He sounded so reasonable. I was kind of impressed. Having gotten the photos they wanted, the others took off out of the alleyway, and Lupo opened the door for us. Kacey climbed out first, giving the guy scrabbling in the dumpster the evil eye. Akio and I slid out after him, the rest of our Pack following behind, then we hustled into the Superior Court building.

I smiled at the guard who let us through, who'd completely ignored Lupo's come-to-Jesus chat with the paparazzi. I hoped both sides of his pillow case were cool and that he got that promotion he wanted.

We met Keisha in the grand hall of the courthouse, and I noticed the DoDA lawyer was conspicuously absent. As soon as Keisha saw Lupo and Tommy, her eyes went wide, the grin on her face spreading so big that it was a wonder it didn't crack her face clean in half.

"Oh my god, look what the cat dragged in." She stepped forward and Tommy picked her up, spinning her in a circle. "I should have known you two would show up eventually. I was surprised when Kace didn't arrive with you the first time."

Tommy gave her a big smacking kiss on the cheek, and then Lupo stepped forward, hugging her just as tightly. "He was keeping us a dirty little secret."

Keisha slapped him on the arm, then seemed to regain her professional composure. "It's good to see you, Tryst. Bondmates," she greeted pleasantly.

I waved. "You too. I see you know our new bodyguards."

"Know? Keisha stole Lupo's girlfriend when she was sixteen. He never got over that, you know."

Keisha raised an eyebrow. "Well then, he should have been a better boyfriend. She was embarrassingly easy to lure away. Besides, then I married her so you should be thanking me for freeing up your wingman."

"Tell Chloe I said hello," Lupo muttered, but in a good-natured way.

Keisha looked at her watch. "We better go." Her face fell into a more serious expression, and it made her look older, maybe a little scarier. "I've got to warn you, Tryst, it isn't looking fantastic. Despite both parties being in agreement about the termination of the bond, the court has dug in its heels and is making it... difficult. We can argue points of law and precedents all day long, but what it comes down to is that this is a unique situation and an unheard-of point of law. Prepare yourself for this case to not go the way you'd hoped."

What the fuck did that mean?

I couldn't ask though, because we were being ushered through the doors of the courtroom and every single person in the gallery was staring at me like I was a bug under a glass. Both my Alphas flanked me on either side, protective and in Kacey's case, kind of feral. I looked over my shoulder at Jak, who was directly behind me, and then back to Grady and Corrin. Corrin gave me a thumbs up, and Grady shot me a reassuring smile.

I sat down at my prescribed spot, Keisha sliding into the chair beside me. Right down the end was the DoDA lawyer, whose name I still didn't know, and the air was definitely frosty between him and Keisha.

The judge banged his gavel. "Court is in session.

Alpha Hart, Omega Hart, the court appreciates you both being with us in the courtroom today, and we also applaud the professionalism of your respective legal teams."

Okay, good start.

"However, we are of the opinion that the bond between an Alpha and Omega—and indeed the metaphysical bond between a person of designation and any of their bondmates—is not something that can be ruled upon by this court. It is not so much as a legally binding agreement, but more of a morally and spiritually binding agreement between parties, and as such, we deny the applicant's motion for a severance of the matebond and its responsibilities."

The sudden buzz around the room was so loud that it filled my skull, churning until it morphed into a high-pitched buzz in my ears.

The judge banged his gavel. "Order!" The room settled down again, though it was still electric with shock and excitement. "Furthermore, we conclude that an Alpha is legally obligated to reside with his Omega, as codified in Federal Statute, *Designations and Reproductive Rights Act of 2027*. Therefore, the court is ordering the full Pack Hart to return to Alpha Remzi Hart's home, or a home agreed to by the Pack or provided by the Department of Designation Associations..." He continued, but I couldn't breathe. I was being bombarded from all sides by noise, by the emotions of my bondmates and of Remzi.

Keisha was standing now, arguing with the judge, which didn't seem very wise from a career standpoint for her. She was also arguing fiercely with the DoDA lawyer beside me.

I looked to my right, and Remzi's eyes were on me for once. I wished they weren't; he looked so fucking sad. It didn't seem to be for himself, though. He was looking at me with a pity in his eyes that didn't make sense.

"...the world still stands on the precipice of a back-slide into extinction, and therefore, we have to judge the comforts of a few against the good of the many. Much like our military, we thank you for your sacrifices, but ultimately we have conducted this with all the fairness and self-determination we could provide while still balancing the needs of the millions of other Americans."

Remzi stood. "This is bullshit! She isn't a brood-mare. She isn't fucking livestock. She is a human being who should be afforded the same respect that purport-edly underpins all our laws and society as a whole."

The judge banged the gavel again. "Another outburst like that, Mr. Hart, and I will charge you with contempt." He started to rattle off all the case prece-dents that didn't make sense to me but were somehow deciding my life. Finally, he banged that stupid hammer once more. "Case dismissed."

A hand wrapped around my arm, and I looked up into the furious face of Keisha. "Let's go, Tryst."

I stood, stumbling toward Grady. Always Grady. He tucked me into his side and snapped at anyone who came close.

"I'm so sorry, Tryst. This is not okay," Corrin whispered beside me as they hustled me out of the room and down the long halls.

We were met at the back entrance by Remzi Hart's lawyer. She looked furious too. I felt like she was flaying me alive; her eyes were blazing with anger. She thrust a business card at me. "Alpha Hart requests the presence of you and the Pack at his home."

Akio accepted the card from her, drawing the woman's eyes from me. "Thank you." His tone was polite, but it was still a clear dismissal. Jak glared at the card like he was trying to set it on fire with his mind.

The lawyer grimaced, but looked at me once more. "For what it's worth, I'm sorry. I agree with Remzi." I tried not to growl at her familiarity with my Alpha. "Your life and your choices should be your own. I don't have to be an Omega to hate the fact that you have no rights. We'll take this higher if we can. As high as possible." Her face was passionate and almost predatory, and I was glad I wasn't the one in her sights.

She strode off, and I watched her go. She looked like she was going to karate kick that judge in the nuts. I wished her the best of luck.

Keisha also said goodbye. "This isn't over, Tryst. Not by a long shot."

But this was the Superior Court. There was nowhere else to go from here. So I gave her a crooked smile instead of stating that fact. "Thanks for trying." She hugged me tight, then strode off after the other lawyer.

I looked around at my bondmates. "Let's get the hell out of here."

Chapter Thirty-Three
Tryst

When they said that they were enforcing it, they weren't kidding. DoDA Officials and Federal Marshals met us at the back entrance of the courthouse, parked both in front of and behind Kacey's car.

Tommy and Lupo were tense, and I was fairly sure it was because they were both carrying concealed weapons. But they were just our security, so no one had any reason to look any closer than that.

A DoDA Official who looked vaguely familiar stepped in front of me. "Omega Hart, we're here to escort you to Alpha Hart's residence."

Kacey scowled. "Did Remzi fucking Hart get an escort home too? Because if you think Tryst is the one who's going to abscond, you have a short fucking memory."

The Official slid his eyes to Kacey. "Alpha Hart also got an escort home for his own safety."

"Oh, now I know why I remember you. Denozo, right? I kicked you in the balls. Sorry about that." No I wasn't. I hated this and I hated him. "Whatever. Where's RJ?"

The other Official's face went instantly blank. "Official Hicks was needed at the East Coast office. I'll be your liason for future needs."

"And your name is?" Jak demanded, his tone not even close to polite.

"Official John Smith."

Jak snorted. "So your parents hated you. Good to know."

The Official gave him a dead-eyed stare and waved a hand at the car. "If you'll hurry, we can deliver you to your Alpha."

Kacey flipped him the bird. "Fuck off. We don't work for you." But still, Akio gently moved me toward the car with a hand low on my back.

He seemed tense, as did Jak. I guess they'd never officially met Remzi, and didn't share the same residual hatred toward my first Alpha. Grady and Corrin hated him for noble enough reasons—they'd borne the brunt of his decision to abandon me during my heat.

Kacey hated him because... well, they'd just gotten

off on the wrong foot and then hopped around on it until it was irreparably ruined.

And now they wanted us all to live in the same house? We were so screwed.

As we drove around the front of the courthouse, crowds surged toward the car, the cops barely keeping them back, even though a NYPD squad car slowly moved them out of the way.

Obviously, they'd heard the verdict, because the pro-Omega protestors were livid. They were screaming red-faced at the anti-designation protesters. It was clearly getting violent in there as tear gas drifted up through the crowd, and I could see armored riot vehicles rolling down the street toward them.

Holy hell. "I didn't realize the case was going to have such an impact."

It was Corrin who answered. "It's been a long time since Omega rights have been addressed. Last time was after the Mud Maidens, way back after we discovered the different designations. Your divorce case was seen as some kind of turning point for society, where we stopped being reactive to what's happened and started moving forward to a more civilized society. The fact that the court just said 'Fuck you' is a big deal. #OmegaRightsAreHumanRights is trending on the internet, along with #HaveAHart and #FreeTryst."

"Catchy," Jak mused. Despite his flippant words,

he looked so fucking concerned. I laced my fingers through his, squeezing them tightly. Actually, both he and Akio looked more worried than normal, so I pushed some of that calming Omega love juice down the bond.

"What's wrong?"

Jak gave me a lopsided smile. I'd forgotten how handsome he was until it slapped me in the face like this. "It's nothing, just the situation."

"And?"

He raised an eyebrow at me. "And a twin thing. Akio's Alpha is disturbed because this isn't how it's supposed to be."

"Jak," Akio hissed.

Jak frowned at his twin. "No, man. I mightn't know Tryst as well as these guys, but I know her enough to be one hundred percent certain she cares about our feelings. We aren't background noise to her."

I sucked in a breath. "Of course not. Have I made you feel that way?"

I mean, I probably had, but this shit had been one thing after another. On those rare days that were drama free, I just wanted to breathe, not deep dive into the psyche of my newest bondmates. That was on me. "I'm so sorry."

Akio gave Jak a furious look. "This is why I didn't say anything," he growled, and if that aggression had been directed at a person other than his twin, they'd probably be shitting themselves. "It's nothing you've done, love. You've been perfect. It isn't your job to juggle us like we're ticking timebombs." He sighed, casting one more sour look at Jak. "When I was taught about the Alpha and Omega relationships, it was drilled into me—into us—that your comfort of the utmost importance. We were to make you a good home that was stress free, complete with a nest and everything you needed to be happy. We'd provide for you and in return, your happiness would trickle down your bond to us." He waved a hand at the armored car and everyone's grim faces. "I feel like I'm failing you, even though logically I know that there's nothing I, or any one of us, could do to shield you from this."

"That's so fucking dumb," Kacey scoffed, and I hissed at him. Actually hissed. It made him pull back, his eyes wide, and then he laughed.

Taking a deep breath, I looked around at them all. "It's over now. It is what it is, and we'll just deal with it the best we can. Remember, we have to live with Remzi for the foreseeable future, and I'd be a lot *happier* if we didn't fist fight every five seconds." I turned back to Akio and Jak. "I know this isn't what you dreamed of, and it isn't what I wanted either, but just in case I haven't told you enough, I'm glad you guys were chosen. You balance us out as a Pack. We'll have years to get to know each other. Decades, even."

Akio reached out and stroked a hand down my face, his eyes inscrutable. "I look forward to it, Tryst. This will all pass, I promise. We'll both get our wish soon enough."

For the first time since we met, I wanted to curl up on the lap of my Alpha, or stay pressed between him and Jak, secure and safe.

My Omega keened for it. *Soon,* I told her. *We just have one hurdle left.*

That 'hurdle' met us in the foyer of a beautiful Art Deco building that overlooked Central Park. Corrin whistled between his teeth. "I mean, I knew he was rich..." he said in a low voice, and I looked over at him with wide eyes.

This wasn't rich. This was insanely wealthy.

I was hiding behind Corrin's shoulders—though I'd never admit that out loud—because standing in front of Remzi Hart, looking him in the eye, felt like too much right now. Everything felt like too much. And what was the point of having a gazillion mates if I couldn't use them as human shields when I felt uncomfortable?

"Come this way," Remzi said, his tone just shy of an Alpha bark. It was still enough to make Corrin grunt with the force of the command, but his feet stayed planted to the ornate marble, like he was proving a point. Grinning at me over his shoulder, he finally followed along behind everyone.

We crowded into an ornate elevator with gold doors right at the end of an elevator bank. "Private elevator entrance. I'll get you all keypasses," Remzi told us, waving a matte black card in front of the reader. "We have the penthouse, but I also own the floor below. If we choose to stay here, I will have the current occupants relocated and we'll subsume that floor too."

"Choose to stay? He has to be crazy, right?" Grady whispered in my ear, so quietly that I was sure no one else would hear over the soft whoosh of the elevator car rocketing upwards. I had to agree. This luxury was ridiculous, and we hadn't even gotten into the apartment yet.

My opinion didn't change even a little as we stepped out into an open foyer and took in Remzi's home. There were hardly any walls, just huge panes of glass that opened up to the sky. My breath stuck in my lungs at the view over Central Park and the skyline of the city. Everything was in neutral tones, which made it cozy. Cream overstuffed couches complemented the warm wood floors. A round pendant light hung over a low coffee table scattered with tech magazines and business papers, like Remzi had walked away from it only moments ago.

The whole place was open plan, with a large dining table under a crystal chandelier, and a kitchen that would make a chef weep with joy.

But that view.

"Omega."

I stiffened, my eyes still on the window.

"Tryst."

I sucked in a deep breath, steeling my spine. I turned to look at Remzi, my eyes on his chest.

It was a damn nice chest.

"Look at me, Omega." Again, just shy of a command, but my eyes still dragged up. A choked sound broke from my lips at the expression on his face. He looked like he'd been through the wringer, his curly hair wild, dark circles sinking below his eyes. His dress shirt was wrinkled and the sleeves rolled up his forearms.

But his eyes. They were soft and filled with something indescribable. Pain? Pity? Maybe even fear.

He rubbed a hand down his face. "I'm sorry. You have to know that this was never about you. You're fine. Better than fine. It's the system that's broken, and I finally had the opportunity to do something about it. But I blew it."

I'd thought hearing those words would fix something in my chest, but it didn't. His rejection still hurt, and I would never forget the pain and the emotional meat grinder he'd put me through. But I could forgive, because holding onto this festering hatred wasn't healthy for any of us.

"I understand." That was all I could give him right now.

"Thank you." He looked past me at the rest of the group. "I don't expect you to understand or forgive me for the court case, but I promise that I was doing it with Tryst's—and all other Omegas'—interests at heart. I never wanted this, but I hope that we can all work together and get along for Tryst's sake."

"We're already working together for Tryst. We've been figuring out *our* shit for *our* Omega this whole fucking time. You're the only one not getting along, so don't make it sound like it's an *us* problem, asshole. It's a *you* problem," Kacey snapped, and Grady put a steadying hand on his arm. I pushed some Omega chill out vibes down the bond at him, and he slid his eyes at me, frowning slightly. I was glad Tommy and Lupo weren't here, otherwise this might have ended badly.

"Kacey..." I warned, and Remzi raised a hand.

"No, Tryst, he's right. This whole situation is of my making, but I'd like it if we could start again." He looked down at me, his eyes filled with something indescribable that made my heart thump harder in my chest. Fuck, he had some big Alpha presence. It made it hard to breathe. "Would you introduce me to your—I mean, *our*—new bondmates?"

I sucked in air through my nose, hoping it would give me enough oxygen that I didn't feel so light-headed. Stepping to the side, I smiled at my two newest bondmates. "Remzi Hart, I'd like you to meet Jak and Akio Bell, my bondmates."

Jak stepped forward first, shaking hands, his eyes flicking appraisingly over the man. "Nice to meet you."

Then Akio stepped forward, and I bit my lip. Akio was the most personable, even-tempered of my Alphas, but he was still an Alpha. They sized each other up, neither dropping their gaze, and I didn't move, didn't even breathe, until a smile spread across Akio's face.

"Good to meet you, finally. Gotta say, we use your name like a curse word, so be prepared for that." His smile widened. "But also, just so you know, you hurt Tryst like that again and I'll help Kacey smash your pretty face to pieces."

He said it in the same way people told you that your milk was about to expire.

Both of Remzi's eyebrows rose. "Understood."

Corrin rolled his eyes. "Alpha Hart. How about we get on with this before the amount of Big Dick Energy in here throws Tryst into heat again?"

Remzi's lips quirked. "Of course. Please, call me Remzi."

Corrin winked, grabbing my hand as he walked past. "I will, when you're more than just another stranger."

Chapter Thirty-Four
Tryst

Remzi only had three spare bedrooms, so we were all bunking together again. Although they'd wanted to give me my own room, I decided it was easier for me to float around from bed to bed. I mean, it wasn't like I came with much stuff, plus it would help me connect with the guys better. My bondmates.

That didn't mean everyone was impressed with the idea, least of all Akio. And surprisingly, Remzi seemed opposed to it too.

"You deserve your own space, Tryst. You aren't property to be passed around from man to man because you feel some kind of obligation," Akio argued.

I gave him a narrow-eyed look. "Thanks for that wisdom, and the backhanded insinuation that I'm basically a sex toy, but it's fine. It strengthens the bonds, and those already feel strained. It'd make me feel more settled."

Akio flushed. "That's not what I meant. I'm sorry, Omega." I sighed, stroking a hand down his arm. I knew that wasn't what he meant, but I was feeling irritable.

Remzi continued to watch me. "I'll take care of it," he decreed, like that was that.

Fucking rich people.

He grabbed his phone, and his fingers flew wildly across the screen. I motioned Akio and Jak into the last room. "Get settled. Have a break. If it's okay with you guys, I'd like to stay in here with you tonight?"

Jak's answering grin sent pleasure straight down south. "Hell yeah."

Akio rolled his eyes at his brother. "We'd be honored, Omega." He stepped forward, dipping his head until his lips brushed my ear. "I intend to make you come so hard that Remzi Hart will cry himself to sleep about what he's been missing." With that, he kissed my cheek and carried his bags into the room. I shamelessly watched his ass as he went.

Silver linings, right?

Remzi interrupted my butt gazing. "Omega... Tryst. I would like to show you something, if you'd agree?"

We had to get past this stiffness, otherwise my time here was going to be unbearable. "Of course."

The sun was beginning to set, casting the skyline a beautiful orange. I'd definitely never get sick of the view at least.

"I'm getting food sent in for us all; it should be here soon," Remzi said, leading me to a door at the end of the hall. "This is my room here, if you need anything." He pointed to the master bedroom on my left, and I got a glimpse of a low bed with moss-colored bedding. We walked past it and he opened a door right at the very end, revealing a beautiful wooden spiral staircase.

"Akio is right—you deserve your own space. This can be purely your domain. I will give you the key."

He led me up the stairs, which opened into a sitting room that stole my breath. There were no walls, just large glass windows that met in the center. We were obviously in the atrium of the building because I could see the night sky spread right across me, the moon heavy behind clouds. Below it, there was nothing but a sea of lights.

Inside the atrium was a large, voluminous couch, its cushions deep and overstuffed. A faux fireplace was built into the wall below a television, and there was a fluffy rug made of something soft and white in front of it. A door at the very back of the room opened onto a small patio. Books ran along the wall beside me, wrapping up and around the door we'd just entered through.

The whole space was gorgeous, and I fell instantly in love with it.

"You can invite whoever you like up here, or no one at all. This is your space and you're free to decorate it however you like."

"It's too beautiful. I wouldn't change a thing." And it was. I saw an open book on a wingback by the fireplace, a remote control sitting on the arm of the couch. "Are you sure? You obviously use this space. We are already encroaching on your home so much."

Remzi was shaking his head. "I've done this all wrong." He reached out, gently placing his hands on my upper arms. "This is rightfully your home now too. *Our* home. You've been given so damn little in life, Tryst, that you believe you deserve only scraps, but it's not true. You, and Omegas like you, deserve so much more than what the government gives you to keep you docile. You deserve freedom. You deserve a choice. None of us *deserve* you just because we're men and somehow that makes us more entitled. I hate it. I hate what it did to my mother. I hate what it's done to countless other Omegas before you. I hate what it's done to you, even though I know that I'm the cause of most of your pain."

He sucked in a deep breath. "So this is yours.

Anything else you desire, I'll give to you to the best of my ability." He pulled me closer. "Tell me, what do you want, Tryst?"

My brain whirled at his words, at his complete one-eighty. I didn't even know what I wanted, because up until this point, what I wanted had never mattered.

"I'd like some plants," I blurted out, blood rushing to my cheeks. "I like plants. But I never got many because I knew that I'd just be moved when my Allot-ment came and I probably couldn't take them with me."

Remzi gave me a smile tinged with sadness. "Tomorrow, we'll go plant shopping." He held out a hand, and I stared at it. It was a peace offering. I placed my palm in his, swallowing hard at the tingle that raced across my skin. I sighed with relief, or maybe it was my Omega who did that, because for the first time, the ache in my chest eased completely.

His hand tightened around mine, and I gazed up into his face, trying to read him. I'd gotten used to looking at his Adam's apple, like if I didn't see the emotion in his eyes, it wouldn't hurt as much. But I forced myself to look now, and what I saw was a punch in the gut.

Desire. Burning hot need. I knew it was the Alpha looking out at me, that incomparable wild feeling that rose between us was exactly what the judge had described: a metaphysical bond that was stretched tight between us, intangible but sometimes as corporeal as if he was stroking my body with his actual hands.

I held my breath as he stared, his eyes falling from my eyes to my lips. "I want to kiss you so badly right now, it's a physical ache."

My lips parted. "Please, Alpha."

He groaned, his hand tightening. He stooped down and brushed his lips along mine, and every ounce of yearning, the ghosts that had haunted me since the heat, all rushed back to the surface.

Scraping his teeth over my bottom lip, he pulled away. "My knot aches every night remembering the feel of you. I fuck my hand and hate myself for it. Hate how much I want you. Hate that you make me feel like an animal," he breathed against my lips. "I hate that you're a fucking abyss in my chest that is completely empty if you aren't beside me. But most of all, I've hated myself. Hated that I inflicted that same feeling onto you day after day after day. Never again," he ground out, a promise to me, or maybe a warning to the universe.

He straightened, and I watched him stuff the Alpha away behind a visage of politeness. "We should go back down. Dinner will arrive in a moment." He looked around the room once more. "I'll have stuff delivered to make a nest tomorrow."

He walked toward the spiral staircase, but my feet were stuck like I was glued to the floor. Our arms stretched across the distance between us, until just our fingers remained connected.

He looked back at me, his face open and soft for once. "Come, Omega. I'm not letting you go now." My feet moved toward him like they had a mind of their own, and I held his hand tightly as he tucked behind him and led me down the stairs.

We'd healed something, but somehow, I felt just as confused as before.

The concierge called up just as we made it down to the first level, and the rest of my bondmates eyed us warily. I couldn't blame them; the whole situation was like a fireworks factory ready to go up in a spectacular, colorful blaze.

As Remzi spoke to the doorman, Kacey sidled up beside me. "Are you okay? Want me to beat his face in? My hand is feeling better."

I tilted my face toward him for a kiss, which he happily provided. With tongue, naturally. Finally, when I drew back for air, I answered his question. "I think everything will be as it should now, Kace. I think we can put all this shit behind us."

God, I hoped so.

. . .

Dinner had been slightly awkward, but with what I assumed was really expensive gin, boutique beer, and pasta so good it would have made angels sing, everyone relaxed a little. The guys fell into their easy camaraderie they'd developed over the last few weeks, and Akio, bless his fucking heart, made an effort to draw Remzi into the conversation. I was giving him the best blowjob ever tonight, just because he was a nice guy.

It was going well, until the conversation turned to where we should all live again.

"I vote we make the DoDA pay out the ass for something fancy," Jak muttered, downing his beer. "Swimming pools and a stable filled with prancy-looking horses."

Grady snorted. "The DoDA isn't going to pay for a crack shack at this rate. No, we shouldn't rely on those fucks for any longer than we need to. They've proved they're happy to screw us over and over. And not even in a fun way," he said, winking at me. It turned out Grady couldn't handle his gin.

"We can't stay here," Remzi said, holding his crystal tumbler with ease. I held mine like it was about to shatter into diamonds and fairy dust at any moment.

Kacey frowned. "Why? Don't want the riffraff in your fancy house?"

I kicked him under the table. Contentious bastard.

Kacey gave me a look that said I'd be in trouble for that later, and my Omega purred at the thought.

"No. You'll just always feel like guests here, like somehow it's my territory, and it'll make you, and Akio, more unsettled to be somewhere neutral. The best thing for Tryst is that we're happy and settled. I know what a house filled with Alphas jostling for prime position looks like, and it isn't a situation that I want to recreate for Tryst." His voice was soft but raw. I wanted to reassure him that it would be fine, but I didn't know that. Not really.

Corrin was grinning goofily. "Bet you feel like a fucking jerk now, Kacey Boyd. Or are we all Harts now? A Pack of Harts," he giggled. "Jesus, this shit is strong. Not like the bathtub moonshine we have back home. How much does this stuff cost a bottle?"

"Four hundred dollars," Remzi said offhandedly.

"Holy hell," Corrin gasped, choking on his drink. "Is it made in golden bathtubs by Omega virgins?"

Remzi gave him a soft smile. "Something like that." He tilted his head as he thought about what Corrin had said. "I really don't mind the Pack name. It should be up to Tryst."

Corrin pouted. "I like Corrin Hart. Makes me sound mysterious, or like the main character in a romance novel."

Everyone was looking at me, and I shrugged. "It

should definitely be a group discussion. Is anyone particularly attached to their surname?" I looked at Akio and Jak. "There's two of you, so we're already a third of the way there. Grady was my first mate. Hart is our legally recognized Pack name."

Grady shrugged. "Let's just hyphenate. Hart sounds fine, and it will save a lot of red tape in the long run. The Hart name will also give you the most protection." He looked at Kacey. "No offense, man. I know your family is very, uh, protected in certain circles."

Kacey shook his head. "No. My family was right. Tryst shouldn't be associated with them at all. It would make her a target."

I was going to ignore the questions that statement raised and just enjoy my gin. Kacey's family drama was an issue for another day.

I looked at Akio and Jak. They were the most family-orientated, and if anyone would want to have their name attached to our Pack forever, it would be the twins.

Jak shrugged. "We came into the mating knowing that you already had an Alpha. It's fine with us—well, me at least?" He looked over at Akio, who nodded.

"Our family has brothers to carry on the family name," he stated simply, and I realized I hadn't even asked them if they had siblings. We'd obviously skipped the first date, small talk portion of our courtship.

Remzi looked at us like we were all aliens. He must have thought this would be more of a fight. "I would be honored for you all to remain Pack Hart," he said finally, his voice rough.

I placed my hand over his, giving it a soft squeeze. "Our Pack will be different from what you know, Remzi. I can't guarantee it'll be easy all the time, but we aren't your parents." I looked around at the apartment. "The government won't pay for anything like this, though." I wasn't sure they *could* pay for something like this. The Department didn't have a lot of excess funds, definitely not as much as private industry.

"The less we take from them, the better. I agree with Grady on that."

Kacey sighed. "Fuck it. None of us can contribute this kind of money anyway, so anything we get is going to be bought and paid for by you. Let's just stay here for now. We'll settle into the apartment downstairs like you said, and then we can figure out other homes later, or when we decide to have kids."

Awkward. That wasn't a conversation I wanted to have... Wait, what was the date?

Oh fuck. Oh fuck. Oh fuck.

I stretched a smile across my face. *Don't panic, Tryst. Don't fucking panic. Could be nothing.*

"I think I'm ready for bed." I stretched and yawned, and everyone watched me cautiously. I flooded the bonds with shiny happiness, which was probably fairly brittle if anyone examined it too closely. No one pushed though, for which I would be eternally grateful.

"How about you guys?" I asked the twins, and Jak grinned.

"Babe, I couldn't be more ready." The two of them stood and followed me out of the room.

I pushed the nagging thought to the back of my brain. I'd worry about it later.

Chapter Thirty-Five
Jak

Was it odd that I was nervous to get naked with a woman I'd already been naked with several times? Seriously, every single time I worried that she'd be disappointed in how I performed and would kick me out of the Pack, like this was some kind of reality show and not our life.

She looked stressed. Hell, she even *felt* stressed in the bond.

"You know, we don't have to do anything. I'm more than happy to hold you and tell you super boring stories in a monotone voice until you go to sleep."

Akio laughed from the walk-in closet. "He really can. Get him to tell you about the glory days of Ducati and how the 1950s were the golden years for motorcycles." He gave an exaggerated yawn that I could hear even from here.

Tryst laughed, crawling into the bed beside me. "I'm sorry. I know I've been a terrible mate to you." She snuggled into my side, like she needed the kind of comfort only I could give. It was heady stuff, and none of it was sexual.

"Babe, your worth as a bondmate and an Omega isn't in how many times a week you put out." I squeezed her tighter to my body. "This right here? It's more than enough for us."

She looked up at me, really looked at me, and for the first time in my life, I felt like someone saw me, Jak, and not just one of the Bell twins.

We'd basically been a sideshow in high school, and although it meant we got our pick of girlfriends—and boyfriends in my case, because I liked to keep my options open—I knew it wasn't ever really for me. It was for us. And especially for Akio since he was an Alpha.

It hadn't even occurred to me to care until I was in my twenties, when my first serious girlfriend screamed at me that she only wanted me as a pathway to Akio. She wanted a real man. An Alpha.

Didn't even matter that Akio hated her guts and always had. If anything, it'd made it worse.

Tryst reached up, her fingers tracing across my cheekbones gently, her eyes intent like she was memorizing them. "Heavy thoughts, Jak?"

I turned my cheek into her hand. "The opposite. Just thinking how lucky I am."

I pulled her onto my chest, enjoying the way her weight spread across me. I ran my hands up and down her back either side of her spine, putting pressure on the places I'd learned about during my research.

When she purred, I had to think of naked turtles and every Yamaha produced in 2017 to keep my dick under control. I hummed low in my chest, at the vibration that was almost like a purr, which Omegas enjoyed.

I wondered if deep down, I'd had some kind of foreshadowing that I'd end up with an Omega, or if that was just wishful thinking. Manifestation, maybe.

The tension left Tryst's body almost in a wave, and I was stupidly proud of myself. I looked over her head at Akio, who was leaning against the door of the closet, just watching me with our Omega.

Our Omega. Honestly, I still pinched myself thinking about it. We'd gotten so lucky, or maybe it was a rort of the system like Grady had suggested, but I didn't care.

He didn't need to say anything—it was all there on his face. His happiness, not just for himself, but for us. "Want me to go?" he mouthed, and I shook my head. I didn't, not really. Soon I'd like one-on-one time to get to know her properly, for her to get to know me too. But she had so little time that I didn't want to be selfish. I didn't actually mind sharing with my brother—it came as naturally as breathing—but I just didn't like being a booby prize. The Bell twin you got when you couldn't bag an Alpha.

Tryst's hand came up and tangled in my hair, which was getting a little long on the top. I hadn't been in for a haircut for awhile when the DoDA had picked us up. But if she wanted to use it as a handle, I was here for it.

"Stop or I'll fall asleep. I wanted to spend time with you guys," she said with a yawn, but I didn't stop stroking her spine.

"You're exhausted. We have plenty of time. Sleep, Omega."

But she set her jaw to a stubborn line and rolled off me. "Nope. You deserve better." She looked over her shoulder at Akio. "You too. Get in here." She crawled beneath the blankets with more speed than grace, then lifted the other side for Akio. He kissed her forehead before sliding in on her other side. She snuggled down further, but despite her stubborn declaration, her eyes were heavy. "Would you still want me if I was a gummy worm?"

I frowned down at her. "Would you still have a personality?"

"Mmhmm."

"Would you disappear if I licked you?"

She shook her head. "I'd just be tasty."

I pretended to think it over, giving her a few test licks. "You're pretty tasty now too." She let out an adorable squeak and wiggled back into Akio, but I chased her, nibbling at her lips. "Okay, I have my answer."

"Yes?" she breathed.

"Tryst, I would want you even if you were a gummy worm that had been rolled around in the dirt and then tossed in the sun to melt."

She beamed at me, her lazy happiness healing my soul. Akio kissed the top of her head softly, and I was glad she couldn't see his expression. She'd freak out at the longing look, the devoted affection that was already there.

Corrin kept saying she was easy to love, and he wasn't wrong.

"If I was a gummy worm, and I was the last edible thing left on the planet, would you eat me?"

I snorted a laugh, and she frowned at me seriously. I schooled my features back into the gravitas the question deserved. "While I think you're a total snack, I wouldn't eat you, even if you were the last edible thing on the planet. I would protect you from the ravenous hordes of gummy worm-eating zombies, and then we'd eat Remzi Hart, because he's big and beefy, and I'm pretty sure he'd be like wagyu since he's so rich."

She closed her eyes, but her lips were still curled in a smile. "Can't eat Remzi. He's my mate. Just have to learn to cook zombie fricassee." Then she was asleep, and I was a little more in love than when I climbed into bed. We sat silent and still, scared of waking her up.

I knew we'd come in at the tail end of her dramas, but I was tired of them already. I just wanted peace enough to explore Tryst and our new bond, to feed her and make her laugh. Carefully, I shifted her so her head was pillowed on my arm, holding her as close as I could without it being weird.

"What do you think of Remzi Hart?" Akio whispered softly.

I shrugged, because I didn't think he really wanted to know *exactly* what I thought of Remzi. We were so alike in so many ways, but Akio had always been perplexed by my attraction to the same sex. Not disapproving, but he wouldn't understand the physical appeal of the huge Alpha. Akio would only see him as a potential threat.

He wouldn't think the way the huge Alpha moved was like a choreographed dance of strength, or appreciate the long, muscular legs and that jaw. Holy shit. He made my mouth water, which made his betrayal of Tryst so much worse.

I could understand why Grady and Corrin still looked at him with distrust. From what I'd heard, they'd borne the brunt of her heat craze. I mean, five days of sex seemed amazing to me, but seeing her in pain all the time, knowing there was nothing I could do to really stop it? That would have been torture.

"I'm reserving judgment. He seems to be genuinely trying."

"And changing your name to Hart?"

I shrugged. "I meant what I said. I'm cool with it. I'd be Jak Trystmate if she let me."

He pinched my arm where it was over Tryst's waist. "Simp. I thought it was Alphas who were meant to turn into mush for their Omegas."

I shot him the finger. "I'm connected to you too, asshole. I feel your big goo-goo eyes whenever you look at her."

"I feel the other big 'feelings' you get when you look at the rest of her mates too. It kind of worked out well for you, didn't it?"

I buried my face, and my blushing cheeks, in her hair. "Don't be jealous that I'll never have to go to bed alone."

He rolled onto his front, shoving his face in her pillow just to get a whiff of her scent. "I'd never be jealous of you, Jak. I'm glad that there are more people to love you how you deserve to be loved."

Fucking Akio. That was the real reason I could never be jealous enough of him to hate him, no matter what golden light shone on his head due to the freak luck of our birth.

I could never be mad at him, because he was so goddamn genuine and sweet. He honestly wanted my happiness more than his own, the self-sacrificing bastard.

"Go to sleep, you big fucking marshmallow."

"Love you too, bro."

Chapter Thirty-Six
Tryst

I crawled from between the sleeping bodies of Akio and Jak as quietly as possible. Akio stirred briefly, and I stilled like I was being hunted, but he eventually settled back into sleep. I pulled on a pair of Jak's sweats and Akio's hoodie, and opened the door softly, grabbing my phone and the keyfob for the elevator.

The light flashed green and the doors opened. It was a soft whoosh, but it sounded like a gunshot in the silence of the apartment. I pulled up my contacts. Tommy and Lupo? Or RJ?

I wanted to call RJ, but he was on the East Coast, so I dialed Lupo's number.

He answered on the second ring. "Tryst, what's wrong?" He sounded groggy. It was three a.m., so he definitely would have been asleep.

"Nothing," I said quickly. "Are you or Tommy busy right now? I need something."

"At three a.m.."

"Yes."

"Okay. Hang on." The phone muffled, like he was holding it to his chest. "Tommy, get up, we gotta go."

Hang on, wait. "Were you guys in bed together?"

There was silence at the other end of the line. "Two beds in the same hotel room," Lupo said gruffly. "We aren't all living it up in the penthouse suite."

Sounded like a deflect to me, but I let it go. "I'll get that fixed, I promise. I just need you to come and pick me up." I paused, holding the doors closed button as the elevator reached the ground floor.

"Tryst..."

"I swear it's nothing bad. You can return me safe and sound in like thirty minutes, tops."

He sighed heavily. "We'll be there in two minutes."

"Lupo?"

"Yes?"

"Can you grab a pregnancy test on the way?"

The silence at the other end of the phone was deafening, before he cleared his throat. "Okay. Make it five minutes."

He hung up, and I held the door closed for a moment more, then grew some lady balls and let go of the button. The doors slid open on the well-lit foyer. I knew the concierge desk was over in the corner, and I knew it would be manned. These high-end apartments always had a twenty-four hour doorman.

Should I sneak out like I was doing something bad? Or just walk out like I owned the place—which, granted, I probably was entitled to half of anyway, by law. Decision made, I pushed back my shoulders and lifted my chin.

The nightman looked up immediately as I walked from the elevator, his eyes widening. "Omega Hart, is everything all right?"

I gave him a tight smile. "Of course. I just felt like pancakes."

He gave me a shocked look. "Would you like me to order you some?"

"No, there's a twenty-four hour diner around the corner. I'm sure they'll have some."

The guy looked like he was three seconds away from strong-arming me back into the elevator. "Omega Hart, it's really not safe to be walking around at night."

As if summoned by the Goddess of Impeccable Timing, Lupo and Tommy walked into the foyer. I smiled at the doorman. "It's okay. My security is here. They're scarier than anything the city has to offer." I gave him a hard look. "I appreciate your discretion"—I looked down at his badge—"Dwayne."

The guy still looked like he wanted to protest, but

that was always the way it was when you were an Omega. People thought I couldn't look after myself without a man at my side, which was bullshit. They'd always second-guessed my decisions, undermined my opinions and generally treated me like I was stupid.

"Of course, ma'am."

As I turned to the door, I let my fake smile drop. Lupo walked out ahead of me, and Tommy stood at my back. I hadn't really thought this next part through, but luckily Lupo had. "Come on, we're only staying a street back. You can take the test in our hotel room."

We walked quickly and silently, and when he stopped in front of a five-star hotel, I whacked him in the back. "You asshole. You're out here giving me the guilt treatment like you're in a roach motel while you're staying in a fucking luxury resort. I thought you'd have to be renting a place by the hour or something."

Tommy laughed. "We aren't exactly hard up for cash ourselves. The family lets you keep a cut, and Kacey always went big." He cleared his throat. "Or at least, he did. Not anymore. Plus, Lupo knows how to invest and shit, so it's not like we'll be hurting anytime soon."

Lupo looked over his shoulder at his friend as they led me to the elevators. "I won't miss holding your bleeding body as we wait for the paramedics."

Tommy rolled his eyes. "Don't be such a fucking whiner. It was one time, and it was basically a flesh wound."

"You had *six hours* of surgery."

They bickered back and forth, making me grin despite the gravity of the situation. They stopped at the end of a hall, and I briefly wondered if I was making a good decision walking into a hotel room with two men who'd been strangers two weeks ago. But Kacey trusted these men, and I trusted Kacey. Besides, nothing they'd ever said to me had been less than completely respectful, and I was fairly sure that Kacey would castrate them—best friends or not—if he thought they'd harm me.

Their hotel room wasn't huge, but it was beautifully furnished. It definitely felt high-end. There were two beds, though only one of them was unmade. I pointedly didn't mention anything. Maybe they liked to spoon? Maybe they were a couple? Didn't matter to me either way. Kacey didn't seem like the kind of person to care either; he was cool with Corrin and Grady. Maybe the rest of his Irish Catholic family wasn't so open-minded.

Tommy pulled a white box from the inside pocket of his jacket, handing it to me with uncharacteristic solemnity. "I'd ask if you needed help, but watching a girl pee isn't my kink," he deadpanned.

I laughed, but I didn't think he was joking. "I should be fine. Thanks for the offer, though."

Lupo nodded to the opposite corner of the room. "The bathroom is through there." He opened his mouth like he was going to say something else, but snapped it closed again. That was fine with me. There wasn't much that empty platitudes could do for me in this situation.

I walked into the bathroom and closed the door. Reading the instructions, I followed each step with pinpoint accuracy, like I was trying to defuse a bomb rather than just pee on a stick.

Capping the end, I stared at it. And stared some more. It said I had to wait five minutes, and these last fifteen seconds had felt like years already. Putting the test down on the vanity, I walked back out into the hotel room.

Tommy jumped to his feet. "What's it say?"

"For fuck's sake Tommy, it's only been like three minutes. How quick do you think these things are?" Lupo muttered.

Tommy shrugged. "How the fuck should I know? I don't make it a mission to go around fucking girls unprotected. Best way to get yourself shackled down for life, or you know, with dick rot."

I snorted. "That's unexpectedly mature of you."

He frowned. "What's that supposed to mean?"

Lupo wrapped an arm around his friend's shoulder. "That you're like a horny teenager with no filter."

Tommy frowned, then gave me a lopsided grin. "Fair."

"Are you going to tell Kacey about this?" I couldn't help but ask. I wouldn't tell them not to, and I wouldn't make them choose because that would be stupid. Their loyalty was to Kacey, and it always would be. They were closer than friends; they were brothers. They hadn't even hesitated to follow Kacey into the unknowns of polite society.

"About sneaking you out of the apartment, or the pregnancy test?" Lupo asked.

I shrugged. "Either? Both?"

Tommy shrugged. "Probably. We don't keep shit from each other. If it's negative, it's no big deal. We can sneak you back in and no harm, no foul. But if it's positive, hiding it from them isn't going to help anything anyway, right? Unless you intend to, you know…"

"Not that we'd judge you for it. You have to do what's right for you, and dropping a baby into the middle of your life while you're still consolidating your Pack, plus all that anti-Omega bullshit, would be really tough. And the DoDA will probably be all up in your ass for a while yet. It's stressful—we understand that."

Tommy nodded. "We do. And so would your bondmates, I think. You have plenty of time for kids, hopefully when things are less crazy. You get so few fucking choices, but this one is all yours. We know people." He cleared his throat, that grin coming back. "Besides, all your mates seem to have a crazy amount of Daddy issues that they should probably get worked out before they become fathers themselves." He spun his finger around his temple, indicating he thought they were crazy. I couldn't help but laugh. They were right, though—the guys would tell me the choice was mine.

"It wouldn't be perfect timing, but I wouldn't get rid of it."

Tommy let out a breath between his teeth. "Okay. That's good. But can you go and check now? The suspense is fucking killing me."

I laughed, suddenly realizing how much I liked these guys. Not the way I viscerally liked RJ, the last man I'd tried to friendzone. I had none of that primal attraction with these two, despite them both being handsome as hell. Maybe they were gay and my Omega picked up on that?

I walked into the bathroom and stalled at the door, looking back out into the main room at them. "I can't. One of you guys check it."

They rock-paper-scissored for it, with Tommy coming out the winner. Or the loser, in my opinion. He slipped past me and grabbed the stick, while Lupo gave my shoulder a reassuring squeeze.

Tommy stared down at it. "Just talk me through how the line thing works again?"

"Oh for fuck's sake," Lupo growled, grabbing the stick. He stared at it for a long moment, and then handed it to me. "Congrats, Omega. You're pregnant."

Chapter Thirty-Seven
Tryst

Turns out, sneaking back in wasn't even an option. Lupo's words were still echoing in my ears when Tommy's phone rang.

"Hey. Yeah, no, calm down, man. She's here with us." Whatever Kacey was saying on the other end of the phone made Tommy's eyebrows shoot to his hairline. "I know you're just worried about your girl right now, so I'm going to pretend you didn't just suggest Lupo and I were spitroasting your Omega." I could hear yelling, but not what was being said. "I didn't say it! You're the one who suggested—" Tommy took a deep breath. "You know what, now isn't the time. We're bringing her back. We'll be there in, like, ten minutes." He gave me a look like 'See how mature I am?' which honestly was kinda cute. He grunted out a

320

bunch more non-committal answers, then hung up. "Come on. I give him two minutes until he's on his way here. May as well meet him in the foyer."

I grabbed the capped pregnancy test and stuck it in the front pocket of my hoodie. No one said anything else as they picked up their guns and tucked them into their waistbands, and Lupo grabbed the room key. I followed them downstairs, ignoring the raised eyebrows of the desk attendant. Guess it did kind of did look like I'd gone upstairs, had sex, and now we were leaving again less than thirty minutes later.

What the fuck ever. Other people's opinions didn't matter.

We made it out onto the street and all the way back to the apartment building before we ran into Kacey. He gave the guys looks that would cut most people like a knife, and grabbed me up into his arms. "Holy fucking shit, Princess. You scared the shit out of me."

He led us back to the elevator, and Dwayne the Doorman gave me a bland look, like 'See, I didn't rat you out for disappearing with two unsavory-looking men in the middle of the night.' I gave him a small salute and could've sworn he cracked a smile.

Kacey didn't talk to us the whole time the elevator went up, and when I stepped into the apartment, everyone was there and wide awake. Well, Corrin was almost awake. Akio looked so fucking panicked that I momentarily felt bad for sneaking out. It wasn't that I didn't think Akio or Jak would take me to get a pregnancy test, but I guess they had a vested interest in the result. Not so much Tommy and Lupo.

My eyes went to Grady and Corrin. Logically, having fucked me through my heat, they were the most likely candidates to be the father, and right now, Grady looked pissed.

"Tryst, you can't go off by yourself in the middle of the night. This is goddamn New York City, and you're an Omega."

"I know, Grady. I wasn't by myself. I had these guys and their insane amount of firearms." I shot him a grin, but he didn't smile back. Yeah, he was definitely pissed. "I had something I needed to do."

"At four in the morning?" I looked at the clock on the wall. Oops, we'd been gone longer than I thought.

"So... I'm pregnant."

The silence was so profound, it sounded like the whole city had stopped. I waited for someone to speak. Anyone. But they were all silent, staring at me with open mouths.

It was Jak who broke first. "Why is everyone so surprised? You've been fucking like rabbits. It's not like Tryst is a Beta." He kissed my cheek. "Congratulations, babe."

Jak made a good point. Some Betas didn't even use birth control anymore since the likelihood of getting pregnant was so low. Omegas didn't get the same benefits, I guess.

This seemed to kick everyone into gear a little bit, Kacey first, surprisingly. He bundled me up in his arms, kissing me hard. "A baby Tryst. Not gonna lie, the timing's a little fucked, but I'm going to love that tiny shrimp and give it the whole world."

Well, now I was going to cry.

Akio was next, kissing me, his hands running in a circle over my non-existent belly. "An unexpected gift is still a gift, sweetheart."

Remzi held himself stiff, and I could see the war behind his eyes. This was the worst possible timing. I'd only just reconnected with him, but fate was a fickle bitch. I reached out and grabbed his hand. It was possible the baby was Remzi's, despite not having knotted me. Nature had screwed with me in weirder ways, after all.

"It'll be okay, Alpha."

He frowned. "I'm meant to be telling you that." He sucked in a deep breath. "It could be mine."

I shook my head. "No, Alpha. There's no yours, mine or his. There's only ours. Our baby. The offspring of Pack Hart."

He looked so conflicted, but nodded. "I'm... happy, I think?"

I snorted a laugh. "Welcome to the Uncertain Club. We think we might get t-shirts. Maybe."

He lifted my hands to his lips. "You'll be a great mother."

Yep, definitely tears. They were beginning to overflow my eyelids now. Because when I looked at Corrin and Grady, their faces were equal amounts of awe and horror, joy and fear. And that was exactly how I felt.

"Apparently, my contraceptive couldn't stand the heat, so it got the hell out of the kitchen."

"Babe..." Corrin gave a choked laugh.

I sucked in a shaky breath. "I don't know what to say."

Surprisingly, Grady folded first. He took two huge steps toward me and picked me up in his arms, holding me tightly to his body. He kissed me like he couldn't say the words in his heart, but needed to *show* me.

"I'm sorry," I murmured into his neck, but he shook his head.

"Baby girl, I have no regrets." He held me for a little longer, holding my weight easily against his strong body, Corrin pressed against my back. The tension in my body unraveled in the safety of their arms, and I nuzzled my face into Grady's neck, drawing in deep lungfuls of his soothing scent.

"Not to break up the cuddle pile, but it could totally be mine. I've knotted Princess so many times that I'm pretty sure I've branded the shape of it on her cervix."

I turned my face toward him, giving him a watery smile. "That's not how cervixes work, Kacey."

Grady huffed, lowering me down his body until I was back on my feet, still pressed between them. His eyes were shiny too. "Doesn't matter who the baby biologically belongs to. Tryst is right—it's ours. Baby Hart."

"This definitely calls for champagne. But not for Tryst." Jak said, then frowned. "Do you think all the gin earlier would have hurt the baby?"

Panic raced through my veins. Shit, had I hurt the baby already?

Akio whacked the back of his head. "Don't stress her out, dumbass. It's fine, Tryst. We'll do everything right from now on."

I looked at Remzi again, but he was on his phone, tapping furiously. "What are you doing?"

"Booking you the best obstetrician in the States."

"It's four in the morning."

He looked at me, his jaw set. "I don't care. I'll drag them out of bed myself if you need them."

Well, that was kind of sweet.

"I think it'll wait until morning. I need to sleep." I

paused. "Do you think we can all sleep upstairs in the atrium?"

Everyone looked at Remzi but his eyes were only on me. Those eyes. They saw too much. "Of course, Omega. We'll move up a couple of the mattresses."

The guys disappeared to gather supplies, but Remzi stayed. "Is this too much?" I asked, worried about the answer.

"Nothing is too much, Tryst. Take what you want."

"I don't know how to do this." Not the baby. Not the Pack Omega thing. Not looking after the emotional wellbeing of six other people. None of it.

Remzi reached out, his hand coming out to palm my cheek, his fingers so long that they threaded through my hair too. "Me either. We'll figure it out together." He grabbed my hand and entwined our fingers. "Let's gather all the blankets. We're going to need them, I think." He cleared his throat roughly. "I've never had a sleepover. Or shared anything."

"Never? What about with your siblings?"

He shook his head. "No, they kept us all pretty separate until we were adults."

I tilted my head at him. "I'd like to meet them one day."

He finally gave me a smile, and it was filled with so much joy that I gaped. "They'd love that. They haven't stopped pestering me about meeting you too. The younger ones don't remember our mother really, so they don't have my... hang-ups."

I snuggled into his side, and he was stiff for a moment, before relaxing around me. I was pretty sure we'd be okay. Only time would tell now.

Chapter Thirty-Eight
Tryst

I'd never spent so long trying to formulate a single text message.

Me: RJ, just wanted you to know I'm pregnant.

I deleted the text. That sounded too much like it was his. Too informal.

Me: Hey, hope you're doing good. Wish you were here. Guess what, I'm knocked up. I think Grady and Corrin are the daddies.

Nope. I deleted it again with a huff and threw my phone on my bed. This was ridiculous. I didn't even know why I wanted him to know. I hadn't heard from him in weeks. I needed to just let it go. Let him go. Queen Elsa this bitch.

"Tryst, are you ready?" Kacey called from the other

room, and I grabbed up my phone and stuck it in my pocket.

Remzi was at work, but had arranged for me to go to a preliminary appointment with a specialist Omega obstetrician. I guess there wasn't a huge amount of call for the profession, but only treating Omegas was seriously specialized. Remzi said the doctor even lectured at the university between cases.

It also sounded like he charged an arm and a leg, but I tried not to think about that part. I'd managed to talk them down to one person coming with me, and Kacey won because he had bonus security.

Cheating, in my opinion.

Akio was out anyway, talking to some local businesses about guest consulting. Corrin was checking out a local art collective, organizing some workshop space and firing times for his pottery. He apparently had a backlog on orders while he'd been balls deep in my drama.

Jak and Grady had gone to look at a 1955 Ford Thunderbird that they wanted to restore in the garage below the apartment. Apparently, Jak preferred working on bikes, but he knew his way around a car too, and the way Grady's eyes lit up when they talked shop made my heart feel full.

"I'm coming!"

"Not yet, but if you have a spare five minutes,"

Kacey yelled back, and I laughed. Could you love a man this quickly? Because I felt some serious feelings for Kacey Boyd, and they weren't all lustful.

I walked into the living room to see him reclining on the couch, his legs spread wide and his arms along the back. He looked like a feast, and I wanted nothing more than to crawl on top of him and let him make good on his promise.

Someone cleared their throat, and I realized Lupo and Tommy were also in the room. Yesterday, we'd properly introduced the men to Remzi, and he hadn't even blinked when Kacey suggested that we put them in one of the apartments on the floor below. He hadn't even asked why they had guns. He hadn't asked why they both had that glint in their eye, the one that said they were dangerous despite the dimples and the pretty hair.

Remzi seemed to just be cool with them. I guess having them deliver me and my groundbreaking news the other day kind of bonded people.

I smiled at the duo. "Whoops, sorry."

Tommy raised an eyebrow. "No you're not."

Couldn't argue with that.

Lupo just shook his head. "We should go before you're late."

"Ha! She's already late—that's why she's in this predicament," Tommy joked, and I rolled my eyes.

Kacey groaned beside me. "That was truly fucking terrible. Let's go before he tries any more of his stand-up routine."

There were moving vans in the basement carpark, and it might have been my imagination, but I couldn't help but think they were giving me the stink eye. Probably people from the floor below us. I gave them an apologetic smile, but doubted it would help.

The SUV was parked beside the empty space marked for the penthouse, and the guys herded me in, Kacey climbing in beside me. "You know, I bet I could still make you come before we get there," he whispered in my ear.

I frowned at him, even though my vagina gave a hearty hip-hip-hooray at the idea. "You better not. The obstetrician is going to be looking at my baby-making parts, and I don't want it to look like you've just finger fucked me in the backseat of the car. Besides, your best friends are in the front and they don't want to hear it either."

They all spoke at once.

"No thank you." Lupo's grunted words were emphatic.

"I wouldn't be opposed," Tommy said with a grin.

"Wait, the obstetrician does *what?*" The shock on Kacey's face was hilarious.

"Well, maybe. I guess it depends how far along I

could be. It's hard to tell with Omegas. But I think it's common that they, you know, do an ultrasound."

Lupo pulled into traffic. "I've seen movies. The ultrasound wand thing is on the outside."

"Not all the time. They have one that goes on the inside." I'd been going to government-approved gyne-cologists since I was eighteen. They'd all wanted to check out my reproductive organs to make sure I wasn't a defunct Omega. Assholes.

Kacey just stared at me. "That's it. Turn around. No way is some crusty old fucker putting anything inside you. Jesus."

I raised a single brow at his panicked statement, but still leaned in for a kiss. "Don't be ridiculous. Lupo, keep driving."

"I pay his bills."

"No, you don't," Lupo teased from the front seat.

"You think you'd be used to other dudes being inside her by now," Tommy quipped. Kacey growled low, and everyone went silent. "What? Too soon?"

"Pull over. I'm gonna punch his face in."

"You're a fucking idiot, Tommy," Lupo hissed.

Oh, for fuck's sake. "Lupo, *do not* pull over. Tommy, say something like that again and I'm going to kick you in the nuts so hard they'll call you Tommy Soprano." I looked at Kacey, who was still glaring at his best friend like he wanted to tear his tongue out. "If you didn't expect your best friend to make at least one joke about you being in a Pack, you're dumber than you look."

Lupo seemed to catch on. "Yeah, Kacey. It was a joke, not a dick. No need to take it so hard."

"You'd know all about taking dick, wouldn't you?" Kacey fired back, and we all went silent again.

Well... Okay then. We were doing this now.

Lupo double parked in front of the clinic, and I sighed. "Guys..." We really didn't have time for this, but I had a feeling it was now or never. "You and Tommy, you're a couple?" I asked softly, like I was talking to toddlers.

The two men in the front of the car looked at each other for a long moment, before Lupo nodded. "Yeah."

I looked at Kacey. "Do you have some kind of Irish Catholic guilt that means you can't love your friends if they're gay?"

"Hey, I'm not gay. I like cock *and* pussy," Tommy protested from the front, and I pointed a finger at him.

"That's enough commentary out of you."

"Yes, ma'am." He leaned over to Lupo. "Is it weird that I think her telling me what to do is hot?" he whispered.

Lupo gave him an exasperated look. "It's like you're *trying* to die today."

I kept my eyes on Kacey, whose gaze was bouncing

between his best friends like he was seeing them for the first time. Which was dumb in itself—anyone with half a brain knew there was something going on between them.

"I don't care, I guess. I think I kind of always knew, ever since they were both naked at Tommy's house when I rocked up after a party, back when we were seventeen. I didn't believe it was really just 'too hot to sleep in clothes,'" he quoted.

Lupo gave a lopsided smile. "I couldn't believe you fell for that."

"Obviously, I didn't."

I looked at the clock on the dash. "To summarize quickly, because we're about to be late: Tommy is a dickhead, and while he can't promise to never say anything stupid again, he's really going to try not to antagonize the Alphas, you included. Isn't that right?"

"Scout's honor," Tommy agreed, raising his hand like he was swearing on the Bible.

"They're a couple. You still love them anyway. No big deal, right?" I prompted Kacey, and he nodded. "Well, that's great. Let's go. I want ice cream after this. And Lupo gets a triple scoop for not being a problematic asshole." Lupo whooped, while Tommy pouted.

I climbed out and pulled my phone from my pocket. Opening the messaging app, I pulled up RJ's name.

. . .

Me: Hey, I miss you. I hope you're doing okay. Turns out I'm pregnant, just thought you'd like to know. Might name it RJ in your honor, seeing how you were probably there for the conception. Wish you were here.

I stared at the words for a little longer, then pressed send before I had the chance to delete it one more time. Stuffing my phone back in my pocket, I hooked my arm through Kacey's.

"Everything okay?"

"Yeah. My Omega—and me—just misses him sometimes, you know?"

Kacey, to his credit, just nodded. "I know, Princess. Let's go and see what the crusty old dude has to say about your vagina." He looked at the guys. "Park and I'll message you when we're almost done." Lupo saluted and drove off into the traffic.

The clinic was stereotypical, though you could clearly tell it was on the Upper West Side. The art on the walls looked expensive and the seating was still uncomfortable, but it was designer-level uncomfortable.

The woman at the reception desk stared at us with

wide eyes. "Omega Hart. Alpha. Thank you for choosing our clinic. The doctor is just running a little behind, but if you take a seat, he'll see you as soon as possible."

I smiled and led Kacey to a spot in the corner. There was another couple in the waiting area, although she wasn't an Omega. I wondered what she was having, a boy or a girl? Would it be an Alpha or a Beta? Or even an Omega.

The idea of having an Omega child chilled me to my bones. Kacey looked at me quizzically, feeling my emotions down our bond.

"What if the baby is an Omega? I can't..." I couldn't express the horror of having to let my child go through the Allotment. The pain and the isolation of being an Omega in a world that thought of you as a commodity wasn't something I'd ever want for my child.

Kacey wrapped his arm around my shoulders. "Don't go borrowing trouble, Princess. But if we have an Omega, you can bet your fucking ass there is no way I would let her go through the Allotment. Neither will Remzi. Or the other guys for that matter—we all saw what you went through. No one is going to inflict that on our child," he murmured softly in my ear.

I tilted my head to the side so I could capture his lips. They were so full and soft, and it was possibly the tenderest kiss I'd ever shared with my wild Alpha. "You're a good man, Kacey Boyd."

"Omega Hart?" a nurse called from the doorway. "The doctor is almost ready, and if you'd like to follow me, I'll give you a gown to wear." She looked at Kacey. "Alpha, you can wait in exam room one if you'd like, just over there."

I kissed Kacey's cheek. "Be right back."

I followed the nurse down the corridor, and she handed me a gown. "Just through there, Omega. Come on down to the exam room when you're done."

I opened the door, and it was dark. I searched beside the doorjamb, blindly looking for the switch. When it blinked on, all I saw were shelves of cleaning supplies.

Weird.

I felt a sudden sting in my neck, and my confusion turned to haze. My vision dimmed, and I fell to my knees. My brain was too groggy to even feel panicked when a man appeared in my vision just before everything went black.

Chapter Thirty-Nine
Remzi

I was preoccupied. The head of my R&D department was speaking about a large upgrade to the connectivity for more rural locations in smaller states, but I was having trouble focusing. They could have this meeting without me; the days where I had to oversee everything myself were long gone. I'd hired the brightest minds from the best schools at the beginning, and I paid them in a way no one else could. They were smart, loyal and motivated to succeed. I was just here as a mascot these days.

I wanted to be back home with Tryst, or taking her to the obstetrician appointment. She'd only wanted one person with her, which logically, I understood. All of us together, we could be a lot. I'd stood aside because I was the one she was least comfortable with, but that didn't mean I didn't want to be beside her each step of the way.

That I didn't want to be the first person to see proof of a baby growing inside of Tryst. Inside of my Omega.

Maybe my baby.

I had to hand it to my new bondmates—they'd sworn there was no possessiveness, no tension between them, and I'd thought it was all bullshit. How could you look at Tryst, with her soft Omega beauty, or feel the way she was totally focused on you when you spoke, and not want to hoard it all for yourself?

An odd sensation slithered down the bond, making me frown. I reached out, gently probing the bond, but then there was nothing. No panic. No excitement. Just nothing.

"Excuse me, I have to make a call," I murmured to my team, stepping out of the room. As I strode down to my office, I tried calling her, but there was no answer. I moved on to Kacey.

"Yeah?"

The knot in my stomach loosened slightly. "Is Tryst okay? I picked up a weird sensation through the bond."

"She just went to change into a gown." There was silence at the other end of the line, I assumed because he was checking the bond. "Fuck it, I'm going to check on her." He kept me on the line as he walked somewhere, snapping at the receptionist. "The change room, where is it?"

The stuttering of the employee could have been an effect of the obvious Alpha disgruntlement Kacey was throwing off, but it still had me moving toward my door. I could hear Kacey opening and shutting doors, hear the rising panic in his voice.

"Tryst? Tryst?" I heard him still. "No..." he breathed, and ice filled my veins.

"What is it?" I growled, already jogging down the stairwell of the building, but he just kept chanting the word no. "Kacey, what the *fuck* is it?" I yelled down the line, making employees scatter away from me and my wrath.

"Her stuff—it's scattered on the floor. The back door's ajar, like someone forgot to close it on their way out. Shit's been knocked off the shelves." He sucked in a harsh breath. "Someone has fucking stolen her."

No. This couldn't be happening. I was running before I even registered it, my phone still pressed to my ear.

I could hear Kacey prowling back toward the reception, his breaths coming in loud pants. "WHERE THE FUCK IS SHE?" His roar was visceral, and I could hear the nurse begging for her life with a wail.

I was almost there. I ran harder and faster. The

clinic was just a few blocks away, but it seemed too far. I took a shortcut down an alley, away from the crowds and the traffic, jumping walls like it meant nothing. And it didn't, not when Tryst's safety was on the line.

Finally, I scaled a wall that backed onto the clinic parking lot, just in time to see a woman in scrubs scramble toward her car, looking around like bad guys were going to jump out from behind the parked cars.

It might've been panic from the freakout I could hear Kacey having inside, but I didn't think so. Something was off.

Just before she kicked her car into gear, I jumped down on the hood, creating a large dent. The woman gasped, and I saw several things flash across her face as she tried to decide if I was about to be her death: fear, horror, but most interestingly, regret.

We definitely had to talk with this one.

I put my foot through the windscreen easily, and she screamed as safety glass rained down on her. Jumping down, I moved to the driver's door and wrenched it off its hinges.

Alphas really did get all the best perks.

"Where. Is. My. Omega?" I ground out the words, and the woman just shook in the driver's seat. I reached in and dragged her out, setting her on her feet as she sobbed and wailed. "Be calm!" I growled, and if it hadn't been for the Alpha bark, that would have been a ridiculous statement.

But the woman stopped sobbing, just standing there and staring at me like she'd been shot full of sedation medication.

"Where is the Omega Tryst Hart?" I demanded.

"Gone. Someone came and got her."

I frowned at her words. Had Tryst planned this? Was she making a run for it? On one hand, I wouldn't blame her, but on the other hand, running from six mates? She wouldn't get a single state away until she was a writhing mess.

"Who?"

She shook her head over and over, and I knew I was about to lose her back to the hysterics. "I don't know who, but I can't feed my kids and they just told me that they'd give me fifteen thousand to call when an Omega booked an appointment. I didn't think—" She cut off the lie. She wasn't stupid.

A cold voice echoed from behind me. "I hope your kids have someone to care for them, because I'm going to make you regret selling out my Omega," Kacey growled, and his voice was pitched so low, the woman started wailing again.

I looked over my shoulder. Okay, maybe it wasn't the pitch of his voice but the fact that he looked murderous. He was backed by his boys, and they didn't look any less capable of violence.

I didn't fucking care. This bitch had sold my Omega to someone for what? Pocket change? Tryst could be tortured. Or worse.

"You better tell us everything you know or I swear to fucking god, I am going to let them rip out your traitorous fucking tongue." The violent smirk on Kacey's face didn't reach his eyes, but it promised pain. So much pain. I'd had my difficulties with him, but right now, I was glad that he was wild and violent, because that was exactly what Tryst needed.

"I swear, I don't know anything. They just gave me a card one day while I was in the grocery store. It's still in my purse. I can get it."

I curled my lip, the rage burning through my veins like acid. "Now."

She launched herself into the car, grabbing her purse and pulling out everything, cards and receipts flying. I looked around the parking lot, and Kacey came up beside me, looming over the woman like it would make her work faster.

He pointed to the service entrance. "The room she was in when she was stolen backs onto that door."

There had to be a camera or something around here somewhere, right? I couldn't see anything over the back doors, nor around any of the neighboring businesses. What the fuck was wrong with people?

"Does that apartment look like it has one of those doorbell security cameras?" Tommy, Kacey's gangster friend asked, pointing to the raised stoop of a building beside us. Right beside the security door was a little square doorbell camera.

"Bring it, and whoever owns the building, to me now."

Both guys looked between me and Kacey. "*Now*," the other Alpha hissed, and they ran.

The woman finally came up for air, and she looked panicked as she saw the Betas' disappearing backs. All that was left were enraged Alphas. Yeah, the outlook wasn't good for this traitorous bitch.

She handed me the card, and I looked at its frayed edges, like she'd pulled it out and put it back a lot. Hopefully, that was because of residual guilt and not from overuse, because one I could forgive, and the other would test the very limits of my humanity.

It was just a scrawled number on the torn end of a business card. There were a couple of numbers still on the end, but nothing I could work with. Just the number sixty-eight, the end of a phone number and the letters OR. I blanked my mind and I mulled it over. Paying attention to the small details had always been my thing; it was why I'd been so successful in business.

There was something about this card that was familiar, the strong dark font on shitty subpar cardstock, and it was itching at my memory.

It finally caught in my brain, and I sucked in a ragged breath. "Do you have Tryst's phone?" Kacey frowned at me, but didn't ask why. He just handed it over. I clutched it in my hand. "I need to make a call."

The world had better hope he answered.

Chapter Forty
Tryst

I woke up in a clinic. There were machines everywhere, and a stainless steel bench with glass cabinets above it, holding vials of medicine. Had I fainted?

"You're awake! Sorry about that. I couldn't judge how much you'd need to render you unconscious. Omegas metabolize medicine faster, did you know that? Alphas too, but Omegas even more so. I wish I knew the scientific reason behind that, but one mystery at a time, am I right?"

I looked around for the voice, wincing at the bright lights overhead. Why did my head hurt so much?

Finally, I saw a young man. This guy couldn't be my obstetrician though. He looked like he was fifteen.

I frowned. "You're not my doctor."

He smiled, and somehow it made him look even

younger. "Well no, not *your* doctor. Doctor Schultz is good, but he's pretty old school." He tilted his head at me. "I'm Donald Breddan, but you'll be happy to know I'm *a* doctor. I know, the face is misleading, but I swear I went to med school." He gave a nervous laugh as I just stared. "This is so exciting. I've been waiting for you for so long. You don't understand. Is it weird to be fangirling right now?"

My limbs felt sluggish, and I could feel the terror and rage of my bondmates through our connection. Okay, so I'd been kidnapped. It was hard to be scared when the kid in front of me looked like all his Christmases had come at once, though.

Did he have a Star Wars t-shirt under his lab coat?

"Not to be rude, Donald—"

"Call me Donnie. Donald sounds like a rich old guy."

"Donnie," I said with exaggerated slowness. "I'm going to assume you kidnapped me. You don't appear to be in the 'kill all Omegas' camp, so if I'm being honest, I don't know why I'm here."

I was proud of how calm I sounded.

Donnie looked aghast. "Hate Omegas? No way. Those anti-designation protesters are all close-minded sheep, looking for someone to blame for our own failings, instead of searching for a solution. I've already thought of a solution. I just need a little help making it a reality."

The way he was staring at me had me thinking that maybe I was the help he needed, which made me more panicked rather than less.

"I'm still confused."

"It's probably the drugs. Let me explain." Donnie grinned as he walked around, ripping open packages of medical supplies like a mad scientist. "My oldest sister was an Omega. That's why I could never hate Omegas. She's the best person ever. But she hated being an Omega. Hated being special and then forced to do all this shit she didn't want to do. Hated being sold off during the Allotment."

I cleared my throat, swallowing down the panic. "I can relate."

"Then they found out she couldn't have babies, due to some kind of genetic malformation of her ovaries. They cast her aside like she was used toilet paper. Like she wasn't special anymore. But they didn't find out until after she'd bonded with a Pack, you know? So she had to stay with them, her *bondmates,* because of the connection between them. It was bad." His lips tightened into a disapproving expression. "They all got mistresses, despite the pain it caused her through her bonds, and life went on. I think she's happy now—she's sleeping with her tennis coach—but for years she was depressed, all because she couldn't fulfill the purpose everyone had thrust upon her."

He stopped and stared down at me with fervency burning in his eyes. "But what if *every* woman could be special? What if the solution to the problem isn't trying to go back to how we were, but rather pushing forward with evolution, speeding it up just a little more?"

My eyes went wide. "You want to make every woman an Omega? No offense, Donnie, but it's pretty fucking sucky. No one's signing up for that."

"What if they didn't have a choice?" he said, stepping closer, his voice pitched conspiratorially low. "What if the whole next generation of female children were all born Omegas? And the males were all Alphas? Supply and demand matrices would say you would lose your value, and then the government wouldn't be able to control you quite as well. They'd have to give you your rights back."

I ground my molars. *Entertain the crazy man, Tryst. You need to escape here before he Frankensteins your ass.*

"The government isn't known for just handing back people's rights, Donnie. You'd just be supplying them with more broodmares, not freeing the ones they already have."

He frowned. "You're misunderstanding. You want to be free. You had a whole court case about it. I want to help you achieve that." He grimaced. "Well not *you*, exactly, but Omegas as a whole. I just need your help to perfect the serum. You would have been fine on your own, to be honest. But embryonic stem cells? They would be far more genetically superior for my research."

He looked momentarily troubled. "It would be bad for the embryo, but it's not a fetus yet, not by my calculations anyway. You can always have more; you're obviously fertile. But we could kickstart the human race, help it evolve before it goes extinct. Desperate times call for desperate measures, you know? If I could ensure that no other woman had to go through what you did, wouldn't it be worth it? To be free again?"

I sucked in a breath, horror at what he was proposing hitting me in the chest. "Donnie..." Fuck, how did I say this without telling him he was batshit crazy? I cleared my throat. "I get what you're proposing, Donnie, I do. I understand it's coming from a good place."

Good, if you had no ethics whatsoever.

"But your solution is just stealing more of our choices. You're doing to me exactly what the government did to your sister. Taking away autonomy just because you think you know what's best."

He paused while filling up a second needle with a

clear liquid, his face contorted. Fuck, fuck, fuck. "But sometimes humans don't know what's best for them."

"That's the real problem here—the fact that everyone thinks they know what's best for us, and therefore believe they have the right to choose it for us. We don't need a scientific solution, Donnie. We need a systematic societal solution. Omegas are perfect, as are Alphas. And so are Betas. We're different, but we don't need to be 'fixed.' We're exactly what we are supposed to be, just as nature intended. You're a scientist who obviously believes in evolution—you have to believe in balance, right? You've read studies on what happens when humans fuck around with the natural balance."

He looked at me with big dark eyes, holding up a vial labeled 'No. 486'. "But I made a serum and everything..."

How was this a fucking thing? I thought fast, sifting through my brain for a way to appease the crazy doctor. "Maybe you can adjust it to help with Beta fertility? If women could increase their live birth ratios, Omegas would have more freedom. You're still saving us then, but in a positive way. I'll even help you. But you have to promise you won't try and extract, uh, any embryonic stem cells. Nothing that hurts the baby."

"It doesn't work that way. Science doesn't work that way! I can't just take it and relabel it. It's been years of work and research," he snapped, whirling away.

I watched his back heave as he drew in deep breaths, until his shoulders relaxed a fraction. Then he turned back to me, his eyes calmer.

"I'm sorry for my outburst. You know what, you've given me something to think about. I'll run some numbers and then we can pick this up again tomorrow, okay?" He grabbed me off the bed and placed me gently on the floor. He was stronger than he looked. "Be careful, the tranquilizers will still be affecting your equilibrium."

Even as he said the words, I overbalanced strongly to one side. "You should let me go home. My mates are worried sick."

Donnie frowned. "Why? I don't mean you any harm."

"You stole me from a medical clinic!"

He half carried, half dragged me out of the medical office and down a hallway. "I mean, it's not like I could have just knocked on the door to your apartment. Besides, I knew I only had a short window. When I took a sample of your blood outside the courthouse, it was like an epiphany. But there wasn't a lot of wiggle room when it came to time."

"You did *what?* When?"

Donnie looked a little bashful. "During the riot.

I'm sorry, I just thought it was better to do it stealthily rather than to cause you unnecessary anxiety. Just needed a little scrape of blood, and in that chaos, it wasn't hard." He frowned. "It was harder to maintain the integrity of the sample in the crush."

I noticed that the hall we'd walked down didn't have any windows, the whole place simply lit by the occasional strip light. Where the fuck were we?

He opened a door, and inside was a nice, boring room. Someone's generic spare room in beige and white. But still no windows. "I prepared for your arrival. There's a mini fridge over in the corner with water and food, and the ensuite is through there." He helped me over to the bed, and took off my shoes in a totally professional and officious way. Whatever else I could say about Doctor Donnie, it wasn't that he was lecherous. "You should sleep off the rest of the meds. I'll see you tomorrow."

With that, he left, and the turning of a key in the door, as well as the sliding of a deadlock, sealed me in. Well, that felt annoyingly familiar. Life was nothing if not a consistent bitch.

I lay down on the bed and reached out to my bonds, sending them pulses of reassurance and taking extra care to get every single one. It was harder than I thought; I was far away, but not like across the country. The strain on my bonds was there, but it wasn't the same bone-deep ache I'd had when Remzi and I were on opposite sides of the country.

Their emotions poured back down the bonds at me, and by the time I was done, I was exhausted. They were all various forms of frantic, except Remzi. The only thing that came back from him was complete assurance. I could hear him saying he would get me back and he would punish my abductors, as clear as if he were standing right there in front of me.

I clung to his confidence like a security blanket, and stopped fighting the drugging effects dragging my body down into oblivion.

Chapter Forty-One
Grady

I'd had my share of bad moments.

When my dad died, though I'd been too young to really remember the pain.

The exact moment when, alone in my workshop, elbow-deep in the engine of a 1978 Mustang, my brother called me on the phone to tell me I'd been selected in the Allotment. My heart had broken in an instant, knowing I'd have to leave everyone I loved behind.

I'd honestly thought that was the worst moment of my life.

I was wrong. Kacey's voice at the other end of the phone telling me that someone had taken Tryst—*this* was the worst moment of my life.

I wanted to be sick. My hands shook, and I couldn't hear anything Kacey was saying, no matter how hard I strained to get the words straight in my head. *She needs you. Get it together!* I screamed at myself, but all I heard was Kacey's voice on a loop saying, "She's gone" over and over again.

"Can you hear me?" he shouted down the line, and I winced.

"I heard you! We're coming."

Kacey growled low in his throat, a sound that raised the hairs on my arms. "Go home. No point coming here. Remzi has threatened every single fucking person in this building, and I broke the kneecaps of the obstetrician who was meant to take care of her." He made a choking noise. "I was meant to take care of her."

"Yeah, you fucking were." My voice was ice cold, as I came out of my shock and fell deep into rage. She was meant to be *safe* with him. He was a fucking Alpha.

He let out an enraged roar, and I heard something shattering in the background. "I know!" There was a long silence. "I know," he whispered brokenly.

I felt like a fucking asshole, but I didn't care. Tryst would soothe his hurts when we got her back. Because we *would* get her back.

"I need her, Kace. I can't…" I couldn't even contemplate a life without her now. I clung to the faint feel of her in my chest. It was almost blank, like she was unconscious or something, but it was there.

She was alive.

"I'm going to get her back, Grady, if I have to fucking kill every person in this goddamn city to find her. Remzi has a lead. Meet us at home."

I believed him when he said he'd kill to get her back. He'd killed for less.

I hung up, looking over at Jak, who was driving Remzi's Jaguar like a stuntman. "Kacey says to head home. There's nothing we can do at the clinic."

Jak thumped the steering wheel. "What if they missed something? What if they are so fucking Alpha, they made people run in the other direction? Maybe we can... we can... Fuck, I don't know! I feel so fucking helpless."

I had no platitudes for him. I felt the same way.

Both Corrin and Akio had beaten us home, and when the elevator doors opened, Corrin was there, a look somewhere between hope and fear on his face. Like he'd expected the doors to open and Tryst to just be there. Like he was hoping this was all just a bad joke.

I was wishing for the same thing.

"Any word?" he breathed, and I shook my head. His jaw flexed, and I knew he was trying to hold it together.

I wrapped him up in my arms, soaking in his strength. Or maybe we gave each other strength. We both loved her. I loved her so fucking much. Loved *them* so much.

Jesus, what about the baby? Did whoever took her know she was pregnant?

Of course they fucking knew. They'd stolen her from an obstetrician's office. A fresh wave of fear swept through me at the thought of her scared and alone.

Akio grabbed Jak and hugged him tight. "We'll get her back."

I nodded as his words echoed Kacey's from earlier. But a little voice in the back of my mind whispered that she could be anywhere. Anyone could have taken her. Pro-Omega groups, thinking they were liberating her. Anti-designation groups, who would... Fuck, I didn't want to even think about what she could be going through. I clung to the bond again, its blankness actually reassuring now.

We all stood in silence until the doors of the elevator opened once more, and Kacey stepped out, on the phone. "I don't fucking care what they're doing. They stole her, Doughal! I need them now. Fly them back from LA. I want them with me when I find the fuckers who took her—I want those assholes killed in the most painful way possible. I need Sharp and Lee. Or a fucking army. She's pregnant, brother," he whispered, and I could hear the shouted *"Fuck!"* from down the phone. If I'd learned one thing about Kacey's family, it was that blood came first.

Lupo and Tommy flanked Kacey where he stood, and they looked as enraged as the rest of us. Murderous, even. Good. I wanted them to spill the blood of every single person who'd thought they could take her from us. I would help them.

Remzi stepped out of the elevator, a phone also pressed to his ear. "I know it was one of yours. You have six hours to be here before I let Kacey off the leash and there'll be a trail of bodies for you to clean up." He hung up, throwing his phone across the room. It was only Akio's quick reflexes which stopped it from slamming into one of the windows.

"We need that," Akio chastised, his voice flat and deadly.

Remzi ran his fingers through already mussed hair, looking between us, his eyes filled with impotent anger, as well as a fear that mirrored my own. The rage of an Alpha was a scary thing. The rage of three Alphas was suffocating. My primordial brain was telling me to run, but the man inside me who loved his Omega, well, he was satisfied that whoever did this was going to die a long, painful death.

Remzi carefully laid a scrap of card on the table between us all. It was white. Boring. It had a phone number scrawled on it in rushed, messy handwriting.

Akio picked it up and studied it. "Did you call the number?"

Remzi nodded. "Disconnected. Probably a burner. I have someone chasing down the name it was registered in, and which tower it last pinged from. I'll find out within the hour."

"How accurate is that shit?" Jak said, gently taking the card from his twin.

"A few square miles."

I grimaced. Too large an area, but I'd take it. I would search every house by force if I had to.

Jak passed the card to me, like I'd suddenly get inspiration from the rough edges. I looked at the torn off numbers. It was obviously a business card. I looked back up at Remzi, and his face was a mask of granite. He knew something.

"What's it from?"

He turned on his heel, disappearing deeper into the apartment, down the hall to his office. I could hear smashing as he tore the room apart, looking for something.

He was back in a moment, another card in his hand. Kacey had ended his call, and we all stood around the table. I placed the scrap of card between us again. Remzi placed the one from his hand down beside the scrap, and all the oxygen left my lungs.

It was a match. I knew that without a shadow of a

doubt. The font. The cardstock. The curved edges. We all just stared in silence for a moment, and I could feel my mind scrambling to keep up.

"Did you call RJ?" Akio asked.

Remzi nodded, his face hard. He didn't know RJ like we did. "He was the only one she trusted. But I don't trust any of them."

The cards in front of us were issued by the Department of Designation Associations. There was no doubt in my mind. The DoDA had stolen our Omega.

I jolted as my bond shocked me with fear and horror—but not mine this time.

Tryst. She was awake.

I grabbed the bond tightly, trying to push down my own worry and send her reassurance. We'd get her back. She'd be in my arms again soon, and then I'd never let her go again.

Tryst returned the sensation, filled with comfort, and I choked back a laugh. She'd been kidnapped and she was trying to soothe me? We didn't deserve her. No one did.

Over the course of the next few hours, Tryst reached out to each of us, sending us reassurance that she was okay, clinging to the safety and security of our bonds. I would have swapped places with her in an instant.

Remzi's communications contacts had gotten back

to him, and the phone had been registered to a Mr. John Doe. It had also been found ditched in the dumpster near the clinic where she'd been taken. Dead end.

How would we find her? If we couldn't get a lead soon, I was just going to follow the tugging ache in my chest.

At seven p.m., about six hours after Tryst was taken, Remzi's phone rang. He answered immediately. "What do you know?" His eyes went wide, and he moved his phone from his ear, putting it on speaker and placing it on the coffee table. "Repeat that." An order, not a suggestion.

I recognized RJ's voice instantly. "I know where she is, but I'm going to need help getting her out." He hesitated. "It's dangerous. If you get caught, they're going to throw you in a dark cell in Federal prison and never let you out again."

Kacey let out a rumbling noise that was one hundred percent threat. "There won't be anyone left alive to point the finger. Now tell me where my fucking Omega is!"

There was a long silence. "She's in Connecticut. I'll send you an address. Meet me there ASAP. We're going to need to have a plan, play it safe, otherwise Tryst will end up as collateral damage."

There was no room for error, not when it was Tryst's life on the line.

Chapter Forty-Two
Tryst

I slept on and off all night, oscillating between anxiety and exhaustion. Some of it was coming from the guys, some of it was whatever drug cocktail Donnie had given me, and some of it was complete fear of what might happen tomorrow. I had no idea of the time, or the day, because all the light down here was artificial. I couldn't see the sun, or even any form of natural light. It could be six in the morning, or midnight. I wouldn't know, because the hours felt like they dragged on and on.

Oddly, when the door opened again, I was relieved. Staring at the walls during the longest night of my life was pure torture, so something finally happening was oddly better than the fear of the unknown.

Boy, the Stockholm had set in quick.

Donnie was in a fresh t-shirt—this one with the periodic table on it—and had a paper bag in one hand and a coffee cup in the other. A messenger bag was draped over his shoulder, and he let it fall to the floor beside the door.

"Thought you might want something warm for breakfast. Well, maybe it's an afternoon snack now." He thrust out the bag at me, and I took it suspiciously. "Plus a peppermint tea. Coffee is bad for the embryo."

I didn't know if I should be worried or relieved that he was considering the fact I was pregnant when he gave me meals.

"Is it drugged?" I asked. I mean, I couldn't really trust his answer, but at least I could try and read his body language, right? He didn't seem like the kind of guy who'd managed to develop enough social awareness to fake an answer convincingly.

"Why would I drug you again?" He seemed legitimately confused. "Ingestion is a fine way to dispense medication, but it's pretty redundant for my research."

Well, there went all those good feelings. At least I could be experimented on with a full stomach.

"Where are we?"

"At my lab."

"And where's that?"

"Connecticut."

"You have a house in Connecticut?"

Donnie looked at me like I was slow, like he hadn't

drugged me and abducted me from a clinic. "No. The Department has a research lab here."

I tried to hold in my gasp. I really did. But it burst from my lips like a bullet. "The Department of *Designation Associations?* You work for the DoDA?"

He frowned. "Have you seen me? Do I look like I could deadlift your unconscious body anywhere by myself?" His eyes went wide. "Not that I'm calling you fat! You're not. I mean, aesthetically speaking, your body is just fine, and your BMI is well in the healthy range for an Omega."

I held up a hand, and he fell silent. Well, at least he took direction well.

The DoDA had stolen me. Why? I'd been with them for years. Any blood they wanted, they could have taken a hundred times over.

This made no sense.

Donnie was frowning at me, then went over and shut the door. My heart rate picked up as he locked us in. "I called my sister yesterday." I just blinked at him, the sudden subject change jarring. "I thought about what you said. About how it isn't about Omegas at all, you know, but everyone else? So I asked my sister—she was in Santa Cruz with the tennis coach; she said I should call him Peter and not 'the tennis coach' though—"

I interrupted. "What did you ask her about Omegas, Donnie?"

"I asked if she had the magic ability to turn every woman into an Omega, so she wasn't special anymore, would she use it? She doesn't understand science, so I had to put things in terms of magic. She believes crystals can help constipation." He snorted. "She said she wouldn't bestow it on her worst enemy, let alone a whole bunch of innocent women. She said if she had magic, she would... well, she explained an extremely graphic system of castration for several senators, the DoDA Director and the judges who presided over your case. It involved exploding dicks. Or skinless sausages. I had to stop listening after a while. She has a good imagination, and it was making me feel nauseous."

I was trying to work out what this meant, other than the fact Donnie's sister and I would probably be friends. You know, if her brother hadn't stolen me to experiment on.

"What does your sister say about you working for the DoDA?"

Donnie screwed up his nose. "She doesn't approve, but how can I help if I'm not inside the nucleus of the problem? They have money, resources and the drive to let me do whatever I like, as long as I 'solve their little problem.' Only issue is that no one ever explained in clear terms exactly what the 'problem' is. Charlotte says I don't understand conversational nuance. So I've just been doing whatever I want."

"Trying to turn everyone into Omegas?"

He shrugged. "Basically, but not anymore. Now, I'm going to see if I can reverse engineer the Omega heat cycle without, you know, the panting heat bit, and use that as a fertility drug for the non-designated population. I don't think that was the Director's 'problem' exactly, though. Between you and me, I've always wondered if he wanted me to find a way to turn all designated people back to ordinary humans because he's a closet Anti-Des. That's scientifically impossible, really, without technology that is at least two decades away, though maybe if we used the new gene-splicing drugs and had the approval of the FDA—"

"Donnie!" I interrupted, because I'd been waiting for him to take a breath, but somehow he just... didn't. Was that even humanly possible? Maybe he was a cyborg?

"Oh, sorry. Anyway, nothing good ever comes from moving a species backward. Beta fertility mightn't have been the Director's end goal, but it's the *actual* problem, right?" He shook his head. "I wouldn't be any good at protesting in crowds and stuff. It's too loud. Plus, did you know a study showed 70% of people don't wash their hands with soap after using the bathroom? I had to shower for thirty-seven minutes after collecting your blood sample."

My mouth fell open. He was slightly eccentric, but his suggestion about the Omega heat cycle was actually... not a bad idea. "Will the DoDA be mad?"

He shrugged. "I don't think the DoDA actually knows about my project. It's why I don't have clearance to the Omegas' actual blood samples. I think it's the Director's pet project. Or maybe they do know and I'm *wrong*?" He screwed up his nose like the words actually tasted bad. "Charlotte said something about the womb-to-Allotment pipeline between talk of peeling genitals like a banana and something involving testicles and Jimmy Choos? Who's Jimmy Choo?"

I laughed. I actually laughed. "A shoe designer."

Donnie frowned. "That makes sense when coupled with the concept of popping testes like grapes." He shook his head, like she was the one that made no sense. "And I got to thinking that perhaps that was true, what you said? Would turning every female into an Omega just create more product? Doesn't matter. The Director isn't a man of science," he said, in the same way you'd describe a crack-addicted meth head giving handjobs in back alleyways. "So he'll never know that I'm not really solving his 'problem.' For all he knows, I'm down here creating drugs that would turn us all back to *Homo erectus*."

I realized I was shaking my head. I... just what?

What was happening here? Did I like this weird little bastard? He'd lasted this long, so obviously he was more savvy than he seemed right now, or maybe no one had spent more than ten minutes in his company.

All I knew was that eventually the DoDA would eat him alive.

"Donnie, we need to get the fuck out of here before we both die. I promise that we'll find you a way to continue your research, but doing it under the damn nose of the Government is a form of Russian Roulette neither of us can win."

"I thought you might say that, so I'm already packed." He lifted his chin at the bag beside the door. "All my research. I burned the rest—I like to make things explode in my spare time. Besides, if anyone can fund my studies, it's Remzi Hart. And the technology!" His eyes lit up. "Do you think he'd get me micro-robots for targeted therapies?"

"If you deliver me home, I'm pretty sure he'll get you any kind of robot you want and a fucking pony." I stood up, dragging on my jacket and shoes. "How do we get out of here?"

Donnie smiled. "We don't. We're on full lockdown. I took the liberty of calling the one coworker I like in the Department, and he said he'd be here in... three minutes and fifty-six seconds."

"You told a DoDA Official that you wanted to bust me out? Are you insane?"

He pouted. "Obviously not. Give me some credit. I can read people."

I groaned and flopped back onto the bed. "You're so dead. They are going to drag you up for treason. They're going to put the death penalty back on the table. Fuck, fuck, fuck," I cursed.

He tilted his head. "You didn't need that many fucks. I told you, I'm a good judge of character. Can't you hear all the percussive force above us?"

I tilted my head like his, no matter how dumb I probably looked. Then I felt something that very well could be an explosion, and didn't give a shit if I looked like a fool. I stood up and walked to the door, wrenching it open, running down the hall. There it was again, but now I heard gunshots too.

Holy shit.

Donnie appeared beside me, his satchel over his shoulder and my breakfast bagel in his hand. "For the road."

There was a bang on the doors that led out of this part of the building. A weird bang-bang, three quick soft taps, and another bang-bang. It was code.

"Your rescue has arrived," he beamed with a smug smile. He hit the red button by the door, and it slid open on a blood-covered horror.

Even with arms streaked with blood and unknown gore hanging off his balaclava, I still knew those eyes. Kacey. I'd never been more happy to see a person in my life.

He had a gun pointed at Donnie, whose face had gone pale. Apparently, there was a small amount of common sense buried deep in the doctor.

"Kacey!" I stepped in front of Donnie, and he lowered his gun. "Don't shoot him. We need him, plus I think we're kind of friends now?"

"We are?" Donnie squeaked out, like that was the most novel part of this whole exchange, not the blood-soaked army in front of us.

But yeah, I was shocked too.

I stepped into Kacey's arms, and he squeezed me so tightly I couldn't breathe. Five people appeared behind him. I knew two were Lupo and Tommy by their eyes. There was also a guy with gray eyebrows I didn't know, and another in a ski mask who stood like a merc, but it was the last one who had me sucking air back into my lungs.

"RJ?"

"Hey, Tryst. I missed you too," he said, lifting his phone. The text.

Kacey let me go, and I threw myself at RJ, kissing him so hard, it was a wonder I didn't bond him as mine in that moment. "You can't be here. If they know you helped do this..."

"Oh, you know Riley-James too?" Donnie asked, and I laughed against RJ's lips.

"Not well enough, apparently."

"We need to go. Three minutes until the security backup comes online," Gray Eyebrows grunted. RJ nodded, releasing me. I was scooped up into Kacey's arms the very second RJ's arms dropped.

"Tommy, at my back. Lupo, you got the doctor. I'd like to have a few words with him later." He buried his face in my neck for a second. "Hold on, Princess. I am never letting you go again. Ever."

Tommy patted me between the shoulder blades. "He means it. Pretty sure he's gonna get your doctor over there to make you into conjoined twins."

Donnie frowned. "That wouldn't be possible, by definition."

Lupo laughed. "Nothing is impossible, kid. You should know that."

"I'm twenty-seven, not a kid."

No fucking way. I would never have guessed that.

There was no more time for conversation as I was bundled out of the building. "Hide your face in my neck, Princess. You don't need to see this carnage, but they needed the lesson. They need to remember not to fuck with us ever again."

I looked though, because I never intended to be a victim again either. I took in every blood-soaked body and committed it to memory.

This was vengeance, and the man holding me was my avenging demon.

Chapter Forty-Three
Tryst

D o you know what every great massacre slash unabduction needs? An airtight alibi. And you know what provides the tightest alibi known to man? Rich people charity galas.

And sex.

Which was how I found myself shoved into a sequined dress, my hair piled high on my head, and lipstick haphazardly smeared across my mouth as we cruised down the freeway just below the speed limit.

The Pack couldn't be associated with... ten, maybe fifteen dead DoDA agents. So the majority of the Pack was at a gala for cancer research in Manhattan.

The plan was relatively simple. Lupo was going to drive us around the back of the Met, where the fundraiser was being held, and drop us in the middle of Central Park. Kacey and I would sneak to the rear entrance, then we were going to pretend we were having sex. The wild look in Kacey's eye had me believing there might not be too much pretending involved.

Lupo was going to hang around the paparazzi, subtly dropping hints that we were fucking around the back, and the newspapers would hopefully do the rest by plastering it all over the front page tomorrow. Small price to pay, really. I would streak naked through the party to protect Kacey.

He still held me on his lap, not even loosening his grip when we dropped Tommy off with RJ and Donnie at a dive hotel on the way here. It made trying to squish myself into this dress interesting.

I'd watched RJ out of the corner of my eye the whole way there. I couldn't ignore the relief, and the happiness I'd felt when he appeared. It meant something, because while I was happy to see Lupo and Tommy too, I didn't want to kiss them like I'd found something vital that I'd previously lost. Like a limb or the ability to take a deep breath.

Lupo barely slowed as we reached the drop off point, and Kacey leapt out, still not letting go of me. He hadn't said a word, and I was beginning to worry. It had been RJ who'd told me the plan, with Lupo filling in the gaps when I asked questions. Throughout the whole thing, Kacey had just sat quietly, breathing me in like he'd been deprived of oxygen for too long.

I pulled back enough so I could see his face, no longer covered in blood or hidden by a balaclava. His eyes were blank, and his jaw was so tight, I worried it would shatter like crystal.

"Kace? You have to put me down. You can't carry me there, especially not in this dress. Unless you want half of Manhattan to see my ass?"

He grunted something but let me slide to the ground. Placing his jacket over my shoulders, he led me into the shadows around the building. There were only slivers of darkness on the well-lit grounds, but Kacey navigated them all with ease. The grip of his hand was firm, but not painful.

"Are you okay?" I asked again.

He spun on his heel and grabbed me up in his arms. "Fucking hell, Tryst. Of course I'm not okay. *I lost you.*" He shook my shoulders a little at his hissed words. "Don't you get it? You were my responsibility, both of you, and I lost you almost immediately. I don't fucking deserve you. I'm a fucking monster, and yet I can't even protect you at the fucking doctor's office!"

"It wasn't—"

He put his fingertips against my lips, stopping my words. "Don't even say it wasn't my fault. It was. But never again, Princess. Never a-fucking-gain, because I will kill every fucker on the planet who thinks they can hurt you. Use you."

I tried to kiss his fingertips but he whipped them away. "No, I haven't washed away the blood properly. I don't want even the smallest drop of them on your body."

If I stepped two feet to the left, I'd be lit up like the Fourth of July by floodlights. This was close enough.

I grabbed the front of his shirt and pulled him close. He'd changed from black fatigues into a tux, and he was so fucking handsome I wanted to climb on top of him and kiss him until we were one person. His body pressed me back into rough concrete walls, and I dragged his face down to mine.

His tongue pushed inside my mouth, stroking mine, as he claimed me. His blood-tainted hands slid to my hips and pushed my dress up my thighs until he could put his palms on my ass cheeks.

He pulled back a little, until there was enough space between us to breathe. "I fucking love you, Tryst. I love you so goddamn much it's painful. You're like a knife jammed through my chest cavity and right into my heart."

"Love you too," I gasped as he thrust his hardening cock against my core. "Kiss me, please." He groaned as he recaptured my lips. One hand cupped the back of my head as he moved against me, grinding me into the wall.

The connection between us, this growing bond in my chest, was indescribable. I clung to his shoulders, and tears ran down my cheeks. He kissed them away. "Princess..." he breathed.

"Omega Hart!" someone yelled, and I turned, wincing against the sudden explosions of light. "Enjoying the party?"

Kacey growled at the paparazzi, but I gave them my best Mona Lisa smile. "Enjoying it very much," I murmured, wiggling from Kacey's arms. I straightened my dress, then handed him back his tux jacket. He slipped it on, tugging it across his broad shoulders. I smiled beatifically at the photographers. "It was just a little warm inside." I fanned my face, just so they couldn't tell if the heat I was referring to was the room temperature or this thing between Kacey and myself. "We should return to our bondmates."

I grabbed Kacey's hand, dragging him along behind me as I walked toward what I hoped was an unlocked exit. The whole back of the building was glass panels with alternating doors, so one of them had to be open.

My breath stuck in my throat as I stepped into view. My whole Pack was standing there, waiting for me in front of one of the exits. Remzi opened the right door, his face schooled into an expression of adoring bemusement, but his eyes scanned me quickly for injuries.

Do. Not. Cry, I warned myself.

He glared over my head at the paps, who disappeared under his burning gaze. Then he looked back down at me. "Are you out there enjoying the party, my Omega?" he murmured softly, though the people watching us would have heard.

"Needed some fresh air, Alpha," I said with a saucy wink, stepping into his space. I tilted my lips up for a kiss, and he obliged. His kiss was a soft brush of his lips, and he moved them across my cheeks toward my ear.

"I am so relieved to see you, Tryst."

I smiled up at him, but didn't say anything. He stepped aside, and we all moved further into the room. I felt like a bug under glass, and wanted nothing more than to go home and curl up between my men, but I knew we needed to be here for a few more hours yet.

I brushed my fingers over Grady's hand as I moved past him, soaking in the comfort of the Pack's presence. They all reached out to touch me subtly as Remzi led us over to our table.

Corrin swore beneath his breath. "Fuck this." He grinned in my direction. "Would you like to dance, baby?"

Yes. I wanted to be pressed close to each and every one of them. "I'd be delighted."

"Hope those are dancing shoes, baby girl, because I'm next," Akio murmured with a smile.

Corrin walked me into the middle of the designated dance floor and pulled me close. Pressing his cheek to mine, he led me around the floor without me even thinking about my feet. "Fuck me, Tryst. I was so worried. Are you okay?" he whispered in my ear. He pulled back and looked down at my eyes, searching them for secrets.

"I'm fine, I promise. Scared. But... bewildered, more than anything." He lifted a single eyebrow. "I'll explain later. Just hold me for now."

He pulled me tighter to his body, tucking my head under his chin and leading me in a slow dance around the floor, his arms reassuring. I felt my body slowly relax as he moved it gently, and the adrenaline I'd been running on the last couple of days began to ebb away.

I was just so exhausted.

"May I cut in?" Akio asked halfway through the next song.

Corrin grinned, giving our Alpha a wink. "You know I'm good at sharing," he said a little too loudly. Troublemaker.

I stepped out of Corrin's arms and into Akio's. He moved differently to Corrin, who swayed with natural rhythm but not in any particular pattern. Akio obviously had formal training, because his body flowed from one step to the next, my body held tight against his. He bent down and captured my lips, kissing me hard and making me stumble. Not Akio though, he just took in my misstep and continued on. No one would have known that his lips literally had me tripping.

"Are you all right? Do you need a doctor?"

I knew I was going to have to reassure them all at some point tonight. "I'm good, Alpha. Kacey got me out, and now I'm here in your arms, where I'm meant to be. They didn't *do* anything."

Akio shook his head. "It was the hardest thing I've ever done, not being there when you needed me, not racing to get you from that hellhole as soon as RJ called and said he knew where you were," he said, so softly only I could hear. "We needed to protect him too, and the best way was for us to be here, spread out, shaking hands with all these people, making our presence known separately so people wondered if you were here somewhere or if they were just missing you. Though I am fairly sure everyone in this room thinks they know what you were doing outside now."

The song changed to something even slower. "If that photographer had been two minutes slower, they'd all have been proven correct," I said with a grin, my hand coming up to stroke the sharp line of his jaw.

"Thank you for protecting him. I know it would have been hard to refuse your instincts."

He shook his head. "The hardest thing in the world, but I stood a better chance of keeping it together than Kacey. He was half feral." I couldn't even imagine. Akio bent down and took my lips again, this time less chastely. "When we get home, I am going to brand you as mine, Tryst Hart. I am going to make love to you until I'm tattooed across your body the same way you're branded across my heart."

I made a choked noise, and he kissed me once more before twirling me into another set of arms. The sweet smell of a summer storm washed over me, comforting and exhilarating all at once. Remzi.

His arms wrapped around me tightly, not even trying to keep the framework of a classical dance. "Your hair is coming undone," he murmured, lifting his hand to my hair, his fingers quickly plucking out the pins keeping my wild blonde waves contained. It fell heavily down to my shoulders like a curtain, and Remzi closed his eyes as my scent clouded around us. "Much better," he whispered.

I could feel every set of eyes on us now. High society gossips were trying to determine if everything was happy between the country's richest Alpha and the Omega he didn't want. Maybe they'd leak it as a confidential source to the tabloids, or maybe they'd talk about it at their society luncheons tomorrow. Maybe they'd just forget about it immediately since it didn't affect them the way it would affect the Omegas. We were just an interesting anecdote, not evidence of a systematic failure.

"Everyone is watching," I breathed.

Remzi shook his head. "I don't care. Let them watch." He held my eyes with his stormy gray ones, and the music fell away. The crowds fell away. Nothing but the Alpha in front of me remained. The intensity in his eyes reminded me of the first time we met.

His hand came up to cup my cheek, his body still moving. His thumb rubbed across my bottom lip, and all the air got stuck in my lungs. "I've wanted to do this again for so long," he murmured, leaning forward to kiss me hard. A commanding kiss between an Alpha and an Omega, but more than that. A kiss that was a promise to love and protect, even if we weren't quite there yet.

He continued to kiss me, and despite the hundreds of people in the room, I curled toward him. My Omega wanted to cry with happiness at being his again. She wanted him to lay her on the floor and claim her in front of all these people.

He was more in control, pulling back before we could get indecent on the dance floor. As he tucked me against his chest, I could feel the pounding of his heart beneath my ear.

When I looked up at him though, his eyes weren't on me. They were casting a stormy expression over the top of my head, and I turned to look at where his laser focus was pinpointed. I'd expected a woman, though I don't know why.

What I didn't expect was Remzi trying to mind-obliterate a white-haired man in a nice tux.

"Who's that?" I asked quietly, drawing his gaze back to me.

"The Director of the Department of Designation Associations."

My whole body went cold. Donnie's words about the Director, about 'solving the problem,' rushed back, crushing the air from my lungs. This man had known where I was. He'd been attending this function, probably thinking I was being experimented on by his mad scientist. He'd been eating canapés while Kacey and his men had been killing a dozen of his operatives. He'd been drinking champagne as I escaped back to the arms of my bondmates.

He fucking knew.

Remzi ran a possessive hand down my back, trying to soothe me. It was the most he'd touched me since my heat, and I wasn't sure 'soothing' was the best way to describe it. I was balanced on a knife's edge between freaking out and horny as hell, and my emotions were getting whiplash.

"Don't fret, Tryst. He'll get what's coming to him eventually—I swear it. Now, relax and we'll dance like we're having an amazing time and he means less than fucking nothing. You're safe now." A growl rumbled low in his chest. "Let him try and take you from me again."

It wasn't a threat. It was a promise.

Chapter Forty-Four
Tryst

We stumbled back into the apartment just after midnight. I'd had to reassure them at least six times that I didn't need to be checked out by a proper doctor. The last place I wanted to be right now was in another clinic somewhere. It had been the longest two days of my life, and I was past tired. I was running on raw energy now.

Grady didn't even speak to anyone. He just strode toward me, picking me up in his arms and carrying me to the curling stairs at the end of the hall. He climbed them easily as I clung to his shoulders, my face pressed into his neck, breathing in his familiar scent. He held me easily, like I was made to be in his arms, and when he got to the nest we'd made what felt like a lifetime ago, he placed me on my feet.

I looked around and sucked in a breath. It was a

beautiful sea of green, plants tastefully crowding the edges of the room, the floor covered in bed pallets that were made of expensive silks and linens. It was a sensory playground, and I couldn't have imagined anything more perfect.

"Remzi had it installed while you were at the doctors. Corrin helped pick the colors." Grady sighed, looking around. "Then news of your abduction hit us and we were worried you'd never see it." He kissed me hard, cutting off any words of gratitude I might have had. "I need you, Tryst. I can't..."

I laid my fingers across his lips. "Shh. I'm here, I'm yours." I pushed my finger into his mouth and he sucked it gently, nipping the tip. "I need you too."

His relieved breath cooled my damp finger, and somehow that shot right to my core. I wanted our other bondmates here too. How did I tell him that without it sounding like he wasn't enough?

Turned out, I didn't need to, because Jak appeared behind me, unzipping my dress. "We all need you tonight, baby girl. If you'll have us," he whispered against the skin of my spine.

"Always," I moaned back as he tugged my dress down my shoulders and sucked on one of my claiming marks.

My dress slunk to the floor, until I was clad only in my bra and panties, and Grady was sitting on the couch, dragging me down into his lap. He'd somehow gotten naked while I was distracted by Jak's mouth.

I ran my hands over all his warm skin, against the soft hair of his chest, pinching his nipples and making him curse softly. Banding his arms around my spine, he dragged me further up his body until he could suck a nipple into his mouth. I moaned, throwing my head back as pleasure burst through my extremities like a flood.

I pried my eyes open and looked around at all my bondmates in the room, each in varying states of undress. *Almost* all of my bondmates. Panic seized in my chest when I realized I couldn't see Kacey.

Corrin appeared in front of me, naked as the day he was born. He gripped my chin, raising my face until he could look me in the eye. "Don't worry, baby. He's just gone to shower. He'll be here. He couldn't stay away if he tried." He pushed his thumb into my mouth, and I wrapped my lips around it, sucking hard. "Relax. Let us make you feel good."

He kissed me, and I breathed him in. I wanted more than just his lips. I wanted everything. "I want to taste you..." I ended the word on a hiss as Grady moaned around my nipple and sent vibrations straight to my clit. Jesus.

"Take what you want, Omega," Corrin said, his cock jutting between us. I climbed further up Grady's body, pressing him into the couch cushions so I could suck the head of Corrin's cock into my mouth. He groaned, the grip of his fingers tight against my scalp.

It was all perfect, but something was missing.

Grady felt me tense, and pushed me back. "What's wrong? Is this too much?" His voice was rough, but I knew if I said right now that I wanted to stop, he'd tuck me up in bed and spoon me until I fell asleep.

"No, I want this. It's just..." I sucked in a deep breath. Corrin said to take what I want, right? "I want RJ. The Omega wants RJ." I looked down at Grady, who knew more than anyone else in this room the connection I had with the DoDA Official. "She— I mean, *I* have always wanted RJ."

Grady nodded, his face so open and accepting that I wanted to fall into his comforting arms and never climb out. He was my safety net. But he wasn't the only man I loved.

I made myself look up at Corrin, knowing he would likely be supportive. If Grady was my safety net, then Corrin was my greatest cheerleader. "It's fine with me, Tryst. Besides, I want to know what he's packing in that suit." He gave an exaggerated wink.

Okay. Those two were easy. It only got harder from here.

I looked over my shoulder at Jak, and he shrugged. "It's your choice. We are yours. You aren't ours."

I frowned. "Yes, I am."

"That's not what I meant." A breath rushed out from between his teeth. "Of course you belong with all of us. But you are our center, Tryst. We will always respect your opinion. Give you what you need. If you need the DoDA Official"—his eyes went wide at the very idea—"then take him. Consensually, of course," he added with a laugh.

He made it sound simple. But the three Alphas at the back of the room were less chilled out.

Kacey was freshly clean, his woodsy body wash wafting toward me. He was shirtless, clothed only in low-slung sweats that I wanted to drag off with my teeth. Why was he so fucking hot that he turned my brain to mush?

"Sure, take your little Beta. We *bonded* over the last couple of days."

I looked at Remzi. He inclined his head. "The Official loves you. He might not like it, might fight against it, but when he found out that you'd been taken, he threw away everything he'd worked for to save you. He is a worthy bondmate. If he'll have you, have us, he's welcome."

Akio just smiled with so much support, I wanted to hug him and never let go. My wonderful, unproblematic Alpha. "Me and Jak agree on this, like most things."

Corrin sighed, standing straight. "I can't believe I'm giving up a blowjob to go call a random guy. Lucky I love you, beautiful." He kissed me once more. "I'll be back in two minutes, and then I'm going to drive my cock into that delicious pussy until you scream my name." He took off at a run, not even bothering with clothes, and I could hear him pounding down the stairs.

I looked around at the guys. "Sorry for killing the mood."

I felt Jak's fingers slide through the lips of my pussy. "It takes more than one hard conversation to kill the hard-on I have for you, Omega," he murmured. "Hold her hips, Grady."

Gripping my hips, Grady tilted me up toward Jak, who had one of my thighs in each large hand. Then he slid his tongue through my slit, making me moan. My nipple was back in Grady's mouth, and it was perfect. Almost perfect.

I made a grabby hand toward one of the remaining men in the room, and I wasn't even remotely surprised when Kacey appeared at the back of the couch, his dick in his hand. He rubbed the head over my parted lips. "Are you gonna suck my cock, Princess? While our bondmates lick your pretty pink nipples and that delicious clit?"

I moaned so loudly, it was embarrassing. I hoped

the atrium was soundproof, or Central Park was going to get a new night symphony.

Kacey pushed his cock into my mouth and I swallowed him down. Fun fact: Omegas didn't have a gag reflex. Doctor Donnie would enjoy that factoid.

Jak's clever mouth was wringing pleasure from me one slow stroke at a time, and I was sure that Grady had sucked my nipples until they were so sensitive that even his cool breath made me clench around nothing. I mewled at my emptiness.

"You want a cock inside you, don't you, pretty Omega? You want Grady in that tight little cunt while Jak slides into your other hole? You think you can take that?"

"I know she can," Jak murmured against my pussy, my thighs wrapped around his head like I was a face mask. Legit, he spoke through it like this was Top Gun and he was Maverick with a flight helmet on. All that was missing were the aviators.

Bogey on your six, Goose.

"Lay back on the couch, Grady, so she can still suck my cock while she takes you." I looked down at Grady, and the lust in his eyes was almost enough to set me on fire.

"He's lucky his filthy mouth is as hot as it is bossy," Grady grumbled, but banded his arms around my ribs and took us down to the couch. Then he lifted my hips, sliding me onto his cock with a hiss. Either he had amazing aim or Jak was giving him a hand back there. Literally.

I let my head flop forward with relief at the sensation of the stretch. This was exactly what I needed, and my eyes met Grady's hooded ones. He thrust up until I was impaled completely on his dick. The exhilaration was something else.

Kacey gripped my chin, tilting my face back up. "Come on, Princess. I want to feel the back of that pretty throat."

I parted my lips and he pressed between them, filling my mouth as much as Grady filled my core. One person still hovered beside me, and I wanted to turn my head so I could watch Jak, but I was busy.

Fingers pushed inside my core beside Grady's cock, then used my slick up to lubricate my back entrance. Jak pressed further inside my ass, making me moan and clench down on Grady, who made a strangled grunt. Straddling Grady's thighs, Jak pressed the head of his cock against me. Curling forward, he kissed between my shoulder blades. "Relax Omega, I've got you."

And then he pushed inside me, and the chorus of animalistic sounds that echoed around the room were their own symphony. I didn't know which was mine, and which was Kacey's as I hummed around his dick.

Grady's fingers flexed on my hips, and would definitely leave little bruises—that just excited me more.

"Look at me, Tryst," Kacey growled, and I was helpless to resist. "We are going to use you up until your body is nothing but a quivering mass of pleasure, Omega." His eyes flicked over my head. "They look so fucking good right now, balls touching as they're buried deep in you. Can you feel it? Can you feel how full you are, how stretched your body is as it takes them, the same way you'd take my knot?"

I moaned, my arms shaking as I tried to hold myself up off Grady's chest and take Kacey's cock.

Jak's hand slid between my body and Grady's, flicking blindly against my clit until I came. I came with so much blinding pleasure that a scream tore from my chest, even if it was muffled around Kacey.

He palmed my head in both hands and came down my throat. I swallowed down every drop, even as my body shuddered and shook around Jak and Grady.

"Fuck... Fuck, I'm going to come," Grady grunted beneath me, and I pulled off Kacey, curling down until I could take Grady's lips with mine. He was still pounding in and out of me, the slide perfectly timed with Jak at my back, and he groaned at the taste of Kacey's release on my tongue. He pushed deep and came, holding me tight to his body.

Jak stilled behind me. "Fuck, I can feel him

coming," he groaned. He leaned along my back, gripping the back of the couch and the armrest with a white-knuckled grip as he slid in and out of me, his face right beside Grady.

I moaned as he turned his face and kissed my first bondmate, my shock giving way to pleasure as I watched their tongues tangle. My clit was grinding down against Grady with every thrust from Jak, and soon I was coming once more, the orgasm somehow even more overwhelming than the one before it.

"Oh god," I breathed, and then Jak was coming too.

"Fuck, Tryst, fuck..." he choked out, and I got it. I totally understood.

My whole body went limp as he collapsed on top of me. We were probably crushing Grady, but the look on his face said he didn't care in the slightest.

Jak rolled off first, coming to his knees beside me. He lifted my face to his and kissed me softly. "You're amazing." Another quick kiss. "Such a good girl." Then he flopped backwards onto the mountains of soft blankets and pillows, completely spread-eagle.

I smiled as I took in the lean lines of his body and the smile stretched across his face. Grady's fingers ran lightly up and down my spine, their calouses having softened over the last few months. "I promise to love and honor you for the rest of my life, Tryst," he murmured into my hair. "To be with you in the good times and the bad. To love you and our baby so hard every day that you'll never doubt how I feel about either of you."

I turned my face and kissed his chest. "I'm thankful every day your number came up first, Grady Davis. I couldn't have done any of this without you."

And I meant it with every piece of my now-crowded heart.

Chapter Forty-Five
RJ

"I don't get the point of this," Donnie declared, and I resisted the urge to laugh at him.

Tommy handed him a knife. "There's no point to Five Finger Fillet except to see who has the biggest balls."

Donnie continued to frown as he took it. "Wouldn't a tape measure be better for that purpose?"

I shook my head, taking the knife off him. "Not your actual balls, Donnie. Your spirit balls." I stabbed the knife between my fingers quickly and easily into the rough wooden countertop that was already filled with gouges.

This wasn't a great hotel, but it had no cameras and the desk attendant didn't ask questions. We'd hide out here for a couple of days, then Kacey would arrange for his family to smuggle Donnie somewhere safe. Probably Canada, or maybe down to Mexico. Remzi Hart had said he'd fund his research, and quite frankly, Donnie was giddy at the very idea.

Donnie was still staring at Tommy's hands. "The amount of cuts on your hands would suggest you don't have very big balls, Thomas."

Donnie had decided Tommy was too close to his own name, so he'd taken to calling him Thomas, which was amusing as hell, because the man in question hated it. I was fairly sure if it had been anyone but Donnie, he would have knocked them out.

But there was something disarmingly pure about Donnie and the way he saw the world, which was why we'd become friends in the first place. We'd gone through DoDA induction together, and despite being in different branches, we'd remained friends.

When he'd called me a few weeks ago to tell me that the Director was trying to experiment on Omegas, I'd freaked the fuck out.

When he'd called me last night and told me he had an Omega and could I come and collect them, please? Well, my asshole had almost fallen out.

Especially since I loved that Omega so much that it was a fucking permanent ache in my soul.

Tommy was still gaping at Donnie. Then he unzipped his pants, whipping out his balls. I ran a hand over my face. I should have seen that one coming.

"My balls are huge. You take that back."

Donnie shrugged. "Seems average sized to me." Did his lips just twitch? Was Donnie teasing the fucking mobster? He reached out, and I swear to fucking god, cupped Tommy's balls in his hands. "Average weight too."

I slapped his wrists, making him pull his hands away from Tommy's testicles. "For fuck's sake, you can't touch someone's balls without permission! Jesus fucking Christ, how are you not dead?"

"I just figured that if he was showing them to me, the offer to touch was implicit."

I just blinked at him, my mouth open in shock. "What? No. That's not how this shit works." My eyes shot to Tommy's face, and he looked just as shocked as I did.

"Why not? All Tommy's physiological indicators suggest he has sexual interest in me, plus I *wanted* to touch his balls, plus he presented them to me. By the actual laws of nature, he wanted me to touch his testes too."

Donnie was naive, but he wasn't stupid. He saw the world in a very black and white kind of way, having spent way too much time in a lab which made him a bit blind to general social niceties, and sometimes that made me almost consider him youthful. Coupled with that baby face, I was guilty of forgetting that he was a man in his late twenties, with an insane amount of curiosity and an obviously broken danger-meter.

"Implicit or not, physiological responses or not, you have to *ask* first. With words. Hell, maybe you should even get it in writing before you grab the wrong man's dick and end up in a coma." I hadn't even realized he liked men.

Donnie rolled his eyes at me, then turned to Tommy. "Sorry for touching your testicles without your permission, Thomas. I think I might like to do it again one day—with your permission, of course."

I threw my hands in the air, but was saved from watching Donnie's gruesome murder by my phone ringing. I looked imploringly at Tommy. "Don't hurt him; he doesn't mean it."

Tommy smirked at me. "He's fine. If I gutted every person who wanted to touch my dick, there'd be no one left in the world," he said with a shrug.

I pulled out my phone and walked to the other side of the hotel room. "Hello?"

"RJ, it's Corrin. How's things?" His casual opening made the stress levels subside slightly. She was okay.

I cleared my throat, realizing he was waiting for an answer. "Well, Tommy just got his balls fondled."

Corrin snorted. "So just another Saturday night then?" He sucked in a deep breath. "I had a whole speech planned, like you'd just won an Academy

Award, but it's disappeared from my brain. She's asking for you, RJ."

My heart stuttered to a complete stop in my chest. Blood rushed in my ears, and my mind was filled with Tryst.

"Did you hear me? This is your moment, RJ. Fucking take it with both hands, because if you fuck it up right now, there won't be another chance. She wants you in the Pack. She wants you as a bondmate, and we've all agreed."

"Are you sure?" Why wasn't she asking me herself?

"I'm definitely sure. I left a fucking orgy where I was getting my dick sucked for this, so trust me when I say I'm one hundred percent certain everyone is on board with this. The only person standing in your way now is yourself."

Silence stretched down the line, and I didn't know what to say.

Corrin gave a heavy sigh. "Lupo will be there in five minutes with the car. He'll relieve you of babysitting duty. I'll give you another fifteen to get your ass back here, but if you don't, I'm going back upstairs to make love to the most beautiful woman in the world, with or without you."

My brain was whirling, but I could only think of one thing. "Yes. I'm coming. I need thirty minutes though—I have to stop and get something. But I'm coming."

Corrin laughed. "Not yet, but I bet that you'll be coming real soon. I know I will be." I could almost imagine his lascivious wink. That man was a walking pick-up line. He heaved out a sigh. "Fine, I'll wait. But just know that I hate you." He hung up, and I just stared at the phone in my hand.

"Everything okay?" Tommy asked, his eyes flicking between me and Donnie.

"More than okay. I've gotta go. Lupo will be here in a minute. Don't... I don't know." I looked at Donnie. "Don't do anything without thinking through the possible outcomes first, okay? Relationships aren't the place to start being spontaneous, you know?"

He gave me a droll look. "I'm not an idiot, Riley-James. Give me some credit."

He'd just grabbed the junk of a guy who'd definitely killed at least six people in the last ten hours. Sorry if I doubted his decision-making skills.

"It's fine, RJ. I won't do anything either of us regret," Tommy said with a grin, and I wasn't sure I believed him. "Promise. On Kacey's life."

Okay, that made me feel slightly better.

Lights flashed through the curtained windows as a car pulled into the parking spot. Lupo stepped out of the driver's seat, not even bothering to turn it off. "Go get her," he said with a grin, slapping me on the ass as I climbed into the driver's seat.

I shifted it into reverse. "Make good choices."

Lupo just raised an eyebrow but nodded. I sped through the streets and prayed that she didn't change her mind before I got there.

Corrin let me up and when the elevator doors slid open, he was standing in the foyer, naked as hell. He had his eyes closed, a pained expression on his face.

"Are you having a stroke?"

He opened a single eye. "Don't test me, asshole. Listen to what I'm missing just so you can join the damn fold."

I cocked my head, and then I heard it. The sound of Tryst orgasming somewhere inside the building. I'd know the cadence of her screams anywhere.

I was hard between one breath and the next. It was a residual ache that I knew all too well.

"Come on, you lucky son of a bitch. This time you don't have to stand outside the door." Corrin looked down at the thing I held in my hands, surprise lighting his face. The reason for my detour. "That's what you stopped to get?"

I nodded. "It's important. I left it with someone

safe in the city when I was transferred back to the East Coast. Just in case."

He dragged me toward the stairs, and I didn't even care that he was naked or that his dick was pointing at me like it had its own agenda. Because when I stepped into the glass room and saw Tryst spread out on Remzi's lap, I knew that I'd no longer have to be a spectator.

Not that I minded watching. Seeing Tryst claim and enamour her mates one after the other had really been the greatest joy of my life. It was like I'd gotten to witness something beautiful and almost mystical as she tied them to her.

She didn't realize I was here yet, but Remzi Hart did. She'd obviously forgiven him, because she was riding his cock where he lay on the floor, her hands pressed into his broad chest, her movements slow and leisurely. His eyes caught on mine, and a world of bad feelings passed between us.

He'd never told anyone that I'd punched him in the face the day he left during Tryst's first heat. She'd been in so much pain, and there'd been so much anguish on her face, that I couldn't comprehend anyone with a heart doing that to her. He'd taken it, both jabs I aimed at that pretty face, and the one I threw into his midsection. Then he'd just turned and left.

He gave me a meaningful look, then turned his

expression back to watching Tryst, his thumb playing with her clit. God, she was so damn beautiful that it hurt. His face was reverent now, and I realized he wasn't as impervious to her as he pretended.

"Remzi," she breathed, pleasure making her body both tense and languid. It was hard to describe, but I could see the way her spine straightened as her orgasm pushed her over the edge.

"Bite me, Omega. Make me yours again."

The noise she made was almost animalistic, a sweet note that was better than any music. She curled down and bit high on his neck, a place that was clearly visible, claiming him for all the world to see.

He let out his own low moan, and this whole process felt like emotional voyeurism, but as I looked around the room, the whole Pack was watching their Omega take their primary Alpha with hungry eyes.

"Once more, Tryst. One more for me," he murmured in her ear, then rolled her onto her back. She clung to his shoulders, her nails scoring long stripes down his golden skin, and he pounded into her, their lovemaking losing the languid edge and turning into something frantic and needy.

"Alpha..." she whined, and I'd listened to her come enough to know that she was almost there again. Already.

Remzi leaned forward and bit her other breast, the

exact mirror image of his first claiming mark. Tryst exploded again, and this time Remzi was coming too, his shout of pleasure muffled by her delicate flesh between his teeth. He lapped at it, cleaning up the blood, then rolled beside her, gathering his Omega in his arms protectively.

"You mean everything to me, Tryst Hart." I believed him, and given the soft kiss Tryst bestowed on him, she believed him too. "I believe you have a visitor."

She turned her head to look at me, and the sheer joy on her face was like a band around my heart, tying me to her as surely as any matebond. She looked down at my mating gift, and her eyes went wide, drawing everyone else's attention to the bowl in my hand.

"Did you bring a goldfish to your mating? That's kinky even by Pack standards," Jak joked, though I could see he was confused.

Grady looked at me and smiled, his eyes filled with pride. Or happiness. "Huckleberry Finns."

Tryst climbed to her feet, wincing slightly, and grabbed the nearest dress shirt to wrap around her shoulders, covering most of her nakedness. When she made it closer, I realized she had soft tears tracking down her cheeks. "You saved my fish?"

I swallowed back the lump in my throat. "You obviously cared about him, and I thought I'd just keep him safe until you and the Pack settled into a home of your own, then I was going to give him back to you as a housewarming gift." It all ran out in one nervous, long sentence.

She sucked her lip between her teeth, blinking those eyelashes that haunted my dreams rapidly.

"Give the fish to one of our Packmates, RJ."

Akio quickly reached out and took the small tank. Huckleberry Finns would need a bigger one soon; I'd been reading up on goldfish care. But now was not the time to discuss it because Tryst was throwing herself into my arms and kissing me in the way I'd always dreamed she would. I held her easily and kissed her back, pouring everything I could into it.

All the longing. All the pain. All the unrequited need I'd felt for her over the last couple of months.

She wrapped her legs around my waist, and I could feel the warmth of her core against me. I walked her to a fluffy rug that was illuminated by the soft glow of a faux fireplace. As I laid her down, the shirt she was wearing spread apart like it was offering me the greatest gift I'd ever received. I tore my own t-shirt over my head, and scrambled out of my sweats with no grace whatsoever. I wanted as little between us as possible. I'd been dreaming about this moment.

"I'm going to make you so deliriously happy, Tryst. I swear it."

She smiled, and it stole my heart for good. I was never getting it back. It was hers now. "You already do." She gripped my hips between her legs and pulled me down. "Make me yours, RJ. We've waited long enough," she whispered.

As I slid inside her, I knew I was home. This was the purpose of my life. To make her happy. To give her all the love she could handle.

I continued to kiss her, rocking gently against her, learning her body. Her breathing was heavy, and when she slipped a hand between us and played with her clit, I almost came on the spot. But if I was ever going to do something right, it was going to be this.

I snapped my hips harder, pulling one of her legs higher on my hip until I was grinding down into her, hitting deeper spots and also hitting her finger-covered clit.

"RJ..." she breathed, drawing out my two-syllable name into ten, and then her body clenched around me in a way that surpassed anything I'd ever felt before. It was like I belonged there. She curled her head to the side and bit me, marking me as hers even though as I came, the bond itself snapped into place and she was everywhere. Around me. Inside me.

If this wasn't heaven, I didn't want to go.

Chapter Forty-Six
Tryst

I couldn't remember the last time I'd felt this way. Not the 'fucked so hard I had to walk like a cowboy' feeling, though that was certainly nice.

No, I felt completely and utterly content. My Omega didn't feel restless or needy. I didn't feel like I was missing something, or waiting for the other shoe to drop. Despite the fact that we'd definitely pissed off the DoDA—and of course, I was still pregnant—I just felt... happy.

I was sitting at the table on RJ's lap, his cheek pressed between my shoulder blades as we watched Jak make pancakes. Remzi was reading the paper on the couch, and I'd left Grady and Corrin curled together in my nest. Akio was doing calisthenics in a clear space in the living room, and it was like watching art, the way his body flexed and moved.

"That can't be healthy," Kacey grumbled into his coffee, watching Akio move from a push-up into a handstand like it was no big deal. I eyed his mug with longing. I needed the caffeine, but I was determined to have the healthiest, most banal goddamn pregnancy known to Omegas. I'd had enough drama; I didn't want any more.

"From what I can see, it looks perfectly healthy. Deliciously healthy, even."

Akio chuckled as he rolled into another push-up. "Thank you, Tryst. If you come over here, I can do an ab workout that I promise you'll enjoy." He rolled his hips erotically in his plank position, and my mouth went dry.

I went to scramble from RJ's lap, because who would turn down an offer like that? Despite the fact that my vagina felt like it needed an ice bath. Or a heat pack. Maybe I needed to try out Remzi's hot tub.

"Before you start a second orgy in twenty-four hours, I thought perhaps we should have a conversation about your abduction and possible future prevention." It was weird to hear Remzi tell jokes. Weird but nice.

Akio flopped down onto his stomach with a grunt, making me pout. "Corrin and Grady are still asleep. We have time."

Grady walked out shirtless, and I was mesmerized by the line of his hip as he stretched. "Time for what?"

He came over to kiss me, then headed to the coffee machine.

I flopped my head back against RJ's shoulder. "Nothing. Akio was going to show me how he does push-ups."

Corrin walked out, his hair adorably mussed, and looked over at Akio. "Was he going to do it naked? Because we can go back to bed." He winked at me. "I got your back, lover."

I blew him a kiss. "I know you do. No, Remzi needs to talk to us."

Corrin waggled his eyebrows at Remzi. "Oh, Pack Daddy needs to have a word? I better be caffeinated for this."

Remzi looked horrified. "Do not call me Pack Daddy."

Corrin took a cup of coffee from Grady, taking a deep sip and heaving a sigh. "Fine. Just Daddy then."

I elbowed him as he came over to me and RJ. He leaned down and kissed me, and I sucked his bottom lip between my teeth. He groaned out a noise filled with pleasure, and maybe a touch of amusement. "I know you're just trying to suck the caffeine from my lips, baby girl."

I gasped with mock-horror. "Was not."

"Don't make Kacey spank you for telling lies. I know for a fact he'll like it."

I looked over at my Alpha, who was smirking around his coffee mug. "Lie to me, baby," he purred, and I squirmed on RJ's lap.

"Jesus fucking Christ, how do you guys function with this much sexual tension all the time?" RJ groaned, pushing me onto one thigh so he could adjust the cock hardening beneath my ass.

Grady sat beside Kacey as Jak put a massive platter of pancakes on the table. There must have been fifty in the pile. "We don't. I walked around with a hard-on for a week when we first arrived," Jak quipped. "Food's ready."

Everyone came over, and I sat down in the seat between RJ and Grady. We all fit perfectly around the table now; it was nice. Like all the pieces were where they were supposed to be. Grady loaded up my plate with more pancakes than I could possibly consume, and then his own, passing the platter around the table.

Kacey waved a fork at Remzi. "You were talking about Tryst's"—he cleared his throat—"abduction?"

Remzi nodded. "I think we should leave the US. After talking to Tryst's new doctor friend this morning, in addition to the conversations we've had with RJ, we should assume that the DoDA has plans to use Omegas, though no one can tell me for what exactly. I would prefer if our Omega, and our child, weren't in constant mortal peril."

"It's bad for digestion," Corrin added.

God, I loved that man.

Akio's brows drew together in a frown. "I hate to be a naysayer, but they aren't just going to let Tryst leave the country. They have really strong travel restrictions on Omegas, otherwise they all would have left at the first Allotment. They'll stop her at the border."

Remzi nodded, sipping his coffee. "I don't intend for us to ask permission."

Everyone spoke at once.

"They'll just extradite us."

"Where would we even go?"

"What about everything we have back here? We could never return."

I watched Remzi's face, his calm confidence assuring me that he'd thought this through and determined it was the best course of action. But we were a team, which meant it was a group decision.

I wasn't particularly tied to the US, and an escape sounded amazing. However, the guys had families and lives here, businesses that would suffer if we were in a different country. I couldn't ask them to tear themselves away because of me.

Remzi raised a hand. "Fortunately for us, the DoDA aren't particularly thorough in their approval process." He waved a hand at Kacey, like he was the case in point. "My father was Canadian."

RJ sucked in a breath. "You're going to relinquish your US citizenship? What about HartWire?"

Remzi shrugged. "It's controlled by a board. It pays its taxes. If they have an issue, I'll move it north as well. Not to sound cocky, but they need me far more than I need them."

Grady frowned. "In layman's terms?"

RJ cleared his throat, his fingers tracing over the bondmark on his bicep subconsciously. "A Pack is considered the citizens of whatever country the controlling Alpha is from. If Remzi has dual citizenship, and we can get across the border, he can relinquish his US citizenship and become a purely Canadian citizen. And so would the rest of Pack Hart."

"They couldn't make Tryst come back?" Kacey clarified.

RJ shook his head. "No. They'd no longer have any rights to extradite us."

I looked around the table, at the men I loved. "It has to be unanimous. I can't—I *won't* drag you away from everything and everyone, unless we're all on board."

I looked at Akio and Jak, who obviously loved their family. They were frowning, looking adorably twin-like. I wasn't sure when I'd stopped thinking of them as identical, but their personalities were so different that I now forgot until moments like these.

Except when they were naked.

They were having some kind of conversation with their eyes, or their twin bond, or something. Finally, Akio looked at Remzi, then smiled gently at me. "You don't need to be a martyr, Tryst. It isn't our safety that's at risk."

Jak shrugged. "Besides, it's Canada, not Africa. None of our family are Omegas, so they can come and visit whenever they want."

Grady kissed my temple. "My mother would skin me alive if I even suggested putting my feelings above your wellbeing. And Jak is right; she'll visit. They all will."

"My family already disowned me when I started dating Grady, so I'm good," Corrin added, drowning his pile of pancakes in maple syrup until it was like a log in the bottom of a river. Sheesh.

I looked at a frowning Kacey. He was close to his family too. "It's okay to say no, Kace."

He shook his head. "I would never put you in danger again, Princess. Never." He rubbed a thumb down his shadowed jaw. "I'd like to ask Lupo and Tommy to come, but I'll leave their decisions up to them. They probably won't want to follow us to Canada."

Remzi nodded. "If they want to come, they're welcome. I owe them a debt that I can't ever repay."

Akio nodded. "We all do."

Kacey waved a hand. "They're my brothers." He gave me a lopsided grin. "Plus, they like Tryst better than me anyway."

I turned to RJ with a grimace. "We probably should have had this conversation before I tied us together forever," I murmured, stroking my fingers over the still raw mark on his arm, making him shiver.

"Remzi isn't known for his great timing after bonding," Corrin joked, but underneath was a gentle chastisement. I wasn't sure they'd fully forgive Remzi for a long time.

RJ grabbed my fingers and kissed them. "I burned all my bridges here. I'll come." He screwed up his nose. "We're gonna have to bring Donnie though."

"I'm going to have to insist on it," Remzi said cryptically.

I frowned at him. "What about you and your family? I know you weren't really raised together when you were younger, but you made it sound like you're closer now."

Remzi cleared his throat. "It won't be a problem. We should leave as soon as possible."

Chapter Forty-Seven
Tryst

Twenty-four hours later, we got off a twelve-seater private plane in the middle of nowhere. A group of people met us on the runway, all huddled against the cold mountain breeze.

I couldn't see a single building in the distance. Even calling it a runway was being generous. It was a mowed stretch of grass on an open plain. But it was the exact color green of freedom, and for that, I'd walk another six hundred miles through it.

"Remzi!"

I frowned as a small woman burst through the group standing off to the side. There was something about her...

Kacey and Akio's spines went ramrod straight, and that told me what my brain already knew. She was an Omega.

An Omega running toward *my* Alpha. When she threw herself into his arms, he caught her and hugged her tightly.

"What in the actual fuck?" Grady muttered, and I wholeheartedly agreed.

The girl wiggled from Remzi's hug and turned toward me, her face stretched in a wide, innocent smile. "Oh my god, it's you!" She raced toward me and wrapped me in a hug too. "I've waited so long to meet you, but Remzi kept saying no, no, no. You know what he's like. And then he went through that whole stupid divorce charade, and I was sure you'd never forgive him." She frowned disapprovingly. "I know I wouldn't have. Honestly, I gave him what-for. Of all the stupid bullshit—"

"Daisy," someone interrupted.

I looked over the girl's head, because she was *tiny*. The guy behind her looked a little familiar, but it wasn't until he frowned at the Omega in front of me that I realized why. He looked like Remzi.

The woman's big eyes stared up at me, her dark curly hair and storm gray eyes finally registering over the raging jealousy.

"Holy shit, you're his siblings."

"Duh!" She slapped her head, looking between me and the rest of my bondmates. "Ohhhh. Shitballs-hackeysack. You thought I was hitting on your Alpha. No way. Alphas are the worst. No offense, guys," she said to my Alphas, who bracketed me. "Remzi excepted, but he gets a free pass, being my brother and all."

The man in question came up and stood behind me, both hands on my shoulders as I rocked back into his body. "Daisy, this is my Omega, Tryst, and our bondmates Akio, Jak, Grady, Kacey, Corrin and RJ." He turned a little to my left. "Also, this is Lupo and Tommy, Kacey's brothers, and Doctor Donald Breddan."

"Call me Donnie," the doctor piped up, his face flushed pink.

"Donnie," Daisy said softly, like she was tasting his name on her tongue. "We sure could use a doctor around here, so you're very welcome."

"And us?" Tommy asked, the smirk on his face way too bold for a man who was obviously surrounded by the Omega's brothers.

Daisy fluttered her eyelashes at him. "Your kind is always welcome."

Someone cleared their throat aggressively, and Daisy grinned. "Oh, I should introduce you to my brothers. Trey and Dustin over there, and Joseph by the car." I waved at Remzi's siblings, and they all nodded at me respectfully, Dustin giving me a grin that was the exact replica of Remzi's. Daisy linked her arm in mine. "Come on, we should get home before   dinner   is   ruined.   Welcome   to   the Underground."

I looked at Remzi with wide eyes and mouthed, "The Underground?"

He shrugged and mouthed, "Sorry."

Oh he wasn't yet, but he totally would be.

Turns out, after about ten minutes down what appeared to be a deserted road, you made it to the world's smallest town. It was literally a church and a bar which doubled as a grocery store during the day. The bar was run by Trey and his pretty Beta wife, Samantha.

There were five large houses along the single road, and I'd met the inhabitants of most of them at dinner. They were all in the Underground, a secret Omega-smuggling ring that they'd discovered after Remzi and his brothers had smuggled Daisy—who was their youngest sibling—out of the US when she presented as Omega at sixteen. She'd never even had time to be picked up by the DoDA because she was dead and gone in the eyes of the government, her headstone declaring her just a normal old Beta.

Now they ferried new Omegas, unmated Omegas or Omegas escaping bad matches across the border. They were just a waypoint, albeit an important one close to the border, and with an airstrip. Apparently, it was a complex network, and you only knew the points either side of you, and no one knew where the Omegas ended up.

They knew they ended up happy though, because more than a few came back after years of safety to say thank you, according to Daisy.

She was a powerhouse, and honestly, I'd never seen Donnie so flustered. His cheeks seemed to be permanently pink, and he stumbled over his words like the dictionary inside his head had burned to ashes.

It didn't help that Tommy flirted with both Donnie and Daisy, making jokes about how they were meant to be together, and their last name should be Duck. Lupo had explained the joke to Donnie. They were kind of cute together, like Tommy and Lupo had adopted the extremely strange man as a pet project.

Unfortunately, no matter how much I liked Daisy and the rest of the townspeople, the town of Lightning Falls wasn't where we were staying. We were going to move further into the center of Ontario, to a house that had been vetted by Remzi's people for safety.

As we drove there the following day in an SUV Remzi's brothers had bought for us, I tried to grill my tight-lipped Alpha for information. "Do you have pictures?" I asked for the thirtieth time.

Remzi shook his head. "Not on me, no."

Grady was grinning, so I knew he'd seen it. "Are you going to tell me what it's like?" I said, poking him in the side closest to me.

"It's a surprise."

I crossed my arms and pouted. "We're meant to make decisions together." Okay, that was a low blow, but I wasn't above guilt-tripping at this point.

Grady wrapped an arm around my shoulder. "If I thought you would anything but one hundred percent love this place, I would have insisted Remzi consult you." He kissed my cheek, then moved his lips to my ear. "He wants to do this for you. Let him have it. He's still groveling."

He didn't need to grovel now. He'd upended his entire life for me, taken a serious blow to his stocks for me, and if that wasn't commitment, I didn't know what was.

We'd left Tommy and Lupo back at Wawa, the closest major town to Daisy's outpost. Calling it a major town was probably a stretch. But apparently, they were going to grab a car to go check some things out, and Remzi's little sister had offered to be tour guide. They might have been as smitten with Daisy as Donnie was.

You could never tell with those two.

We headed north-east, further into Ontario, and up past Timmins toward Iroquois Falls. Snow dotted the landscape, like it hadn't quite committed to winter just yet.

"Is it too late to tell you that I don't know if I like snow? Or bears?" Corrin asked, and Kacey rolled his eyes from the passenger seat.

"Yes."

"Damn. Note to self: get bear spray and a pair of ear muffs."

I looked over my shoulder to Corrin in the back seat. "I volunteer my thighs," I purred.

"I eagerly accept your offer. Actually, since you mention it, my ears are a little chilly right now," he announced, unbuckling his seatbelt.

Remzi looked into the rearview mirror. "Seat belt back on. We're almost there."

Corrin pouted but buckled himself back in. "Pack Daddy is no fun."

"Don't call me that," Remzi growled, and Corrin's eyes sparkled with mischief.

Turned out Remzi hadn't been lying though, as he turned the car down a dirt road. Trees rose up immediately to surround the car, like we'd somehow left civilization and turned straight into the wilderness.

"The closest town has all the amenities you may need, including a hospital and a Tim Hortons, which is apparently a big deal in Canada. But our closest neighbors are a couple of miles away, so all you can see right now is ours."

Through the trees, I kept catching glimpses of water, so I knew the land must have backed onto a river or a lake or something. Excitement built in my chest. I'd never lived somewhere so rural, but already I felt free.

"You should close your eyes," Akio whispered from beside me, and I smiled as I slammed my eyelids shut. We bounced around for a few more minutes and Jak's whispered, "Fuck," let me know we'd arrived long before the car rolled to a stop.

"Keep them closed, Omega," Remzi commanded softly, and I did.

I heard the doors opening and closing, and then someone unbuckled me, lifting me out of the car. I knew immediately it was Remzi; his presence was a full-body experience. Not only his scent—that light, woodsy smell that seemed so primal—but the way his Alpha made my skin prickle with awareness.

He carried me easily a few steps and then set me down. "Open your eyes," he breathed against my cheek, his body pressed tightly to mine.

I sucked in a gasp as I took in our home. And it was our home. I felt it immediately in my soul. A large two-story house was built into the side of a steep rise, backing right into the woods. It had a peaked gable roof, with large windows on all sides. Big stone steps led up to the front door and a stone patio, and on the other side was a tiered vegetable garden, with a greenhouse at the top. Several large workshops were off to the side, and as I spun in a circle, I saw a small boatshed at the end of a large front yard.

"It's perfect," I breathed, and I felt Remzi's pride in our bond. And Grady's smug satisfaction too. Fine, he'd been right. I turned in Remzi's arms, my hands sliding up over his shoulders until I could hook them around his neck and drag him down to my level. "Thank you. I love it."

He kissed me softly. "You never have to thank me for anything, Tryst." He picked me up so he didn't have to stoop, and I wrapped my legs around his waist. "This is where we'll be a Pack, and where we'll raise our children. We can fix or change anything you want —just say the word."

I kissed him hard, pouring all my affection into the embrace and pushing love down our bond. We weren't ready for the words; we still had a lot of things to work through, but it was there. We both knew it.

"This is really nice. Reminds me of my grandparents' house back home." RJ whistled beneath his breath as he took it all in. "I'm going to have to take up fishing, considering I don't have a job up here."

Well, no one but Corrin and Remzi did, but that

was something we'd figure out slowly. Remzi was going to start proceedings to relinquish his US citizenship next week, and register our Pack as citizens of Canada, and there'd probably be a ceremony or something.

But then we'd get on with our lives, and honestly, that's all I wanted.

A life, with my Pack, filled with love.

Notes from the author

Anyone who has ever read one of my books before knows that on top of orgies and surprise pregnancies, sticking it to 'The Man' has been a recurring theme in my stories. Sometimes 'The Man' is a ruling council, or an unfair social order, or just the rich and powerful in general, but they all inevitably fall to the strength of the female main character and her willingness to do what's right and just. Because this is fiction, and it should inspire and empower.

However, despite the recurring theme, I try not to use my books as a soapbox to preach my beliefs (except for the benefit of orgies—I'll die on that hill, dammit! Orgies for all!).

I hear you say, "What are you getting at already, Grace?"

I was about 75% of the way through writing this

book when the US Supreme Court overturned Roe v. Wade. The plot was already done, but I would've been blind not to see the parallels between Tryst's fight for Omega autonomy in the Superior Court, and the rights of women to their bodily autonomy in the here and now.

Sure, I'm pro-choice, but I'm also pro-your-right-to-your-own-opinion, even if I don't personally agree with it.

I guess what I'm trying to say is that this isn't an abortion rights manifesto. It was a coincidence in timing, but not one I'm mad about. You should have the right to govern your own body and make your own choices, whether you're an Omega, LGBTQI+, a person with a uterus, or any flavor of religion under the sun. What makes you different is what makes you perfect.

Be kind to one another, and to yourselves.

Love Grace x

About the Author

Grace McGinty is eclectic. She has worked as a chocolatier, a librarian, a forensic accountant and finally a writer. Like her professional career, the genres she writes are also eclectic. She writes romance, reverse harem romance, fantasy, contemporary young adult and new adult books.

She lives in rural Australia with her crazy family, an entire menagerie of pets, and will one day be crushed by the giant piles of books that litter every room.

Head over to www.gracemcginty.com and join my mailing list for sneak previews into what I am working on and to stay up-to-date with new releases and giveaways!